The Magician's Redemption

Naomi Boyd

Fisher King Publishing

THE MAGICIAN'S REDEMPTION

PRINT ISBN 978-1-913170-38-7

Published by

Fisher King Publishing
The Studio
Arthington Lane
Pool in Wharfedale
LS21 1JZ
England

www.fisherkingpublishing.co.uk

It is the pleasure of the bee to sip the honey from the flower
It is the pleasure of the flower to give its honey to the bee
For to the bee, the flower is the fountain of life
And to the flower, the bee is the messenger of love

Kahlil Gibran 1883 – 1931

Prologue

The world we see is only a fraction of the life we live. Many worlds exist side by side, invisible yet real nonetheless, and in focusing on our physical world, we close our eyes to the greater part of creation.

There is much more that is unknown than is known, especially within ourselves and, whether we realise it or not, our souls partake in a much richer life.

All that is required to see it is to change our point of view. Even a simple deck of cards can help us to see within ourselves, to access the deeper memories that symbols trigger within us.

Great forces move through our world, yet they are not of our world, they stand apart. There are two points at which all of our simple lives touch eternity, death and love.

But the greater of the two by far is love.

THE FOOL.

You want me to do what?

The train journey hadn't been good. Multiple delays meant they now risked running into colleagues who would be congregating at the hotel to check-in. To make matters worse, although they were seated side by side, he couldn't hold her the way he ached to so they sat, occasionally touching one another's knees. Putting his head back, he closed his eyes, smiling to himself as he reminisced about what had been a late night and a very early morning.

It was the hottest September day on record in London. After a journey on the underground and lugging suitcases through the streets, they were both hot and sweaty. Arriving at the hotel, he asked if their colleagues had checked in. Thankfully they hadn't.

If they bumped into them now, they would have no choice but to accompany them on their various appointments when all they both really wanted to do was go straight to a bedroom, any bedroom, to make love.

"Could you do me a favour please, give me a room as far away from the others as possible?" Graeme asked the clerk at the desk.

"I'll do my best sir," she said.

Taking their luggage to their respective rooms, Graeme jumped in the shower. A few moments later, he heard a light tap on the door. Opening it, he pulled Katie inside, he was kissing her before she could speak and she responded eagerly, her tongue exploring his.

Pulling away, she turned on the air conditioning then went into the bathroom while Graeme took off his towel and climbed into bed, pulling the sheet up to his face. He pretended to be shy, peeking over the top, when really it was the aircon blowing like the Mistral making it a little chilly. Katie liked the cold air and, by the time they were in full swing of making love, he knew that he'd appreciate it too.

A moment later, she stood at the end of the bed starting to undress, taking off her favourite light blue t-shirt covered in love hearts, followed by her jeans. She was stunning in just a bra and tiny knickers leaving little to the imagination. Graeme felt the blood coursing faster in his veins as she removed her bra before joining him in bed. They were indeed learning about each other as Katie had promised they would all those months ago and now they both knew their lovemaking would last for several hours.

The feel of her hair on his cheek, her soft skin next to his, her breasts against his chest were all now familiar and delightful. He kissed her forehead, face and neck, working his way around her cheeks as he whispered, "Te amo Katie, I love you."

Katie responded with a moan of pleasure as Graeme began to gently explore her body. He could feel her even before his hands made contact with her skin, such was the presence she exuded. He ran his fingers over her cheeks, her brow then down her neck. She spread her arms wide as he caressed and kissed them from the tips of her fingers to the curve of her breast, being careful not to touch them, not yet.

Turning her over, he gently massaged her back running his fingers up either side of her spine; then with his hands spread wide he massaged her from her shoulders down to her buttocks before gently peeling off her knickers on his journey. Next, he worked his way down each leg, kissing and stroking her, being careful not to miss an inch. Sitting astride her, he ran his hands up from her thighs, over her buttocks and up her back, then leant forward to kiss her, mirroring the journey with his lips and tongue, that his hands had just taken.

Graeme was hard and wet now, the head of his shaft glistening as it ran over her buttocks. He couldn't resist stroking her, gently massaging her thighs and as he did so, her legs parted just enough to feel that she too was wet. Supporting his body with his arms, he gently explored the gap, probing with his manhood until he felt the warmth of her surround him. They writhed together for a few moments before he reached underneath her to fondle her breasts knowing he had to stop, to withdraw from her so that he could take more time to enjoy all she had to offer.

He turned her over again until she was prone beneath him, her legs open wide, waiting for him to return to her. No, not yet, he thought, as he began to work Katie's breasts gently, first from the sides, then underneath and on top, being careful not to touch her nipples, his tongue would do that, lightly tracing the circle of her aureoles. Then he flicked his tongue across her nipples, alternately sucking them, licking them before blowing cool air across them until they stood erect in anticipation of what was to come.

Graeme looked down at Katie. Almost totally shaven, except for the small area surrounding the lips of her vulva, she was a joy to behold, the tip of her clitoris just visible as he ran the head of his penis up and down against it, gently pushing her lips apart. As he did so, he could not help himself, slipping inside her once more, relishing her tightness around him, grasping him eagerly. She worked her hips back and forth, relaxing, becoming wetter as her body prepared to receive him. Feeling himself filling up, getting tighter, he ached for a release from the torment, but he had to resist.

Pulling away once more, he started working Katie gently with his fingers, before going down on her, licking her gently, tasting her delights. He kissed her belly letting his tongue roll down her mons pubis, then he kissed the inside of her thighs before running his tongue around either side of her vulva. She moaned softly as he ran his fingers from inside her, up along the ridge of her vulva to her clitoris then back inside her in a gentle, rhythmic movement, attuned to her body.

Now eager for her touch too he shifted his position to lay next to Katie, continuing to explore her with his fingers, aching to be inside her again while she gently caressed him. She continued to moan gently, her head turned into him, eyes closed until he could feel the excitement mounting under the gentle motion of his fingers as she explored new boundaries. As he pulled away slightly Katie lifted her thighs to follow his fingers. "Oh don't stop," she whispered and as he continued his caress, her body shuddered, waves of pleasure spreading over her.

Holding her tightly, he whispered, "I have got you babe. I love you Katie."

As she sighed contentedly, still holding her tightly, he could feel her heart beating against his chest.

When she had composed herself, she pushed him back, sat astride him, her hair gently playing on his chest as she worked herself up and down on him. He could feel the cool air from the conditioning unit running down her body as his hands caressed her back. He could wait no longer; his hips pressed hard against her, he released his seed then they both collapsed together, slipping into a loving embrace in each other's arms.

"That was fantastic," she said. "I think I'm learning to make love."

"Oh you are," said Graeme

"We should write a book," she said, as they both started laughing.

"I'd be no good at that sort of thing, besides who

reads books these days. I'd love to read your memoirs though, Katie."

"Let's worry about it tomorrow," she said as she kissed him one last time

"I will you give you a wake-up call - about six am."

Hmm, tomorrow, thought Graeme, as he drifted off to sleep in her arms, with a song gently playing in his head, *The Rose*, the most beautiful song he'd ever heard. 'How appropriate.'

The next morning Katie asked again. "Write a book for me."

"What?"

"Write a book for me. You make me laugh."

They lay together, naked in bed as he looked at her. She was so beautiful. He looked into her dark brown eyes, like deep pools he could fall into and drown in; he knew he could refuse her nothing. But a book? That's no small undertaking, it could take years.

She was persistent. "Write a book for me."

"Okay. I will, if you help me."

As he looked around the bare room, Graeme had no idea then that this journey would lead them through worlds and lives undreamt of by either of them.

"This has to be the worst hotel I've ever stayed in and I've stayed in some dumps," he said.

It looked like the sort of place you rented by the hour. The 'wardrobe' consisted of two hooks on the wall at the end of the bed. There were no tea or coffee facilities and nothing to stand a cup on even if there had been. Walking into the room the previous afternoon it was so spartan he'd doubted that there was actually even a window behind the grey blind pulled down to the floor. He'd opened the blind and, although there was a window, had he been able to open it he could have reached across to the next building as the gap was so small.

On the plus side, it was cheap. God knows it was cheap - in every sense, and it had aircon which definitely had its uses. This was a business trip so, while the company would be grateful for the thrift, the colleague who booked it was going to get some stick over this when they met for dinner later.

" Oh, I think it's been fab here," said Katie.

He had to agree, it had been wonderful, although he couldn't put the reasons why on Trip Advisor.

"What sort of book?" he asked.

"You can write about my life, about making love… with me. I like the way you make love to me. You take me to a place I haven't been to before, it's just fabulous."

Oh God, she certainly does know how to flatter a guy.

"What, you mean like mummy porn?" he asked.

Her smile and laughter transformed the whole drab room as she began to giggle. Graeme felt his heart singing. Knowing he loved her, in that moment he also realised that there was no hope for him.

"Okay," he said, "how about something like this... She walked out of the bathroom, standing at the end of the bed wrapped in a small, white towel. Her pendulous breasts heaving as she breathed slowly, rhythmically, he couldn't take his eyes off her. Her nipples were standing proud in the air-conditioned room, like bullets ready to impale him to the bed. "

She started laughing again and he couldn't help joining

in, as he continued with the scenario. "The bottom of the towel, hanging like a pussy pelmet revealing a glimpse of her very tidy downstairs…"

They both collapsed in a fit of giggles.

"I've no idea what a pussy pelmet is," he said. "I thought old people used pelmets for curtains."

"Write about my life… and how you make love to me," she repeated.

"Okay. If you think of the things you want me to include, when I see you next we can make a start."

They cuddled up closer. Then before making love again, Graeme asked her if she was happy.

"Yes. I didn't think you would like me as much as you do."

You have got to be kidding, he thought, as his mind drifted back to the first afternoon in December 2015 when this life's adventure began.

The Alchemist

Lately, Graeme had taken to walking in the evening for a breath of fresh air before bed so he had been sleeping well. He was getting over a recent bout of man flu, but, despite his improving health, the small voices in his head hadn't stopped. They'd been building for a long time and lately had begun to shout.

"What are you doing with your life?"

Despite a full life, family, friends, even a great career - in truth, the answer was, "Nothing."

Just marking time with a routine of getting up, going to work, coming home, a brief walk then bed. Monotony can be a blessing to help one cope, as well as a curse to underline the meaninglessness of things.

"How the fuck do people become tax lawyers?" he

wondered.

Fortunately, Graeme wasn't a lawyer. He was a jovial guy in his fifties with a paunch and fair hair, tinged grey at the edges. Although he wasn't bad looking, the tracks of his life were etched on his face and hands. He was industrious, intelligent and had worked diligently for over thirty years before suddenly abandoning his career to join a new tech company. In the last few years, his home city of Edinburgh had become alive with new possibilities bringing him to a sudden realisation that it was now or never if he was going to grab his life with both hands.

Having made the jump, he needed a team to help him, people with financial industry experience, who also had some imagination. Fortunately, with the world still reeling from the worst financial crisis in history, there was no shortage of candidates, but it wasn't just anyone Graeme wanted, he needed experienced people who could also adapt to the new world that was emerging. He wanted Katie.

He didn't really know Katie, they'd only met once briefly, almost a decade earlier, though he'd followed her career. She worked over two hundred miles away in Manchester and had carved out a reputation as a high calibre businesswoman. The fact that she was stunning was a distinct bonus and he spent far longer than he should have staring at the picture on her LinkedIn profile.

She was smiling, as she always seemed to be, with a friend in a bar, along with a guy in the background trying to photobomb what looked like a selfie. Katie was in her fifties too, petite, with brown eyes and brown hair with blond highlights. She had the figure of a model, even now she could have any man she wanted.

What on earth made Graeme think he could persuade her to join him in a start-up business in a different country?

Well, he thought, nothing ventured and all that. He sent her a message to ask if she fancied meeting for a coffee. He knew that a lot was going on at her current workplace and somehow he timed it just right to pique her interest. She agreed to coffee on December 30th at The Alchemist in Manchester.

When the day came, Graeme was unsure if he would make the meeting due to widespread flooding which had disrupted the trains, particularly on both sides of the Pennines, but he reflected that fate has a plan for all of us.

The train was initially delayed but as his journey progressed, the carriages seemed to be gliding over the sea; there was so much water in the fields on either side of the tracks. It was an almost surreal, dreamlike journey.

My very own journey to Avalon, he thought. Had he known then where this train would eventually lead him, his thoughts might have been very different, but, for now, he was enjoying his own mystical journey.

Arriving in Manchester and realising he was early for his meeting, he headed to a cafe to think about what he would say to Katie. Sitting with his coffee, he looked through the window at the rain bouncing off the concrete and running like a river down the hill towards him. He smiled as he pondered on the symbolism of it, washing away the past, leaving a clean slate for new beginnings

- a good omen.

At the appointed time, through a break in the rain, he made his way to The Alchemist bar, ordered a glass of red wine then settled down to wait for Katie.

Katie had suspected nothing when Graeme's message dropped into her inbox. Hmm, she thought. That's interesting.

Guys her own age didn't light her candle, but she had quite fancied Graeme when they'd met some years earlier. Looking at his profile on LinkedIn, he's still quite good looking, she thought. The picture stirred memories of that night when she had felt that some kind of spark had passed between them even though their meeting was brief and conversation short.

She remembered that he had attractive blue eyes, a cheeky grin and she'd found the soft burr of his Scottish accent sexy. She pondered the message for a few moments. Why does he want to see me?

She did a little digging on his new company and half an hour later, none the wiser, she thought, a coffee can't hurt.

She smiled. "besides, I'd like to see him again, if only for the cheeky banter.

Donna, a colleague and one of her best friends, asked, "What's up?"

"Do you remember Graeme? He wants to meet me for a coffee."

"Uh oh," said Donna.

She'd also been present that night when they'd met all those years ago.

"You fancied him, didn't you?"

They both laughed.

When the day came to meet, Katie was surprised at how excited she felt. Whether she had wanted Graeme to fancy her, or just wanted to tease him, she wasn't sure as she dressed provocatively in sexy little boots, a short skirt, a matching low cut top and, despite being a little nervous, she set off to The Alchemist.

As she entered the bar, she felt the warmth of Graeme's smile then, saying 'hello' she leant towards him as he bent to kiss her on the cheek.

He's still cute, she thought and, from the outset, it felt more like a date than a business meeting. They made their way to a table, ordered a bottle of wine and started to relax. The conversation was wide-ranging, catching up on gossip or sharing news about mutual acquaintances as they sought common ground. They discussed Graeme's new venture, Katie's aspirations, and, as the afternoon wore on, they ate lunch then ordered more wine. A lot more wine in fact as Katie took in less and less about the business Graeme had come to discuss.

Suddenly she realised that she was more interested in him.

She wanted to know if he'd shared that strange feeling the first time they'd met.

"Do you remember the night we met?" she asked.

Of course, he did, how could he forget? The sparks that had jumped between them would have been visible to anyone watching. Yet, the strangest thing of all, was that nothing had happened between them. Their conversation had been brief, yet almost a decade later, despite the time that had elapsed, they both remembered every word, every detail, every feeling.

"I've had too much to drink and I'm worried about the weather, I think I'll stay here tonight," said Graeme. "Can you recommend a hotel?"

Katie was streetwise immediately wondering what Graeme had in mind, but he did live a long way away, so she dismissed her concerns and recommended The Johan Hotel offering to show him where it was.

Half an hour later, after a painless check-in, Graeme relaxed now that he had somewhere to stay.

KNIGHT of SWORDS.

Making War not Love

Although he had intended to stay the night, several hours later, almost politely rather than passionately, Graeme kissed Katie goodbye at Piccadilly station then headed off to find his train. Even as they parted, Graeme knew he had to see her again, no matter what the cost. He was almost in shock at the thoughts running through his head. She was beautiful and her experience with men was evident from the time they'd just spent together, yet something bothered him as he reviewed the events that had occurred earlier in the hotel bedroom.

He'd bought a bottle of wine, borrowed two glasses from the bar downstairs and headed back to the room where he'd left Katie. He needed a shower and, when he came out of the bathroom, he found her laid on the bed.

He lay beside her in nothing but a towel as they started to kiss and fondle one another.

Like an inexperienced teenager, he struggled to undress her, removing her top, her skirt, then he fumbled hopelessly with her bra. Katie was well endowed so it was fastened tightly; she slowly removed it for him revealing her breasts in all their glory then she reached under his towel and began working him. She had a very tight grip which belied her petite size as she squeezed him harder and harder.

It had the desired effect. He couldn't wait to slip off her knickers, she pulled him on top of her and the sex began almost immediately, with only a brief pause for her to turn over, rest on her knees; raising her perfect buttocks in the air so that he could take her from behind. She reached around holding onto his balls as he penetrated her pulling him deeper, all the time squeezing him hard.

Too soon he was spent; it hadn't lasted more than half an hour.

Standing on the station platform a few hours later, he suddenly realised what was bothering him. For all her boyfriends, years of marriage and the occasional 'bit of fun,' men had always desired her for their own pleasure, to possess her and enjoy her. She had never been with a man who really wanted to make love to her - a gentle lover, one who would make love to Katie, for Katie.

Graeme considered himself a gentle lover but, as he took his seat on the train, he felt as though he'd just been in a battle. His feeling was confirmed when; having arrived home several hours later he undressed for bed.

His nether regions were black and blue and the shaft of his penis ached. For sure, it had been pleasurable in a physical sense, but the sex was mechanical, pornographic almost, lacking the sensitivity of lovers exploring one another.

He would have work to do, but he smiled as he drifted off to sleep thinking to himself, I can make love better than that.

Katie meanwhile was heading back to her home in Cheshire having her own reflections on the evening's events. She couldn't remember who'd made the first move. The sex had been raw, needy, driven by lust and fuelled by alcohol but, when Graeme had suddenly decided to take the train home, alarm bells had started ringing. Her concerns magnified as he said a quick goodbye at the station. Oh God she thought, he's regretting what's just happened between us.

Although she had no way of knowing it, the only reason Graeme had left was so that he didn't have to leave at 4 am the following morning to face a long, challenging commute back to Edinburgh on Hogmanay, the busiest day of the year.

When she woke the next morning, a sense of dread washed over her. Did she regret what she'd done? No, but she didn't want Graeme to think that she made a habit of that sort of thing. Thinking she wouldn't hear from him again, she decided to file the whole episode in a mental box and closed the lid firmly. She felt sad, knowing that for a business meeting they'd both overstepped the mark, by some considerable distance.

Two hundred and fifty miles away, Graeme knew it too, but he had to speak to Katie and reassure her. So, first thing in the morning, he sent a brief message promising to call her later. Although the conversation was stilted he promised to contact her when he'd developed his plans for the business further. He wanted her to give some serious thought to what he'd said about joining the company.

Katie settled back into her routine at work. It was over a month before Graeme contacted her again, asking if they could meet in February when he would be in Manchester again. She'd been discussing the job with Donna and had decided that she wouldn't be joining him in his new venture, although she felt that she owed it to him to tell him face to face.

Graeme knew nothing of the conversations Katie had been having but had already accepted it was a long shot that she would join him so he was delighted when she agreed to meet him again. He made a day of it, catching up with old business contacts and, about three in the afternoon, made his way to his hotel to check in.

More in hope than expectation, he wandered out to a nearby supermarket for a bottle of white wine to take back to his room. He also bought some condoms. Last time they'd taken chances and, while Graeme hated the things, if he was lucky enough to be that close to Katie again, they'd be there if she wanted him to use them.

As he paid, a pretty young girl at the till, perhaps in her mid-twenties examined him closely, clearly wondering what someone of his age was doing with a shopping basket that consisted of just wine, condoms and a corkscrew bottle opener. He gave her a rather withering look back then; in response to her silent questioning, he said out loud, "I'm practising drinking responsibly."

Laughing quietly to himself, he left the shop, returning to the hotel to put his shopping in his room before heading to the bar. He ordered an expensive bottle of Chablis then sat down to wait for Katie.

Walking into the bar, when Katie saw Graeme with the ice bucket, wine and glasses her feelings caught her off balance. Sensing that instant attraction once more, even before she sat down she knew that they'd end up in bed again. When they'd finished the wine, he mentioned that there was another bottle on ice in his room and the idea of a new job faded from Katie's mind. At that moment, all of her interest focused on what Graeme could offer in the bedroom.

Once inside his room, there were few preliminaries before they lay almost naked on the bed. Contemplating the perfect curves of her body, Graeme was conscious of his feelings from the last encounter and he wanted to treat Katie gently, as a woman should be treated.

"What do you like Katie?"

"We'll find out what each other likes, won't we."

It was as if she was unsure herself, waiting to find something she'd searched for all her life but had never found.

This time Katie made the first move, sitting astride Graeme letting her long hair tickle his face and neck as she moved further down his body until she was at last in the position to explore him with her tongue, tasting him for the first time.

"Be gentle with me," he whispered, but she was eager, too eager.

Again, it was as though Katie was acting out a sex scene to please an audience that didn't exist, rather than to satisfy the lover she was with.

Graeme pulled her up to him, quickly reciprocating as he listened to her moan gently, but he was also too eager. All too soon they were making love and he was spent.

"Stay with me," he said.

"I can't stay the night. I don't have to leave until about nine though. We have time for a repeat performance."

Graeme reminded her of the condoms they hadn't used. Katie just smiled, poured them each a glass of wine and ten minutes later they were once again engaged in a sexual battle.

At the appointed time, Katie left. Graeme wanted to walk her to the station but she refused. She simply kissed him, walked out and, as the door closed in front of him, he felt a strange feeling welling up from deep inside, struggling to make itself known. He wondered if he'd ever see her again.

As she left, Katie took stock of her thoughts. The last train home was at 9.30pm so she'd pushed it to the limit already. She'd had a fab time with Graeme and on the work front, he'd said enough to encourage her to meet with her prospective new colleagues, Bruce and Paul. Although he'd offered to walk her to the station, an independent Katie knew where she was going and, after several glasses of wine, felt capable of looking after herself. She'd kissed him then sped away, and as she marched to the station, her head spun.

Will I ever see him again? Guess if I get the job I will, but how will that work? I'm sleeping with the bloody Director. You don't do things by halves do you Katie?

Anyway, it's not up to him it's up to Bruce, as, technically, he'll be my boss. Will he like me? Let's meet Bruce, see if I think I can work with him then make a choice. Then where does that leave me with Graeme? I'm probably just a bit of fun. I wonder if he has sex with others on a regular basis? Oh, God, I've made the situation totally confusing and I really like him. I hope I get to see him again, but if not, I'll just have to put it down to a nice experience.

The station was deathly quiet. As she sat alone on the platform, she received a text from **Karen**. They'd been friends for many years and she now lived in the house that her friend had sold her in 2002.

Katie replied, saying, *I've just had another meeting with Graeme.*

Karen immediately called, wanting to know all the details and if she wanted the job.

I really don't know. I guess I need to know more about the role, the salary, most importantly, whether I can work with my new boss.

Katie said that her meeting had just been with the Director Graeme, that he was nice and they'd chatted over a bottle of wine although she wasn't ready to discuss anything else.

Karen wished her luck and said that the job sounded perfect for her.

Over the hill and far away

Boarding the train home, Katie still wasn't sure. A career change was a big thing at her time of life. As *the* top performer she was under no pressure where she was, she had to be sure she wasn't making a mistake. Graeme had suggested that she meet a couple of the team who were due to be in the city soon to get their take on life in the emerging world of fintech, so she agreed.

Although years of practice meant she never showed it, Katie felt nervous at the upcoming meeting. She put on her mask of makeup, a brightly coloured new dress and set off. An early text from Graeme asked if she was okay and for her to call him later, which calmed her nerves a little, realising that he must want her to do well. An hour later, she stepped off the train in Manchester, walked to a cafe called The Kettle and waited for Bruce and Paul.

When they arrived, they weren't how she'd imagined them. Both were casually dressed, Bruce was tall with glasses, Paul was pale with bleach blond hair. Bruce did most of the talking, only coming up for air occasionally. Paul was quiet; altogether more serious, still, they both seemed to be decent guys.

They told Katie about the business. Although she'd heard it before from Graeme, what really struck her was their enthusiasm, leaving her excited at the prospect of working for a new business and being able to make a difference. An hour or so later, she said goodbye then made her way along King Street to the office where she'd been summoned by her boss because her sales records weren't up to date. Yes, she thought, if they ask me for an interview I'll go. Why not? I'm consistently the top performer yet I'm about to get bollocked for not having completed a few entries on a bloody stupid system.

Bruce and Paul had both formed a favourable opinion of Katie. They had common ground as they too had once worked for the same company albeit in London, so after a quick chat with Graeme the following day, an appointment was made for a formal interview in Edinburgh.

The day of the interview Katie awoke early from an uncomfortable sleep. She took competitive situations seriously. She had bought a new dress, booked her hotel and set off with time to spare. Paul had given her a steer on some oddball questions that might get thrown in so she felt relaxed. She thought about what animal she would be and decided on a dolphin. What colour would she choose if that was asked? She wasn't sure. If it was a question about what fruit, she'd say she'd be an apple.

How had this had become the norm? How had corporate life become so silly? she wondered.

Gradually though, these thoughts faded. As her mind drifted back to Graeme she smiled at the prospect of seeing him again.

Their last meeting had been a month ago. She knew he'd be there, involved in a small part of the interview and that she'd feel self-conscious answering questions in front of him, but she smiled. "He must like me, or he wouldn't have given me the opportunity."

He already knew that she could do the job, even so there was a procedure to follow. They'd had a brief conversation in which Katie had asked candidly if he might be around afterwards. Although he'd said yes, she really wasn't sure if he was just being polite. The nearer she got to her destination, the more nervous she felt. She was unsure whether it was the interview that was bothering her or seeing Graeme again. There was something about him she couldn't put her finger on, she could feel the pull of 'something' drawing her to him.

Arriving in Edinburgh she checked into the hotel, changed quickly then set out again for the company's head office in St Andrews Square. As she sat nervously in reception, Graeme arrived and said hello. It felt so surreal, she wondered if she had dreamt of their previous encounters because this was so business-like. Then she pulled her mind back into focus. Had she really expected anything else?

The interview was split. First, with her prospective line manager and HR followed by a second with two of the directors, one of whom was Graeme.

Katie struggled with the second part, feeling it hadn't gone well. Although Graeme's questions were familiar because they had similar work backgrounds, this was not the case with the second participant, his questions threw her.

Afterwards, Graeme walked her to her car promising to catch up later. Katie returned to her hotel on the outskirts of the city pondering on the events of the afternoon, her competitive nature revealing itself in her thoughts. Was she bothered how it had gone? Of course she was, and there was something else. What had Graeme thought about her? Would he still come to see her at the hotel as he had promised?

If he did text to say he couldn't make it, then so be it. Eventually, pushing her concerns aside, she put on a fresh dress, touched up her lipstick, went into the bar and ordered a bottle of wine.

Around 6.30pm, Graeme walked in and he didn't seem relaxed. He suggested getting a bite to eat, so they crossed the road to a Chinese restaurant where neither of them ate much. She knew he had a cold, that he was feeling rough but Katie's insecurities were starting to emerge. Added to her concerns over how the interview had gone, she was wondering if it would be his excuse to make a run for it.

Graeme had no such thoughts. He asked for the bill and they returned to the hotel. She wanted him to stay but was still waiting for him to say he'd better go. He didn't. Instead, he got his bag from his car. He was so gentle, so caring as if he had all the time in the world to make Katie feel special.

In truth, Graeme felt as though he did indeed have all the time in the world. With Katie, time just seemed to fade away as he entered another world.

It was hot in the room that night and the air conditioning wasn't working. Katie usually slept on the edge of the bed with no contact and, every time she woke, she was aware of this person who wanted to touch her, hold her, feel her, and it felt strange. Waking in the morning next to a man she didn't know that well made her a little nervous but he held her, stroked her gently, making that morning an experience that she would not forget.

Later, back in the office, Graeme argued with his colleague. With a small team, he could take no chances, he wanted Katie because she was proven, she was a winner. His colleague favoured younger people, digital natives, not someone who had always worked for large companies.

"I need the experience to sell our systems," said Graeme. Big finance companies won't buy from kids"

Graeme knew that although big companies often paid well, they weren't good at valuing their people. They did, however, invest heavily in training and development, so many of their staff had strong transferable skills, he himself was proof of that. In the end they compromised asking Katie back to meet the wider team a few weeks later.

Graeme wasn't in the office that day, but he wanted to

meet Katie afterwards. If he was honest with himself, his reasons were mixed. He had missed her and he wanted to understand how she felt afterwards, to see if she had changed her mind. His attraction to her was deeper than he understood, he too could feel the inexorable pull, like gravity, drawing him to her.

After her meeting, Bruce walked Katie to her car. They chatted and he said he'd be in touch once Graeme returned from his holiday. Katie got into her car, thinking, that was a strange meeting. Although she knew it was more about whether they could work with her.

Graeme had already been in touch and agreed to meet Katie at 4 pm at the Crown Hotel in Peebles, which was on her route home. Setting off with butterflies in her stomach, eager to see him, still she could not help wondering if this might be the last time. Since the first interview, Katie had thrown herself back into her current job. Donna had even commented over her refound focus, assuming that she was going to stay put regardless. Speeding down the country lanes, she thought it might not be a bad thing, at least this, - whatever it is - can't go any further.

On the other hand, she really was becoming quite fond of Graeme.

"Let's see what happens when I get there."

Half an hour later, she was surprised to see him waiting just inside the doorway as she entered the hotel. Graeme's eyes lit up as he smiled. She was taken off guard by his passionate kiss, yet reciprocated without hesitation.

Katie was still wondering, where this would go if

they do offer her a job? Should she take it, or did she need to consider how this relationship might develop? Yes, working for the same company would be exciting, it allow her to see him more but what unforeseen dangers would that bring?

Graeme's feelings mirrored Katie's. Was this really a good idea? He felt as though he couldn't bear to let her go, but after a few pleasant hours together, she drove away to consider her future.

A week later, she took the opportunity to meet Bruce again in Manchester. It was this meeting, rather than the encounters with Graeme that finally allayed her fears. It was obvious that Bruce loved his work, so, when she was offered the job, Katie said yes. Her life was being remoulded, reborn and, although she didn't realise it, she was being given a chance to change tracks in more ways than one; to lay to rest ghosts that had been unsettled for untold ages.

Through the Garden Gate

Three months of gardening leave between jobs was new to Katie and it coincided with her annual girls' trip to Ayia Napa with her best friend Jenny plus four other girls. Few people knew how to party like Katie and she enjoyed a solid week of fun in the sun. The days consisted of falling out of bed at midday, 'breakfast' on the beach then winding back up with strawberry daiquiris before heading to 'Mambo's' for lots more drinks.

Childhood friends, Jenny and Katie had been inseparable at school. Although they had followed different career paths, with Jenny going into nursing, they partied together most weekends and were closer than sisters, sharing even their most secret thoughts.

Jenny was pretty too, a little over five feet tall, slim

build, blonde hair with blue eyes, so it was little wonder they stood out from the crowd. The bars were always full of men with all eyes on Katie who dressed provocatively and loved being the centre of attention. She always brought the girls into the conversations, but this was only a warm-up, she was simply surveying the scene in anticipation of the main event. After the afternoon party, they would head back to their hotel for a short nap before getting 'scrubbed up' in anticipation of the long night ahead.

Katie knew that she scrubbed up well.

Ayia Napa's wild reputation is well-founded. Lots of hen and, stag parties, bright lights, numerous bars, boys and girls on every corner offering free shots or cheap drinks, to attract people into their bars, particularly parties of women. Jenny knew that Katie loved to dance, that she would want to go up The Strip, the main street, before heading to the Revolution Bar where the black midget drummer played every night. Although it wasn't really the other girls' scene, they humoured her for an hour or two each night so that she could get her music fix.

The nights always ended up in the same place, 'The Plaza', a 'copping off' place full of men and women looking to pull at the end of a drink-fuelled night.

Well into the early hours, when she could take no more alcohol, she'd go home, usually alone. The hotel was nearby so Katie, being independent, would just say "Right, I'm off, have fun." then off she'd trot.

At least that's how it seemed in Katie's head, although the truth was far darker.

Over the years she'd had some unpleasant, very scary experiences. In time she'd need to share these with Graeme for the sake of her own sanity, but, for the moment, she couldn't conceive of baring her soul like that to any man.

She told Jenny about Graeme. Showing her pictures of him, describing their affair as 'just a bit of fun'. They discussed their home lives and their relationships with their husbands. Katie wondered why she'd started something with Graeme and where it might lead.

It's not uncommon, she thought. She knew Jenny and her husband had been having problems for the past few years which had resulted in them both seeking comfort elsewhere. Jenny was in love with a guy from Birmingham she had met in Ayia Napa a few years ago. He was normally in Cyprus at the same time as her, but this last year he hadn't been and Jenny now knew why.

Social media is a remarkable thing when you want to share, but not everything is meant for sharing. Jenny was linked with her lover on Facebook. She'd spotted that he'd had a stag-do in Prague a month earlier which meant that he was recently married. Even though he'd never promised her anything, saying that he was happy with his life she was hurt. Now that she was back in Ayia Napa Jenny was feeling it more intensely, she was really missing him.

Katie too found herself distracted with thoughts of Graeme. She texted him regularly, sent him pictures and hoped it wouldn't be too long before she could see him again.

The rest of her leave seemed to pass all too quickly. She would get up late, sit in the sunshine weather permitting, go drinking with friends, shop or walk her dog. She enjoyed it although feeling the days were short, she was wondering how she would fit in her full-time job when she eventually got back to it. There was another major event occurring in her life too, which would also have a far-reaching effect on her.

Her son Tom's girlfriend Carly had given birth to a daughter, Helen. Their joy at her arrival was tempered due to complications and Helen's introduction to the world was via an operating theatre. Katie had rushed to the hospital where she cried tears of joy when she saw Tom with a massive grin on his face.

He said, "I'm a Dad, Helen is here." He was waiting for an update from the doctors, but Carly would be in hospital for a few more days.

Katie spent the next few weeks going back and forth, providing support and supplies. Fortunately Carly made good progress leaving Katie relieved as her date to start work with her new employer was fast approaching.

When she told Graeme about her new granddaughter, he had congratulated her.

She thought it strange when he added, "She will be a great comfort to you, a light in the darkness."

"Why do you say that?"

"Her name - it means bright shining one."

Graeme had arranged for the new recruits to meet in Newcastle for an inaugural team meeting towards the end of May and he invited Katie. He would understand if she was conflicted as technically she still had a few weeks before her start date, never the less he hoped she could make it. It would be low key, just to meet the team, and of course, a chance to see him again so she agreed.

He travelled to Newcastle with Bruce. They met Paul at the station and they had just parked up when Katie arrived. Unable to find a space, she absent-mindedly rolled around the car park almost running them over. Oh God! she thought. How nervous am I? Eventually, she found a space, got out of the car, acting casually, said, "Hello," then apologised, laughing it off as their fault for being in her way but she was embarrassed leaving her throat dry.

The meeting was a relaxed affair, an opportunity to lay out the basic strategy and get to know one another a little. The intention was to have dinner together later that evening then see where the night took them. There were only three more team members to meet, Anthony from the South-East, Paul from Yorkshire, and David, who ran the operations team in Edinburgh. They formally introduced themselves and Katie felt embarrassed when asked to say a little about herself. Usually confident, Graeme's presence made her uncomfortable. She was feeling like a teenager, shy in front of her lover.

At five, Graeme closed the meeting allowing them to make their way back to the Mount Vernon Hotel. The plan was to meet for a quick drink in the bar at six and then head for a great restaurant in the city called La Paz for about seven.

When Katie entered the bar, Graeme was already there, chatting to a pretty barmaid who managed to extract a large tip because his mind was clearly elsewhere. She was feeling nervous and wondered why. He seemed so relaxed; so calm. That was one of the things she loved about him, he seemed to make all situations calm, no panic.

In fact, his feelings were a mirror of her own.

She wore a black lace top over a black diamanté bra and, one by one, as her male colleagues arrived, Graeme noticed that each in turn had their breath taken away. He thought that Anthony was going to faint, such was the effect she had. As they chatted, he scanned the bar noticing that, without exception everyone was looking at her and he could sense their emotions. The men exuded admiration, tinged with jealousy that she wasn't with them. The women almost disbelief, as they also sensed the sheer sexual magnetism which highlighted their own imagined inadequacies. For anyone who could feel the world the way that Graeme did, it was overwhelming.

They wandered over to the restaurant, ordered food and wine and the dinner was fun, with plenty of laughing, joking and mutual piss-taking. Graeme wanted to cultivate a relaxed atmosphere. Their team would always be small, so they needed to get on well as they'd need to rely on one another for support. The banter was cheeky at times so he always looked to Katie to make sure she was comfortable as the only woman in the team. She was. She gave far more than she took in that regard with the others sparking off her as she brought the group to life. Graeme watched them suss one another out, establishing their respective niches in the group dynamic.

Katie only knew one place in the pecking order, top or nowhere.

She wanted to look at Graeme across the table but knew that if they ended up staring into one another's eyes, the game would be over before it had begun. So she kept her glances furtive and they held one another's gaze only as long as they dared. After the meal Graeme made his excuses, leaving in order to give Bruce a chance to bond with his team. After they had visited a couple more bars, although the guys didn't want her to leave, when a suitable opportunity arose Katie also made her excuses to return to the hotel.

Graeme was happy with his room away from prying eyes on the 14th floor. Katie knew where he was and, as she left the elevator, she took off her shoes tip-toeing towards his door. It was late when Graeme heard a gentle knock. As he opened the door, "Room service," she announced with her broad smile that lit up her face.

"Oh wow!" he said, inviting her in.

He opened the bottle of white wine he had brought and they sat on the bed while Katie chided him for leaving her.

"You know I have to give the team room to bond, give Bruce a chance to assert his authority," he said. "Besides, you wouldn't like me if I were drunk and not at my best would you?"

"No," she laughed, "I wouldn't."

They started to kiss and undress one another.

"So what do you think of false boobs," she asked, shaking them at him.

Obviously, this wasn't the first time he'd seen them

or enjoyed playing with them, but there'd been no discussion so he was caught off balance.

"Er… well, I like them," he said, but honestly, it was because this it was the only way he'd ever known her. Well-endowed or not, it was the intimacy with her he craved so in that context it didn't really matter to him.

Graeme lay on the bed and Katie pushed his legs apart so that she could position herself on her knees between them. It was late, the curtains were open letting in the neon lights from the surrounding city that made the shadows dance across the walls and ceilings. Still, there was no fear of being overlooked. She looked down at Graeme who was now fully erect, "That's a big willy." she said.

He smiled, knowing it wasn't true, that she was just buttering him up. He would have laughed out loud, had it not been impolite. A moment later, all such thoughts faded as she worked her magic. As he looked down, he could see her backside in the air, her skin like china glistened in the reflected neon light. He moved her long blond hair to one side to watch her bearing down on him.

How does she do that? he wondered then his head swam as he drifted off to another place from which he would not return for several hours.

Afterwards, she moved to the edge of the large bed out of habit to drift off to sleep. She slept so quietly, like a small child, as if she was trying to cocoon herself, hiding away in the night which seemed to embrace her. Graeme shivered as he thought of Nyx, the goddess whom the ancient Greeks believed to be the personification of night. It was said that even the king of their gods, the mighty Zeus feared her, along with her three daughters, the Fates, who ruled over all things.

Graeme reached out pulling her closer, he held her all night. If Katie was to be his fate he was content.

The next morning, she arose to return to her room so that she could prepare to meet the team for breakfast before heading home. Watching her dress, Graeme looked at her bra which she didn't put on. It seemed huge, even to hold her ample assets. She in turn was watching him, laughing.

"You can keep it if you like. It would make a great hat."

"Thankfully my ears are too small for it," he said, laughing.

As Katie headed back to her room, she thought, Phew, good sex, wow! Yes, he made my toes curl. How good is that! I'm starting to really like being with this man. I hope that's the best room service he's ever had. Katie needn't have worried, she'd touched him on a level she couldn't yet understand, but she would in time.

Driving homeward, Katie was on cloud nine, singing at the top of her voice. She called Donna, who immediately realised that she was far too happy for this to be an ordinary day. "What's going on Katie? Or, on second thoughts, do I really need to know?"

Katie skated over the question. "It's just starting a new job with nice people, we need a night out to catch up."

THE HIEROPHANT

1633

St Peter's, Rome. The candlelight flickers and, as the shadows dance along the smoke-stained walls, an older man, sixty-nine years of age, hindered by chains hanging from his ankles, shuffles slowly into the grand stone chamber. He has a thick grey beard, his thinning, receding hair is also grey. He is dressed from head to toe in black. The smell of fear taints the air and, to the casual observer, he bears more than a passing resemblance to the disembodied shadows that now seem to be looking down upon him, studying him intently.

This is no ordinary man, this is Galileo Galilei, destined to become a symbol for all those would-be seekers of knowledge that had long been hidden from men. To some a respected scientist, a true renaissance man. To others, he is a magician, a servant of the occult, and a blasphemer. His life hangs in the balance, but the events of this day will reverberate around the world.

The chamber is dimly lit and has a thick choking atmosphere, not only because of the candles and incense burners hanging from the vaulted ceiling, but also from the accumulation of years of terror experienced by those who have trodden this path before him. The shadows live in this place, sustaining themselves on the fears of men.

This council has been convened by the court of the Catholic Church. Galileo has been summoned to stand before it to answer for his heretical pronouncement that the earth revolves around the sun. It matters not if he is right or wrong, at stake is his very life if he does not recant then seek the forgiveness of the Church.

Nor is his accuser an ordinary man, he is not a noble nor even a king. This man, resplendent in fine white linen robes, a red cape and carrying a golden cross, is no less than the most powerful man on earth, Pope Urban VIII.

At his side is the head of the feared Inquisition, Father Vincenzo Maculano da Firenzuola. A Dominican monk from the age of sixteen, father Vincenzo is a stern man, dressed much more austerely in black and white robes. He is known for being efficient - perhaps some would say ruthless - in the execution of his duties, but, fortunately for Galileo, he was also an educated man, a trained architect, who had been responsible for rebuilding the city walls of Genoa. He'd also felt the change in the wind that was beginning to sweep across Europe.

The irony is not lost on Galileo. His only hope of relief from God's voice on earth, if he is to have any, would be from the Devil incarnate - Father Vincenzo.

After many hours of deliberation, Galileo is convicted of heresy and the shadows expand around him as his fears rise. Yet in a remarkable act of mercy, he is sentenced to spend the remaining years of his life under house arrest. He has no choice, he must recant allowing his work to be driven underground on pain of death. It would be 359 years before the Catholic church would admit its mistake. By then too many will have died. No matter, a stream of hidden knowledge born that day was to make its way around Europe through the learned men and nobles who held sway.

Almost fifteen hundred miles away, in the little Cheshire village of Ashton in North West England, the shadows turn their attention to another unfolding drama.

After a difficult labour, a young unmarried girl called Maria gives birth to a baby daughter. She has time to hold her for just a few moments before she smiles; names her Grace with her last breath and then she dies.

The child's father waits outside, unaware until he hears the cries of the maids from inside the chamber. Moments later, a mature servant with tears in her eyes, opens the door, she presents him with the child wrapped in a small woollen shawl. For a moment, he is unable to breathe, his chest heaves as he struggles, feeling that his heart is being torn out. Then, as the realisation dawns that his soul mate has left this world, he utters a haunting cry. He takes the child in his arms, looks into her piercing blue eyes and in an instant his heart is captured.

He is no servant, he is Richard Peak, lord of the

manor of Ashton and the fate of his bastard child now rests entirely on his next words.

The old maid dressed in puritan white, now stained with blood, is Catherine, the head of his household staff. As he hands the child back to her he says, "Find a wet nurse, this child will have an honoured place in my household, she will never know anything of this. Catherine, you have always served me well, will you do me one more great service and protect Grace?

"So much like her mother, she will be no ordinary child and the power she has within her will only bring her misery."

The old maid smiles. "Of course, my lord."

These are hard times when it is not unusual for inconvenient children to be abandoned to their fate by lesser men.

On the other side of Hollins Brook in the Grand Manor House of Renwick Hall, there is another who awaits news of Maria, a young man named Adam Bright.

A weariness begins to overtake Richard but, fighting an urge to rest, he says, "Call the page to send word to Renwick Hall."

"Yes, my Lord," said Catherine.

Though devastated by the events unfolding around him, Richard Peak understands better than most the vagaries of fate. As a dark shadow seems to embrace him, he cannot help wondering, how it had come to this?

The heartache and despair he felt were crushing.

His coarse accent, along with his everyday demeanour betray the fact that, although he is lord of the manor he is not of noble birth. Nevertheless, he is, by any measure of character, a 'noble' man, a warrior, a soldier in the army of King Charles whence he has gained both his fearsome reputation and riches from loyal service.

He had made steady progress through the ranks, becoming part of the young prince's personal bodyguard. Although it was in the war against the Spanish, which the King had commenced in 1625, almost as soon as he had been crowned, that truly changed Richard Peak's life forever.

King Charles was a suitably generous benefactor, greatly in need of allies. On the death of Edward de Hulton his widow, along with his estates, were given to Richard Peak as reward for his loyal service which had not always been easy. Charles was also an arrogant man, inexperienced in the art of kingship. As a youth, he had not been first in line to the throne and so was not tutored as heir until the death of his elder brother in 1612. He had been a spoilt child, aloof, even demanding. He had a knack for creating discord wherever he went that would ultimately see him lose not only the crown but his head with it.

The war with Spain began in the wake of his marriage to the French Catholic princess Henrietta Maria of the house of Bourbon. Henrietta's beauty was the talk of Europe and she had captured his heart with ease. A less petulant king would perhaps have considered the political aspects of a union which his kinship afforded, but not Charles. He followed his heart without hesitation or any thought as to what might follow.

The marriage enraged most of his English Protestant subjects who would resent this for years to come. More pressingly, it also enraged the Spanish King Philip IV, who had been vying for a union between his own daughter Maria Anna and Charles.

Philip was the head of the most powerful family in Europe, the Hapsburgs and, in angering him, there would be consequences that would reverberate well beyond the small islands of Britain.

The Queen in the Tower

A few weeks earlier, Katie had mentioned that she'd been invited to Rome by an old business contact. He'd been successful over the years and wanted to invite those who'd helped him on his journey to a very special party.

Although he had no right, Graeme was jealous of Katie's husband accompanying her on the trip. They did their best to maintain regular contact, she sent him photos or videos and he yearned for her return.

Although Graeme had never met him, it was obvious from the photos that their host on this trip also had feelings for Katie that went beyond business. Had her husband noticed too? he wondered. Graeme was starting to realise that Katie's past was complex; there were unresolved secrets that would only reveal themselves in their own time.

They met in Cardiff in the middle of June resolving to take care of business first before spending the night together when they'd be able to catch up properly. The early evening event would be an opportunity to network and catch up with old friends. Following dinner, they retired to the hotel bar and, after a few drinks, he went to bed, knowing Katie would follow when she could.

It was late when Katie finally arrived. As they lay in bed, he asked if she had enjoyed her time in Rome. Although he had missed her terribly, he wanted her to be happy.

"Yes," she said. "I ended up being chucked in the pool very late at night. I only found out about it the next morning when I woke up with my hair all over the place."

She laughed.

"Someone threw you in the pool? Didn't your husband have something to say about that? I would."

"Oh, it was just a laugh."

Although the conversation moved on, it nagged at him and, whilst he said nothing, he knew there was more to this story. Perhaps she'd tell him one day, but Katie, secretly embarrassed, was glad to change the subject.

"I didn't think you would be so nice," she said, "You have a very unusual way of looking at things."

"I just believe there's more to life than we know," said Graeme then, almost as a throw-away comment, added, " I can read your tarot cards if you like."

"What?"

"One day, I'll read your tarot cards. I used to do it when I was a kid. Although I haven't done a reading for years I am sure I still have the cards somewhere."

Katie wasn't sure she wanted her fortune told, she was enjoying where things were going, but she couldn't resist.

"Ok," she said.

Over the following days, Graeme found many old feelings buried deep within himself starting to emerge. Things he hadn't felt since he was a child, feelings which no one had touched until now. He searched out his old tarot cards.

It wasn't long before they were once again making an excuse to be together. This time, Katie decided that she needed to be in Edinburgh to work with the wider team. Graeme wasn't going to argue and, as she came into the office, he smiled at her, said, "Good morning Katie," and carried on working. That didn't reflect how he was feeling inside. She wore jeans with a tight t-shirt which, when she took off her small brown jacket, showed off her curves to maximum advantage leaving him instantly aroused. He smiled inwardly knowing that they'd be together later, then he began wishing away the hours.

Katie had struggled to decide on a hotel. Eventually, she booked into the Tower then furtively texted Graeme with the details. Strangely even though this was his home city, he didn't recognise the name.

Never mind, he thought, the sat nav will find it.

The hours dragged and, as soon as she could reasonably leave the office, Katie set off for her hotel to check-in with Graeme not far behind.

Parking next to Katie's distinctive cabriolet, he checked his phone. She'd sent him her room number, so he made his way upstairs and knocked on the door. The hotel had been converted from a large historic villa and the room on the second floor was large with a wooden sash window overlooking the lawns. He'd brought two bottles of wine, so Katie called the porter for an ice bucket, two glasses and a corkscrew.

Graeme made a mental note to carry a corkscrew in future.

They settled down on the bed with glasses of wine, laughing at how surreal the day had felt. Speaking to each other just enough to allay any suspicions from the wider team while ignoring one another to the degree that left them both feeling uncomfortable, had seemed so unnatural.

It was not long before Katie was naked and Graeme was kneeling on the bed gently stroking her.

"Where are you going?" he asked, as she started to wriggle.

"Where am I going?" Katie mocked, edging closer to him. He knew full well where she was going. He let out a huge sigh as her mouth closed around him and she started to gently work him with her lips and tongue. Her hands were cool on his thighs and he was unable to move as she took him fully into her mouth.

Not for the first time, Graeme thought, how does she do that? It was immensely pleasurable but frustrating because he was looking down, unable to reach her body. He was facing the headboard, she laid sideways across the bed and, after a few minutes, he could stand it no longer. He eased himself down, pulled her body into a position where he could lay beside her, open her legs reciprocate while she continued to tease him.

He could hear the guests in the next room, which meant they could also hear what was happening here. Soon the headboard was banging so hard against the wall that he had to place a cushion behind it. As she sat upright on top of him, he could feel the cool breeze from the open window. He hoped no one was walking across the manicured lawns below, what she was doing would have been obvious to anyone looking up. He would, for a long time, remember this balmy summer evening.

Before they settled down, Katie phoned her husband. She told Graeme that while her husband loved her, it wasn't the first time she had taken a lover.

Katie was lying but felt guilty, she didn't want to hurt her lover by him hearing her talk to her husband. She had an agreement that whenever she was away, she'd phone home so that he didn't worry. Katie tried to be fair to everyone, blaming herself when anyone got hurt. It had become a pattern, it was easier that way.

Her responsibilities fulfilled, they snuggled up then she asked him about the future, more specifically, their future. Graeme wasn't religious, but he considered everyone as a spiritual being on life's journey. To him, life was a path that each must walk, sometimes alone, at other times with company which could take many forms. Paths crossing many times with fate spinning a web for each human soul seemed like a good analogy to him. The ancients conceived of fate and souls searching for one another from lifetime to lifetime and, to Graeme, this idea was not at all alien.

When they had first met, Katie felt the surge of energy between them, a connection of sorts was established as she had reminded him when they'd met in December. She believed that people were attracted to one another for a reason, even though she wouldn't admit being subject to anything, not even fate. Katie's soul raged against the machine. She would be subject to no one, to nothing except her own will. She alone was the captain of her soul.

"I've brought the cards, " said Graeme. "I'm not sure I believe in things like that," said Katie, but her interest was piqued.

"They are not magic. Our subconscious works differently to the conscious mind. It works in symbols, giving them meaning or taking meaning from them. When we dream about something like a house, for example, this can be a metaphor for our souls, whether they are tidy, full, empty, in need of repair and so on. They help us bring feelings to the surface, they guide but never dictate.

"Playing cards are descended from them. Four suits represent the elements of fire, water, air or earth - clubs, hearts, spades and diamonds. There is one more card in each suit plus twenty-two other picture cards representing the soul's journey through life. Although there are many versions, this one is the most famous.

"How do you see yourself? I need to pick a card to identify with you so that when you ask your question, it relates to you personally. Usually, for a mature woman,

I'd choose a queen."

As he described the characteristics of the four queens, Katie chose the Queen of Pentacles.

The queen of fertility indeed, thought Graeme, smiling to himself, a perfect choice for a woman with black hair and dark, almost black eyes. Graeme had long since discovered that Katie was not really blonde, or indeed fair-haired.

It wouldn't have been Graeme's first choice. The Queen of Swords was more how he saw her. The queen of dreams, on the butterfly throne, with an air of authority about her that said 'approach all who dare'. Katie was yet to understand her true nature so for now the Queen of Pentacles would serve its purpose.

"She is ripe, the queen of fertility, of desire, rich, yet charitable, generous with her gifts, a truly noble soul," he said.

Katie didn't believe she had a noble soul, but that was how Graeme saw her. He was in no doubt on that point so they pressed on. Shuffling the pack she handed the cards back to him.

Speaking slowly, he dealt ten cards:

"This is what covers you, the factors currently working for you.

This is what crosses you, the things which oppose you.

This is behind you, that which is passing away.

This is before you, the factors coming into play.

This is below you, the root of the matter relating to your question.

This is what crowns you, the best that can be hoped

for.

This represents your fears.

This represents your family.

This represents your hopes.

This represents the final outcome."

Not knowing the question she had silently asked, he proceeded to explain the meaning of the cards, allowing her to form her own opinions.

He walked through the reading, explaining their significance; waiting for Katie to take in his comments and relate them to something that was happening in her life so that she could make sense of them.

There were a few moments of reflection. "There aren't many major arcana in the reading," he said, pulling his comments together. "So the answer to your question lies not in the hands of other people, it is largely up to you."

Katie seemed disturbed by the reading picking out four cards.

The three of cups.

"The best that can be hoped for," said Graeme. "Health, abundance, good luck and fortune, if you're true to your task to see through the question at hand. Cups generally relate to questions of love."

She liked that one, the idea that there was better to come.

The three of swords; family attitudes.

"There's sorrow in your family life," Graeme said. "Relationship difficulties, perhaps with you or your immediate family or perhaps the fear of the pain you could cause them."

This struck at Katie's heart in a way he'd only come to understand many months later.

The King of Swords; her hopes. A blue-eyed man of intelligence and authority with many thoughts and ideas.

Is this me? he wondered.

Katie believed it was.

Well, thought Graeme, I'm here for her if she wants me.

The Devil; the final outcome.

"Succumbing to temptation. The card signifies Pan the god of wine and sexual passion, sitting on a cube which means that this, the physical world, is only half of the journey which most of us take without understanding. Many things are hidden from our view in this physical life."

He gathered up the cards. "Did it help you answer your question?"

"Yes," said Katie, still keeping her most intimate self from him. Much was indeed hidden and he had a lot to learn about her. "I want you to do a reading for yourself."

Graeme obliged, shuffling the deck then dealing the cards once more. This time they were both shocked by what the cards revealed. The same four cards that Katie had focused on appeared in Graeme's reading, in exactly the same places. The odds against this are probably the same as winning the lottery, twice.

The Devil card, the final outcome, seemed to look up at them, laughing. They both knew this was where they were heading and that they could not stop.

Graeme said, "It's as though we were two old souls that have been parted for aeons who have once again found one another." Two halves of one whole, completing one another and intoxicated with the feelings it had unleashed in them both. Truly, they were without understanding, but it wouldn't be long before they realised exactly what the cards were trying to tell them. Theirs was still an intensely physical relationship and they needed to seek the deeper meaning of their time together. They had to know one another better, much better.

The hairs stood up on the back of Katie's neck. She didn't believe in things like this she told herself. She was always matter-of-fact. When you're dead, you're dead, but she had lost loved ones and, although she missed them terribly, she also knew she could still sense their presence, even though she found it hard to put into words.

So why should this be any different?

She wondered if she could really bare her soul to Graeme. If she did, what would happen to her, to both of them? But curious, she wanted to know more.

They talked for hours about other worlds and Graeme didn't want to frighten her, so tempering his words, he said, "I like the idea that love echoes through the ages, that it follows us from lifetime to lifetime, it's quite a beautiful way to think about life don't you think?"

"Yes, it is a beautiful way to think about life. How do you know all this?"

"It has been my interest since I was a child."

That much was true, but it wasn't the full story. There had been incidents in his early life that he would share with her one day, but he had shared enough for now, so that she started to understand his gentle nature.

"Many familiar stories we are told as children have deeper meanings. I love exploring them," said Graeme. "You asked me about your star sign earlier, why is the zodiac so popular? It's because it calls to our subconscious, much like the cards do with their symbolism. You're a Libran; air signs are good at abstract thinking, that's why you have no problem getting your mind around new ideas. Let me tell you an ancient story about how the zodiac was created.

"God created the cosmos and every living creature, including the gods and demons that we read about in ancient history. We were created to participate in the act of creation, exalted above all other beings. Even Lucifer the Bright Morning Star with all of the angels were asked to bow to our creation.

"When man first saw Earth, he was spiritual in nature and she was beautiful to behold. She saw the reflection of God in him and, yearning to be together, they stretched out their arms to one another. He became human in this physical form for the love of her, in the process he shut himself off from the spiritual realms. No longer able to see or hear them, he forgot his divine nature. Our whole human condition is based on love and we must find it to remember who we are.

"Mankind retained his inquisitive instinct and, as the worst of his lower animal nature emerged, the gods cried out to heaven saying, 'Mankind will dissect the lower animals, learn all the secrets of creation, he will destroy himself and the universe.' So God created the great wheel in the sky that we call the zodiac, to regulate the lives of men during their time on earth. 'As above so below'; this is why people believe they can find meaning in the stars.

"Each time souls are born, they're given their guide or 'genius' to help them. People take this to mean intellect, but it's not. As we descend to earth, each of the gods gives us a gift, an aspect of our character, like fiery Mars or strict Saturn, to use during our time on earth. We return these gifts when we die, but our souls keep the interest if you like, or the lessons we've learned to take to the next life and so on.

"Sometimes we can glimpse our true nature, it's nothing to be frightened of even though it may seem strange.

"I don't really believe in coincidences, do you? Do you remember when you told me about Helen, that you had no idea where the name came from, but Tom and Carly just knew it was the right name for her?

One daughter of Zeus was better known as Helen of Troy. She's a gift from the sky and her symbol is the moon. Ships sail on the tides which are governed by the moon; what other face could launch a thousand ships? She is a light in the darkness. I told you, she will be a great comfort to you."

If she hadn't just had one of the strangest experiences of her life Katie would have laughed. As she drifted off to sleep in his arms, she decided that she wanted to know more about this strange new way of looking at the world and there was a lot more Graeme could share with her, but he knew she wasn't ready. Although he'd shut them out for many years, he wasn't disconnected from these other worlds, and, as he held her in the darkness, he was afraid of what she would think if he told her.

More surprises were to come and Helen would play a more important role than either of them yet realised.

California Dreaming

A couple of weeks leave gave Graeme a chance to take stock. In spite of feeling the strain of missing Katie every day, Los Angeles was great fun, as was the road trip through Nevada and Southern California. They had spent one more night together before he flew out and now, as he drove, he reflected on the things she had revealed to him.

Needing to be in the Midlands to recruit more team members, he'd arranged for Katie to help him with the interviews. Picking her up in Sandbach gave them plenty of time to talk on the journey. He was waiting in the car park of the Griffin Hotel when she arrived. She parked her car, put her suitcase in his, then they took a few moments for a long deep kiss and they set off.

Graeme was feeling guilty and he wanted to know more about Katie. "Have you done this before" he asked.

"Done what?" she said, teasing him.

"You know what I mean, had an affair?"

"Yes," she said matter of factly. "I had a brief fling with a colleague which lasted a couple of months then it fizzled out. My husband was hurt when he found out about it but it was really just a bit of fun. It actually caused me more grief at work.

"Then, in 2005, I started having an affair with a guy called Andy from Nottingham. I didn't set out to do it, it just happened. I met him on a girl's holiday in Ayia Napa."

"It is not nicknamed Slapper Napa for nothing is it?" he laughed.

"It started out as a bit of fun. I didn't see him again until we were there again the following year, then when we got home we started seeing each other. He was good looking, quite sweet really, he had spent the whole of the previous year in the gym because he didn't think he was good enough for me."

"Oh no," groaned Graeme, "Just to be clear, I ain't spending time in the gym or having chicken fillets inserted into where my chest should be."

She laughed.

"When we got home I made excuses to go to Derby where it was easier to meet occasionally until it got quite serious, he even took a lease on a flat. Although we intended to be together in the end he backed out, he couldn't leave his family. I was really hurt.

It all came to a head when we were in Cyprus again the following year. Always the same week me with the girls, him with his mates. Somehow his wife had found out, she turned up on my doorstep while we were away then told my husband everything. He phoned me to ask how I was; then he asked how Andy was. I pretended not to know what he was talking about, but he knew Andy was with me. Although I had hurt him again, he coldly said, 'Don't worry about it, whatever it is, we'll sort it out when you get home'. The sun was shining; things are always different when you are on holiday then when I got home, things changed."

If Graeme had known what she meant, he would've felt physically sick. That awful feeling would come later, but for now, blissfully unaware, he just listened enjoying her company.

"Was that when you had the boob job done?" he asked.

"Yes, my husband had been encouraging me to have it done for some years, I'd already undergone several consultations. I don't regret it, my breasts weren't full and now I like the way they fill my dresses."

Graeme didn't really understand, although he couldn't argue with that.

It was still early when they arrived at the Montgomery hotel. "I am sorry, I currently don't have a room ready," said the receptionist. "If you could just take a seat I'll call you as soon as one becomes available, it shouldn't be long,"

"Thank you, that's no problem," said Graeme. They found a secluded area, put down their luggage and started attending to their emails and messages.

After a while, Graeme found himself watching Katie. She was standing with her back to him, talking on the telephone, in a blue and green zip-up dress that showed off her figure to stunning effect. Her long hair cascading down her back, he was already imagining holding her in his arms. She was unaware as he took a photograph of her, which, from then on, he always kept with him.

Later that afternoon, when they went to their room, they were hardly through the door before he held her tightly, kissed her, unzipped her dress all the way down until she simply stepped out of it. Letting it fall to the floor, she emerged like the goddess Aphrodite rising from the waves. She took Graeme's breath away.

Making love was slow and passionate now, but it was a warm summer's day and without aircon. Katie liked the way Graeme made love to her more each time they met. On this occasion, once sated, they collapsed together in a sweaty heap, but still, they didn't want to let go of one another.

It was still early and, looking out over the golf course, seeing it was still light outside, they went down to the lounge. They sat on a sofa holding hands, with a bottle of wine, looked at the menu then ordered some bread, olives and chips. The conversation was light, they were continuing to find common ground passing a few pleasant hours before they would go back to bed to continue exploring one another. Before they settled down for bed, not really knowing why, Graeme reminded Katie to phone home.

The next morning over breakfast, they talked

about how they'd handle the upcoming meetings. Two candidates were coming to meet them and Graeme wanted to see Katie's reaction to the prospective new team members and their reaction to her. The morning went well and he liked both candidates, they would chat through their conclusions on the way back up the M6 as they headed for Nantwich to their final meeting together on the trip.

Later that afternoon, their goodbye kiss was tinged with sadness due to his upcoming leave and their enforced separation.

Being in California encouraged Graeme's daydreaming. America was a world away from Edinburgh. For most of his life he'd only seen it on TV in James Bond films where Sean Connery, that other, most famous son of the Edinburgh tenements, would inevitably end up in bed with the beautiful girl and she alas would inevitably end up dead, covered in something unpleasant.

Equal opportunities have come a long way since the 1960s but James Bond is now wearing budgie smugglers leaving Graeme wondering if it had all been for the best.

Driving down Highway 5 to San Diego, he wondered about Katie, about her life as the music he listened to rolled back the years. Although they were both born in the 1960's they were really children of the 1970's, a much-underrated decade in Graeme's opinion. The swinging sixties had bypassed industrial Scotland, which had gone straight from the end of rationing into the oil crisis of 1974, economic hardship with mass unemployment. In short, for a decade or more, it was stuck somewhere between a glorious industrial past and a frankly uncertain future.

He was laughing silently to himself as he reminisced.

The tenements were harsh, central heating non-existent, you could watch the icicles form on the inside of the windows from underneath the warmth of as many blankets as you could take the weight of before the pressure crushed your chest… plus your parent's coats thrown over you for good measure.

Health and safety meant, 'if you get hurt it's your own fault'. There was no compensation culture; the Human Rights act didn't exist. Children were to be "seen; not heard" and we really didn't understand that when Jimmy Saville said he wanted to 'fix it' for you, you were unlikely to be getting something you really wanted for Christmas after all.

Today everything is so readily available, so graphic. Is it any surprise to see young girls acting like cheap showgirls with young men not understanding that we were meant to be curious, discover one another at our own pace; to be gentle? Young people today have unrealistic expectations, they don't really know how to explore and to please one another and the awful predatory instinct rearing its head is truly sickening.

Graeme was glad of his years. He couldn't have lived with the peer pressure of having to have chest implants or a ten-inch willy.

As a small child, with blond hair and blue eyes, angelic-looking in fact, thinking back, he struggled to understand how he had ended up with so much corporal punishment. When he stayed with his grandmother in Fife, she often saw the bruises on his backside and would joke, "you get stripes in the army."

He wasn't fazed nor did he complain. He was far more frightened of his father than he was of his teachers. His father had the famous Celtic temper. He'd been an old fashioned bare-knuckle boxer in his younger days and a manual labourer for most of his life. He was a strong, muscular man right up until the day he died.

Women played a formidable role in shaping his life, his grandmother, his mother and his three older sisters, all of whom he adored, so he always treated girls with respect.

The 'reality stars' of the internet age were still decades away, amusement was homemade and it was possible to find space to be alone. He would roam for hours on the high hills near his home, ride his bike, gaze up at the stars on camping trips in the Highlands where he could travel to other worlds in his head. He read copious numbers of books prompting places like Edinburgh Castle and Arthur's seat to fire his imagination.

Gifted as a child, he had a strange talent in that he always *knew* when something was wrong with someone. He would play with tarot cards and a ouija board with his cousins at his grandmother's house. They were considered little more than simple board games, long before they became the iconic doorway to letting evil shadows into the world, as they were subsequently portrayed in the movies; movies, incidentally, which took years to arrive in Scotland.

If people were lucky their heroes were their parents, who struggled every day to provide the basics of life in a loving home. So it was for both Katie and Graeme, a harsh economic environment where mothers eeked out the housekeeping and fathers worked hard in heavy industries, taking extra shifts whenever they could. The women learned to be wise and, although some looked down on them because they didn't have formal qualifications, the fathers were clever; resourceful men. Life was raw, it was real, brothers and sisters fought like cats and dogs with the young ones wearing the cast-off clothes from their older siblings.

These days he hardly touched spirits, but Graeme started drinking at fourteen which quickly got out of hand. A single malt would be the go-to drink in time, back then however it was vodka because it's lack of odour meant that the teachers couldn't smell it. By the age of eighteen he was developing a liver problem.

Nowadays, most of this would be classed as child abuse although Graeme would take it anytime over the pressures of growing up today. He couldn't recall if being gender fluid was actually illegal or not, but, at the time, it seemed that it wasn't a choice available to just anyone, you had to be a member of the House of Lords, an MP or work for the secret service if you wanted that option.

With all of these thoughts and chuckling to himself, it was hard to believe that he was arriving into such a beautiful place as San Diego. He parked up and headed into town to find a bar with some live music.

That evening Graeme took some pictures as he watched the sun go down over the Pacific from Coronado beach. Later, back in his hotel room he sent them to

Katie. "One day," he said, "I would like to watch the sun go down with you from here."

It was still too early for Katie to entertain any such possibility. She was still playing with Graeme, but her feelings were changing and he was intriguing to her.

Sugar and Salt

Back from America, Graeme sought any opportunity to meet Katie again. He was due to be working in Nottingham for a few days and he hadn't expected her to be able to join him but she'd eagerly made changes to her diary to be nearby. As he drove down the M1, he listened to some music and wondered what Katie saw in him. He'd no doubt that he'd been born lucky and he wondered how she felt.

He considered Katie a queen with a rare beauty that few are ever gifted with. When he'd told her, she'd said, "I don't think I'm beautiful, but you make me feel beautiful." Then she cuddled him tighter.

"When I was a little girl, about nine years old, I remember being sad, looking in the mirror and asking why am I so ugly? I was fat, with short hair, my mum dressed me in the same clothes as my sister which I hated. I was jealous because she was prettier than me. My friends were all pretty so I wanted to be like them."

Digressing, she recalled that she'd also had a crush on Virgil from Thunderbirds, who flew Thunderbird 2. Although lots of things crossed Graeme's mind at this point he just smiled. She had shown him a picture of herself, sitting on the step of a terraced house in Manchester with her younger sister. Graeme had a similar picture of himself somewhere around the same age, sitting on the tenement doorstep wearing short trousers. The old buildings were gone now, having long since been condemned.

He knew Katie was competitive and realised the drive had to have come from somewhere. We all have demons that drive us, he thought.

She continued. "It was then that I set my goal to be the best, to win at whatever I did, to be top of the class. I didn't always succeed but was usually close. My friends were all tall and had lads chasing them. Being the smallest, no one ever looked at me, not until secondary school, even then I never believed they were really interested so I threw myself into sport.

"My friends had secured their places, but I was rejected at trials for the netball team at age eleven so I asked the coach, a large fearful lady, if I could train with the team. She took pity on this small person who was desperate to be part of the team. She said 'okay as long as I didn't get in the way'. I worked hard, waited for that opportunity. When the centre was injured, I got my chance. As soon as I was on the pitch, she knew I could read the game. I was good at most sport and awarded 'school colours' for outstanding sporting achievement. My name's still on the board in the hall of my high school, which is now a sports college."

Yes, they had common ground, they laughed together about things that happened when they were young and he wished he had known her then.

To everything there is a time, thought Graeme with the song, 'Turn! Turn! Turn!' ringing in his ears.

Is this our time? he wondered, I hardly know her.

Although they could relate to one another through shared experience, they were also very different. Katie was always dressed to kill. Graeme, on the other hand, was almost always casual, jeans and a t-shirt or sweatshirt. She always looked fabulous, he looked like a sack of coal tied in the middle with a piece of string, even when wearing a suit. Katie loved shopping and clubbing with her friends. Graeme was more at home watching the match or going to a working men's club with his friends. He could clearly remember the last time he was in a nightclub was in 1987.

As far as music was concerned, he hadn't made it much beyond the 1970s. Katie said she wanted to take him clubbing then laughed when he'd asked if they still played Slade, Rod Stewart, Frankie Miller or T Rex in clubs.

"Only at Christmas," she'd lied, to make him feel better.

She was a modern girl in every sense. Despite being a little older than Graeme, her taste in music had moved on. She still liked great tunes by Vandross, Silvia Tella, Barry White, but she also liked house music, contemporary stuff, anything in the charts that she could dance to. She loved to dance.

Graeme couldn't dance, but the idea of learning to dance with Katie didn't faze him if she was willing to be patient.

When Katie arrived, Graeme was already waiting in the bar with a bottle of wine, an ice bucket and two glasses. He admired the figure hugging blue dress she wore as she leaned over to kiss him passionately.

She seems to have missed me, thought Graeme and, if he could have read her thoughts, he would've heard her say, '"Oh I have.'

Somewhere, over the previous months, they'd lost all inhibitions or ideas about keeping their distance in public. Katie's first kiss was always questioning. Has he missed me? Has anything changed? She knew instantly he had, that nothing had changed between them.

They had a quick drink and Katie went back to the car for her case, then they took the remaining wine to Graeme's room. The hotel was being redecorated leaving behind an intense smell of paint, which, on top of the wine, was making them both feel woozy.

As they hadn't eaten they decided they would come back down later. Of course, they didn't, they hardly ever did as once they were in each other's arms neither wanted to let go, they just enjoyed one another immensely. As the evening went on, Graeme reminded Katie to phone home so she went to the bathroom to make her call. She came back to bed a few moments later and again they made love before falling asleep, then all too soon the dawn came.

Before they got out of bed, Graeme said, "I almost forgot, I have a present for you." Reaching into his rucksack he pulled out a book. She had told him several times that she liked the way he looked at the world and the book was an old Hindu tale of lovers following one another from lifetime to lifetime.

"I hope you like it," he said.

"I am intrigued. I will read it."

Unsure if it was the alcohol or the paint fumes, they both felt worse for wear that morning. "Come on," said Graeme. "We both need to eat something."

They chose the same thing from the menu and Katie thought, it's uncanny how many times we choose the same meal. Some things I just would never imagine he would choose.

This morning they both opted for an omelette. When they arrived, Katie decided that she needed some salt but, as she took the salt cellar in her hand, it came apart, the contents pouring out all over her meal.

"Don't worry," said Graeme. He cleared as much of it off the plate as he could then exchanged some of his food for hers making the best of a bad situation. They ate their food, drank their coffee, ordered more to wash away the salt, then they walked to their cars in the rain, kissed and said goodbye.

"Let me know when you are home safely please," he said.

The weather was miserable and, as Katie drove away,

she knew there was no longer any way that she could keep this on a fun basis. Graeme was totally unaware of this, yet if he had been he would've smiled, he didn't want to be a bit of fun.

It's becoming harder to say goodbye, I'm falling for him, Katie thought. What should I do? What do I want to do? What does he want from me? What does he want to give me, if anything? Where is this going?

In a few hours, Katie was home and she texted Graeme to let him know that she was safe. Graeme had been in meetings all morning and he got her text around lunchtime, just as he was about to set off for home too. He'd had a good morning, both with Katie and workwise, but that was all about to change as he set off home in the bank holiday traffic. It was dreadful leaving him stuck in stationary traffic for long periods. When he finally got home he let Katie know, grabbed a beer from the fridge then he too sat wondering where this was going.

They had always texted one another, usually sparingly to avoid suspicion in their respective homes, but now it was becoming much more frequent. They had to change one another's profile names in their phone directories, particularly Katie, whose phone was provided under her husband's contract.

They were taking more chances now. Graeme used generic photos, Katie however, being a natural poser, always used selfies. He knew it was in her nature and laughed at Katie's reaction, at the feigned look of hurt on her face when he had said so. In the end, they agreed that she would put a picture of her pet dog on her profile page and she would be tagged as Virgil in his phone.

Katie giggled as she teased him. *You can take me for a walk whenever you like. I'm not so good at fetch or carry, but I get ever so excited when I see you. I'm good at licking your face when you wake up in the mornings.*

If only, he thought.

He put a picture of a king on his profile and naturally assumed he would be Graeme King in her directory. He was somewhat disappointed to find he was actually to be called 'Bruce'. Bruce Kay in fact. He should have been flattered, it could have been a reference to Robert the Bruce and Katie had thought it funny but had overlooked the irony that it added a further complication to an already complex situation.

The real Bruce was Katie's boss and they were all due to be in Dublin together in a few weeks.

Oh God, he thought, I hope she doesn't text the wrong Bruce or the shit is really going to hit the fan.

That weekend the weather was lovely so Graeme went cycling. He wasn't big on selfies but he couldn't get the picture of Katie's eyes out of his head, so he sent her a running commentary of his journey. Before he left the house, he took a picture of a single Rolo and sent it to her, knowing she'd understand. Then he set off riding through the grounds of a stately home. She had sent him a picture of her in the garden some time ago and, as he rode, he took a picture of the gardens then sent it to her.

Are you going to buy the house?' she had asked.

No," replied Graeme laughing. *It belongs to the National Trust.*

Next, he rode out through the villages into the

Northumberland countryside, through the forest before heading out towards the coast from where he sent her a picture of the beach.

I would love to walk down that beach with you, she texted.

If he could have reached down the phone line, he would have hugged her. She wasn't too amused, though when he sent her a picture of him eating fish and chips.

How could he without her?

Katie was having a quiet day, she sent him a picture from Tesco's of a very large box of Rolos. She was going to a party later, in fact, she was going to two parties, a dinner party with her friend Karen she had bought her house from, then later to another at a friend's house.

Two parties in one night, how on earth does she do it? thought Graeme but something didn't feel quite right and it ate away at him.

Before she went out, she sent a picture of a single Rolo on the carpet to Graeme and her note read, *I have saved my last Rolo for you.*

He laughed as he replied, *be honest, it looks like the dog's got it.* Katie owned up sending him another picture, clearly showing her dog Virgil enjoying Graeme's Rolo.

Oh well, he thought, I probably deserved that.

The next morning, Katie had a really bad hangover. She sent Graeme a good morning text adding, *When will I grow up and learn to drink responsibly?*

But there had been a lot more to that evening than the hangover alone would suggest.

WHEEL of FORTUNE.

Maria Vazques

It was a cold February night 1633 AD and Richard Peak, lord of the manor of Ashton, lay tossing and turning in his bed, he was sweating and crying out as he struggled with his dreams that seemed to be so vivid. Had he been asked, he would've sworn that he was awake. Yet he couldn't be, for he was talking to Maria, his lover, who had died the previous day.

She was standing before him in a gown of pure white, the most beautiful soul he had ever known, radiant and smiling at him.

"She has your eyes," the apparition said to him.

"She has your strength," he replied. He could feel the warmth of her smile and, as he always had, he ached for her.

"Please don't leave me!" he cried.

The apparition idly fingered the stone amulet she had always worn around her neck, as she said, "I will never leave you and our daughter will be a great comfort to you, but you must remember her purpose, I am here for you always, but she is here for another."

He awoke with a start and in that instant the vision was gone, all he could see in the dark were the last embers of the fire, the flickering shadows that seemed to wander around the room and his grey and white hound lying in front of the fireplace, staring up at him. He rose from his bed, put some wood on the fire, cradled the dog before once again his tears came unbidden. In a few hours he would bury the mother of his child, he would say good bye to Maria.

His manor of Ashton was a beautiful place. Situated on the low hills to the South East of the Parish of Wilmslow, it extended over more than sixteen hundred acres. For the most part it was rich land, with good green pastures, well suited to crops and beasts alike. The many wooded glades, where the dappled sunlight hit the ground, provided nuts, acorns, mushrooms and hiding places for the wild boar, which were especially prized for the feasts and banquets he regularly hosted. But it was in the lower land, a small clearing in the woods, bounded by a brook, where it met with the neighbouring parish of Renwick, that held a special place in his heart. This was where his beloved Maria had always been at her happiest.

The decision he had dreaded came easily. He chose her favourite spot by the stream in the lower pasture where she was laid to rest in a white gown, but without the only possession she had ever owned, the strange stone necklace with what looked like an intricate wheel carved upon it. He removed it gently, ordering a headstone to be made, engraved with the same design. It would forever mark her presence in his lands, in the place where they would often lay in the shade of the trees, cooling their feet in the clear waters of the brook, which had served as a reminder to them both of how fate had brought them together.

The pastures were worked by sixty-two tenant farmers along their extended families, all owing allegiance to their lord of the manor. Many had served with him in the war against the Spanish, some as volunteers, others as mercenaries, but he respected them all for their courage and loyalty. He, in turn, had earned their respect, treating them well and fighting bravely by their side. He knew that land for farming was hard to find in England which meant it was all too easy for a family to starve to death. He also understood that a lord needs loyalty, for the time would inevitably come when he would have to call upon it again.

It was in Spain eight years earlier that he had met the women whom he was to discover was his soul mate - Maria.

Kings, generals and politicians are quick to send men to war, but they never really see its true face. Like most soldiers who have seen battle first hand, Richard knew that there was no glory in war and the attack on the white-walled town of Caceres had in truth been a disaster.

He had led a mixed detachment of some three hundred cavalry and infantry across the border from Castelo de Vide in Portugal with the intention of surprising the small garrison, overwhelming it before sacking the town. They knew that most of the men of fighting age had been conscripted, sent to the border city of Badajoz some sixty miles to the south-west and the Spanish wouldn't be expecting an assault this far into their territory. The town itself had little strategic value, but the King had wanted to make a statement to his rival, his arch-enemy the Hapsburg King Philip IV, that his reach was long and he wouldn't be intimidated. So the intended fate of Caceres, along with everything inside the walled town was to burn, all for the vanity of one man.

The men were eager, anticipating an easy victory and the mercenaries were greedy for gold, for plunder. As they crossed the border, making their way towards Caceres, they reached the first settlement of Aliseda. They sacked the village, the mercenaries taking what they wished, including a dark-haired, dark-eyed young woman who was destined to become a camp girl to provide them with comfort, succour and entertainment during the cold mountain nights.

Fate however had other ideas for both the girl and for Richard. When he saw her, he had an uncomfortable feeling, as if an unseen spark passed between them which troubled him. By his word men lived or died and he decreed that any who touched her would not see the following dawn. He just knew - he did not know how he knew - yet in an instant she had captured his heart and from that day she was devoted to him.

He ordered his men to seek billets in what remained of the village, for tomorrow they'd attack Caceres. As night fell, a strange peace descended over the troops. Usually, they'd be drinking, singing or fornicating into the night, bragging about how they'd spend their plunder or gambling it away, but a strange shadow seemed to lay heavily over the land which the light from the campfires did nothing to disperse.

There was a great deal of intrigue in the court of King Charles. Many of the courtiers were still fervent Catholics who favoured an alliance with the house of Hapsburg and so opposed not only his marriage to a Bourbon Princess but also the war with a Catholic ally. Even many of his Protestant subjects wished to frustrate his efforts. They were unconcerned with the war, yet vehemently opposed to any Catholic influence at court and somehow the Spanish had learned of the impending attack. Unknown to Richard Peak, reinforcements had been sent from Toledo, trained imperial troops, not local conscripts. The garrison had been strengthened and more troops were located just to the south in the town of Merida.

Buoyed by their easy success in the small villages around the town, the attack on Caceres began at dawn on October 8th. Upon meeting heavy resistance, they quickly realised their mistake falling back, They were only surprised that the troops in the garrison didn't follow them, and soon they realised why. The cavalry from Merida were swiftly approaching; they could see the dust rising over the plain to the south. If they couldn't find a defensible position, they'd soon be cut to pieces on the open plain below the town.

There was no longer any prospect of overrunning the town, their only chance was to run, to head north as quickly as they could praying that they would make it to the Alcantara lake, to the wooded valleys of the river Tajo which they could follow back across the border to the safety of their comrades and allies in Portugal. They ran, leaving most of what they had looted as they fled, but as they reached the shores of the lake, the Spanish fell upon them forcing them to fight for their lives.

In the gorge of the river, where the ground was wooded, steep with hard grey granite and scree slopes, the cavalry would no longer be effective, improving their odds of survival.

This was their only chance and soon madness descended like a wave broken on the shore, a wave that left broken bones, severed limbs and screaming men in its wake, with many small groups running, harrying one another amongst the trees until darkness fell when the Spaniards, fearing ambush, eventually retreated. There was no respite, the English had to keep moving, for they knew with certainty that the hunt would begin again with the rising sun. Being outnumbered, tired and lost, nothing would save them except crossing the border.

In the heat of battle with adrenalin fuelling his every move, his every thought, Richard hadn't noticed that during the fighting he'd been wounded, he was losing blood. If the bleeding couldn't be staunched, tomorrow would be of little consequence because he wouldn't live to see the sunrise. In the descending darkness, he'd become separated from his men and he was surprised to see the slave girl who'd been captured in the village the previous day. She hadn't run back to the Spaniards as he'd expected she would in the chaos of battle, instead she'd been watching him closely, studying him, and now she approached with her arms open, offering a ripped cotton shawl to bind his wounds. As he looked into her eyes she smiled and he stumbled, falling down the river bank he hit his head on a rock and consciousness left him.

The Border Heifer

When Graeme arrived at the pub, he was surprised to find Katie already in the bar. Dressed in a revealing light blue dress, she looked gorgeous. As always, he was casual in jeans and a sweatshirt. He pulled her close, kissing her as they checked in. The young girl behind the reception desk was polite but clearly guessed why they were there. She seemed more than a little surprised that anyone their age would be troubled by libido.

Embarrassed, Katie blushed slightly, just enough for Graeme to notice. He smiled as he thought, it's a shame you can't check in as Mr and Mrs Smith anymore as you once had to, to get a double room in a hotel, but paying for everything on cards has put paid to that… what joys the younger generation will never know.

The receptionist smiled back, unaware of his thoughts.

He took the key, ordered two glasses of wine and they sat down at a nearby table to catch up on events since the previous week and to giggle about what the receptionist must have thought. "I don't really care," said Graeme. "I feel sorry for the kids these days. They know all about sex, more than we ever did, but they know nothing about romance and I think we get better as we get older."

Katie wasn't going to argue.

While they were chatting, the receptionist approached, asking them if they'd like to make a dinner reservation. They took a menu and examined it, more in hope than expectation that they'd make it down for dinner. They decided to take a chance, politely declining, it was only 5 o'clock, they didn't stop serving until 10 pm yet still it would be touch and go if they could finish making love in time.

"Where's my Rolo?" asked Katie teasing him, referring to the picture he'd sent just before he'd set off cycling the week before. "It'd better be the same one, I have a photo."

Uh oh, thought Graeme. He hadn't brought it, so he changed the subject.

"Nice dress," he said. "I have a theory that women dress to initiate sex."

Katie laughed. "You're right. I did want to do exactly that. I actually put another one on first but thought it was a bit too revealing."

She laughed again and Graeme joined in. He loved both her laugh and the thought that she wanted to be with him.

A few moments later, as he followed her up to their room with two wine glasses, he was also grateful for the dress noticing how well she filled it. She could've been poured into it. Her arse was a spectacular sight as she sashayed with each step. He wasn't even in the room, yet he was already aroused.

The Border Heifer was a pub with rooms in the beautiful town of Melrose in the Scottish Borders. Each room was individually styled and Graeme was pleasantly surprised to find that the room wasn't the one he had booked. It was larger and the first thing they noticed was the huge roll top bath under the window at the end of the bed. Although enticing, for the time being, these details were unimportant as they stripped to their underwear and headed straight for the bed. They kissed and held each other for a few moments as they finished their wine.

Soon they were exploring one another eagerly but gently. For the first time, they were truly comfortable together. They spent several hours caressing one another, gently kissing, stroking and exploring new feelings. At last, they were ready to lay themselves open to the emotions that would come. Graeme understood that lovemaking was at least as much emotional as physical, that for it to be truly beautiful their minds, bodies and souls needed to be in total harmony. There is an old saying that at the appointed time you can feel the earth move, but it's not this world that moves, there are other worlds that only lovers know.

Katie didn't know it yet, but she was exploring new worlds with Graeme, worlds she hadn't dreamt of. All too soon her body quivered and she shook all over before she closed her legs over his fingers and pulled him close to her.

"It's okay, " he whispered as he held her tightly.

"Oh God, that was fantastic," said Katie.

"Thank you. You do say the nicest things. I adore making love to you."

"It's not what I'm used to." she replied.

He looked down into her soulful brown eyes; she seemed sad.

"Has someone hurt you?"

Katie avoided his gaze, turning her head as a tear formed.

"I won't hurt you," he said and, as she pulled her face into his chest holding him tightly, he could feel her tears on his skin.

When she'd relaxed for a few minutes, Katie sat up and poured another glass of wine. "Let's have a bath," she said .

Graeme got up, pulled down the window blind, ran the bath and they both climbed in. Katie laid in his arms as they finished the wine.

"Where's my Rolo?"

"Uh oh," said Graeme. "To be honest, I'm not a hundred per cent sure. They're surprisingly difficult little buggers to get hold of when you go looking for them."

"Hmm," she said, relaxing into him.

"I'm going to pay for that aren't I?"

It was a lovely feeling, laying together in the soft warm water. Although neither of them wanted it to end, wondering if the restaurant was still open they dressed and went downstairs. The pub was full now, it was late and the kitchen was closed so the best they could get was two bags of crisps and two more glasses of wine.

Although neither of them cared it was obvious to everyone that they were like young lovers, unable to get close enough to one another. They sat drinking, talking and sharing their feast of crisps until last orders were called for non-residents. When Graeme asked if Katie would like to make love again she said, "Let's have just one more drink before bed."

The next morning, they did make it down for breakfast. It was touch and go, they were the last two in the restaurant. They had fruit juice and Katie encouraged Graeme to have a full Scottish breakfast. "You've earned it," she said. Besides, she knew he had a busy day ahead. Katie, on the other hand had booked a day's holiday so she only had to make her way home.

It was a beautiful summer's day. Winding through the Borders countryside, on roads that cars like her Porsche were made for, Katie enjoyed the thrill of the drive. Shadows cast from the trees that lined the country lanes softly caressed the ground, pursuing her and the light seemed to shimmer as she sped homeward. As she drove, her concentration drifted, she was remembering Graeme's touch laying softly on her skin like the shadows touching the world around her.

Graeme had woken early that morning. It was already light, he'd gone to the bathroom, cleaned his teeth then he started to wake Katie with kisses so gentle she felt as though she were still in a dream.

Now that he knew what Katie liked he could reach her in a way no one had before. Running his hands lightly over her body, touching her breasts ever so gently, he lightly touched her nipples and then moved his hands expertly over her body, knowing he was driving her crazy. She yearned for his touch now, she wanted to scream, "Please, touch me!" Her body was trembling, she'd never felt so aroused. When it was over, she had held him tightly and said, "That's the best I've ever had."

Oh God, she had thought. This can't be happening, I'm in love with him.

It was the first time she had admitted it to herself, even though she had already felt it after the night she'd spent with him at the Tower. She'd gone back into the office the next day, they'd both been polite yet pretended to the rest of the world that nothing had passed between them. As the day came to a close, they'd passed on the stairs. As they were not alone, he simply said, "Goodnight Katie, have a safe trip home." Then he walked out into the car park without a look back.

To say goodbye on the stairs had cut her like a knife. She didn't know what to do, where to look, how to behave, just an awful sinking feeling, a desperate want to run after him, but knowing that wasn't possible. She'd packed up, said polite goodbyes and left the office. She walked to her car, wondering what she'd gotten herself into. It was painful, but she knew he'd not deliberately hurt her, it was just how things had to be. Never the less it still bloody hurts, she thought.

She'd sent him a text, which simply said, *Ouch, that kinda hurt.*

She knew she could only feel that way because she loved him.

Yes, it really did, Graeme had replied. *That was awful.*
He too was in no doubt about the way he felt about her.

Ciara and Bruce

Katie was hard working too, constantly seeking opportunities to develop the business and, if it resulted in more time with Graeme, that was a bonus. Having been approached by some contacts in Ireland, Graeme had given her the go-ahead to arrange a number of appointments in Dublin the following Wednesday and Thursday. It required an overnight stay, which they were both looking forward to, but Bruce needed to go with them. He knew nothing of their relationship, so they would need to be careful. He was an easy-going guy though, Katie liked him and he had been friends for many years with Graeme, so they would have a laugh over a beer or two.

Bruce lived not far from Graeme, just over the

border in Northumberland. Although not native to the region, he'd moved there twenty years earlier and liked it so much he now considered it his home. He picked Graeme up at 5.30 am on Wednesday and they set off for Edinburgh airport. They planned to meet Katie at Dublin airport then travel into the city together.

The plan nearly came unstuck at the first hurdle when Graeme was searched at the security gate. It hardly seemed worth checking in luggage when all they needed was one change of clothes and a toothbrush. Graeme intended to have as few clothes on - and for as little time as possible, so he wasn't focused when the security scanners picked something up in his backpack and he was taken aside.

The security guard was large and bearded with little resembling a sense of humour. He asked to search the bag. Graeme smiled. "Of course you can, it's probably just all the connectors or adaptors for my laptop."

"Just unzip the bag and step back please sir," the beard seemed to say.

Graeme's mind wandered, it was early, he was tired and as all he could see was facial hair. He couldn't tell if the lips were moving although there was definitely a noise coming from behind it.

It reminded him of Katie, as most things did these days, but more specifically her childhood crush on the puppet from Thunderbirds, in whose honour she had named her dog, Virgil.

He was horrified when the security guard pulled out the corkscrew that he now habitually carried for when he and Katie shared a bottle of wine in the privacy of their bedroom, which was now every time they were in a bedroom.

"This is an offensive weapon," said the beard. "You can't take that on the plane."

"I'm so sorry," said Graeme, mortified. "I just forgot it was in there."

The guard was clearly thinking, this prick hasn't bothered reading any of the notices adorning all the passageways. He was lenient and binned the offensive 'weapon' then put some sort of radioactive tag on Graeme's bag before putting it back through the scanner.

Great, thought Graeme. I'm going to be searched everywhere I go now.

He got dressed, collected his belongings, found Bruce then they made their way through the duty-free to get some coffee.

"Surely a corkscrew can't be the most offensive thing in Dublin" said Bruce. Their colleague Ciara was from Dublin, she was more offensive than that."

Graeme laughed.

When they arrived at Dublin airport, they went to a café to wait for Katie. They sat admiring a new Jaguar parked inside the arrivals hall. Graeme liked Jags, he was considering buying one. Even though Bruce liked Mercedes, he too had to concede it was a handsome beast, the build quality looked good as well so maybe he could also be tempted in due course.

While they talked, Katie appeared through the security screen wearing jeans, a tight t-shirt and a small brown leather jacket with an ethnic American Indian design. Had she worn a hat she could have passed for a cowboy, albeit a short, pretty and well-endowed cowboy. Nevertheless, it was an interesting look.

Graeme had pretended to wonder where Katie was, but already knew because she had been texting him all morning. She was eagerly looking forward to seeing him.

I wish I was on the same flight as you, not in Manchester, she had said, even though the flight was short. Now, seeing Graeme and Bruce together having a coffee, she felt that uncomfortable feeling again. It was a strange situation; she wanted to hug him, but had to limit herself to a simple, chaste kiss on the cheek. She laughed when Graeme told her she looked like she was on her way to a rodeo. He could usually make her laugh. It was one of his most endearing qualities, complementing his warm smile every time he laid eyes on her.

As they approached the taxi, Graeme hung back, letting Bruce climb in the front. He wasn't interested in exchanging pleasantries with the driver; he just wanted Katie to know he loved her. He silently mouthed the words to her as he climbed into the back beside her. He reached furtively towards her and feeling his hand on hers Katie wanted to jump all over him, but she was conscious of Bruce in the front, feeling he knew something was going on.

They went to Jury's hotel in the city centre where Graeme left Katie and Bruce to go to their appointments. She knew it was the right thing, but it was only ten o'clock and she didn't want to be apart from him so soon.

Graeme went to the desk. "I have a booking for tonight, it's probably too early to check in so I'll just sit working in the lobby, if you can let me know when a room becomes available please."

"Actually sir, there's a room available if you'd like to take it," said the clerk.

Pleasantly surprised; he checked in, asked for a spare key and went to his room on the first floor. He took Katie's case up having offered to look after it. He would have done the same for Bruce, but, like Graeme, he travelled light. Graeme had plenty of work to do, but first he went to the local supermarket to buy water, a bottle of wine and three packets of Rolos.

He wasn't going to be caught out by that again.

Returning to the room, he opened the window then propped the door open with the ironing board to let some air circulate as the room was foisty. He texted Katie to let her know which room he was in, made a coffee then sat at the desk to work diligently all day. As he worked, he ate the first packet of Rolos, careful to save the last one.

Katie and Bruce returned to the hotel at about 3pm and checked in. She let Bruce disappear to his room, then she made her way to Graeme's room.

When she arrived there was a single Rolo and a glass of wine waiting on the bedside table.

Graeme had been on a conference call for the last hour with his phone on mute. He kissed her passionately as they lay on the bed listening to the call.

"Do you understand how exciting my life is?" Graeme asked. Even as she smiled her eyes were glazing over at the background conversation. She started teasing him. It wasn't long before she was stripped of her jeans and Graeme was sitting in wet trousers - not a good look when you have to go to meet someone an hour or so later. They fooled around like teenagers and, at five, Graeme had to leave to meet Brendan, an old colleague.

He left the hotel, turned right, walked past the Europa hotel to the Café next door where he sat down to await his friend who arrived a few moment later. They talked for over an hour, reminiscing before Graeme suggested that they meet up with Bruce and Katie before heading out for dinner.

When they arrived, it was raining. Graeme had no coat but Katie had an umbrella so, as they left for the restaurant, he held her tightly as they hung back behind Brendan and Bruce, huddling together under the available cover. In the restaurant, Katie made sure she was sitting next to him and, for the duration of the meal, played footsie under the table, which kept Graeme's attention on her.

Oh God, she's a tease, he thought.

The meal was lovely, washed down with lots of wine between them, red and white. Graeme alternated but Katie finished most of the white, which left her somewhat tipsy.

Brendan lived out of town and afterwards, he called his daughter for a lift home, arranging to be picked up at the hotel. After saying good night to Bruce and Katie Graeme sat with Brendan in reception, finishing their earlier conversation until his ride arrived half an hour later. He said goodnight to Brendan and went up to his room expecting Katie to be waiting for him but the room was empty. He texted her to see where she was.

In the bar with Bruce came the reply, so he made his way down where he found them drinking spirits. Katie asked Graeme if he wanted a Sambuca. She and Bruce had been on shots before switching to vodka. On top of the wine, the effects were starting to be very noticeable.

"No," said Graeme. "No more. Get yourself off to bed Katie, we have a long day tomorrow."

Dutifully she finished her drink and left.

Graeme stayed with Bruce for a few minutes, catching up on the events of the day so as not to arouse suspicion until his phone vibrated in his pocket.

It's home, he said, as he looked at it. It wasn't, it was Katie.

The key to our room doesn't work, come and make love to me, her text read.

Graeme quickly made his excuses about it being a long day and Bruce was ready to retire too, so they took the lift up together to the first floor. Fortunately their rooms were in opposite directions, because when Graeme approached his, he saw Katie slumped on the floor outside his door. It would have been impossible to pass this one off as an innocent mistake because her room was on the fifth floor, which Bruce knew because they had checked in together.

Katie fell into the room with Graeme and they undressed as quickly as they could, eager to get their hands on one another. Although it had been a long day it would be a few more hours before Graeme would get any sleep. There was no aircon in the room so he had left the window open, but this was a capital city which never seemed to sleep. First he heard the late night revellers, then the even later night revellers, followed by taxis, street cleaners and early morning delivery vans. He didn't seem to get any rest at all yet by 5.30 am he was ready to give Katie her early morning wake up call and she responded as always.

Satiated, he fell asleep, waking just in time to have a shower and get dressed but Katie hadn't finished with him yet, she had other ideas. There was now little time left before they were due to meet Bruce for breakfast although Graeme had no choice as his body responded to Katie who kept urging him on until they made love again.

"That was lovely," said Katie as she lay beside him. "Did we make love last night?"

Oh my God! thought Graeme. Yes, they had, for several hours but she didn't remember. Not sure how to broach that with her, he got up and jumped in the shower again.

He needn't have worried, as a few weeks later he was going to get the shock of his life when Katie was ready to talk.

Graeme went on ahead to meet Bruce for breakfast finding him already sitting in the dining room. "Where's Katie?" he asked.

"No idea," said Bruce. "She was a little tipsy last night, I'm sure she'll be down eventually."

They ordered coffee, took some food from the buffet and, sure enough, about fifteen minutes later, Katie joined them. "Good morning," she said.

"Good morning," they replied.

"Did you sleep okay?" asked Graeme.

"I was disturbed a bit," she answered honestly then the conversation turned towards the more mundane matters that the day had in store.

Coincidentally, another ex-colleague Simon, hearing that they were in Dublin had texted Bruce,. They were fully booked for the morning, but Graeme suggested it wouldn't take three of them to go to the next appointment, that Bruce and Katie should go. He'd stay to meet Simon then they could all meet up later at the most important client meeting of the day at 11.30 am.

Returning to their room to collect their belongings, Graeme slipped a packet of Rolos into Katie's bag so that she would find them when she got home,. They all checked out then sat in the foyer.

When Simon arrived, they explained the plan which he was fine with, then they went their separate ways. Graeme took Simon to the Café where he'd met Brendan the day before, for a catch up which mirrored the conversation he'd had the previous day. He told Simon where he needed to be, at what time and Simon promised he'd get him there, which he duly did a little over an hour later.

Katie and Bruce arrived shortly afterwards and he asked them how their meeting had gone.

"Fine," said Bruce. "Nice people, I think we can do business with them".

Then Katie piped up, " Did you notice that they both had lovely blue eyes."

"They what?" asked Bruce as they began to laugh. Graeme knew this was Katie's coded message that she had been thinking of him and he smiled to himself. After the meeting, they went for a bite of lunch as they had a couple of hours to kill before they needed to be back at the airport for their flights home.

Lunch was entertaining. They sat down, ordered their meals and then their discussions turned to legal work they needed to complete when they got back to Edinburgh.

The legal secretary was a colleague called Ciara, who by sheer coincidence was also from Dublin. Ciara couldn't have been more different from Katie, she terrified people. She had flaming red hair with a temper to match, it was scarcely possible to have a conversation with Ciara before she started jumping down your throat. She often wore short skirts and red shoes that reminded Graeme of the wicked witch in the Wizard of Oz. Dorothy's house had landed on her and all that was left was a pair of legs wearing red shoes sticking our from underneath. Graeme had often wished over the last few years of working with Ciara that he had owned a house like that.

She didn't lack confidence. Charisma yes, charm yes, confidence no. Someone must have once told her she was gorgeous and the words had anchored themselves deep in her psyche so internally this must be how she felt. Externally, however, the picture was far from pretty. She walked like a docker as she approached her prey, - which is really the only word that can describe anyone who attracted her attention, - as though she was stalking them for dinner.

An encounter with Ciara was never pleasant but for some reason she had a rapport with Bruce. He seemed able to get her to do things that no one else could, to help the team when he needed it. She was however efficient. The trouble was, Graeme could only visualise that efficiency in terms of a predator dispatching its victim and, in her presence, he felt more like a small antelope, rather than the boss.

Everyone pulled a face at the mention of Ciara's name, then Graeme started to tease Bruce, creating imaginary scenarios of an encounter between him and Ciara. He put on his best Irish accent.

"I don't know about your legal forms Bruce, but I can do ye good and proper if ye like."

They laughed as Graeme developed his theme.

"Bruce followed Ciara up the steel stairs to her bedroom where she slowly, seductively, took off her clothes to reveal in all her glory her biggest, most comfortable knickers and a big ginger growler sticking out of the sides."

Katie was really laughing now and Bruce wore a pained, almost panicked expression.

"Bruce was remarkably calm, he should have been more like a war veteran suffering from post-traumatic stress disorder who had buried the sights he had seen deep within his subconscious, but the horror just kept clawing its way back into his conscious mind, but instead Bruce, as he surveyed the scene before him, just thought, `That reminds me, I need to get my hedge trimmers sharpened, you need good tools for a big job'."

They were all creased with laughter now. Graeme was giving himself indigestion in the process and Katie looked like she was about to wet herself.

"I am a bit worried about you," said Bruce. "You're fixated with Ciara."

Well, it was just a bit of fun that had passed the time until their taxi took them to the airport.

As on the inbound journey, Graeme and Bruce's flight back to Edinburgh was due about an hour before Katie's flight, so they said goodbye and made their way to the departure lounge. They left more or less on time, but Katie wasn't so lucky. Not long after Graeme had left, her flight was cancelled. She wouldn't have minded being stuck there another night had he been there and she sent Graeme a text, which said, *Flight cancelled, fly back, I promise to make it worth your while.*

Graeme knew that was true, but it was too late. They were already back in Scotland and Bruce was driving them home.

Katie tried get another flight but she was unable to secure a seat on the last flight to Manchester, so she settled down in the executive lounge, ordered some wine and cheese while she wondered what to do next. Eventually, she was offered a flight to Birmingham then a bus back to Cheshire. It wasn't an appealing option, but by the time she boarded the plane, she noted that the second Manchester flight was also delayed, so it wouldn't have been a better alternative after all. Before take-off, she sent Graeme a text which simply said, *I want to cuddle up to you and go to sleep.* Graeme smiled when he read it and asked her to let him know when she was safely home.

A very hard landing

A week later, as Graeme arrived home he checked his phone, as always, hoping for something from Katie and found a message waiting. It read, *Guess I didn't know quite how hard I had fallen for you until this morning.* It was followed by a love heart.

His mind raced over the events of the past 48 hours, which had in turn been some of the best and some of the worst of his time with Katie.

At 8.30 am that morning he had been seated on the edge of the bed in the Benjamin Franklin Hotel as Katie sat on his knee crying.

"I told you I was soft," she said through the tears. "I let you in, I let you in."

Her voice tailed off to a whisper as she continued to

cry.

"Everything has changed, you don't love me."

She paused, composing herself slightly.

"Well, ok," she said. "I will shrug it off."

But, even though Katie was still feeling confused, she knew that she was lying. She could bury emotions deep behind her mask, where she hid all of the aches and pains that she'd accumulated in her life, but she did love Graeme and she could never just shrug that off.

Two nights before, Katie had been staying close by and Graeme had arranged to attend a business dinner. He was to meet her at her hotel room afterwards to resume their affair after a week of enforced abstinence. When she'd checked in, she'd asked for an extra key to be coded so that he could leave his clothes and return unseen while she would be in the bar with their colleagues later that evening. They didn't have long before he left, but had fondled one another passionately, which had left them both aroused.

Half an hour later, he arrived at the venue for his dinner and checked his phone to read Katie's message. *Please drive carefully because I need you back - no pressure but you've left me so f**cking horny. I don't normally swear but...* It was followed by a smiley face. The message held his attention through most of the dinner making the hours pass like a vague dream.

He returned at 9.30 pm, entered the room then send her a text so she could make her excuses to join him. Immediately she entered the room he wrapped her in his arms as they fell together on the bed. Their love making continued to reach new heights, but Katie struggled to let herself go and, as they rested together, they began to talk.

Graeme wanted to know Katie much better. He gently quizzed her about her sexual experiences in an effort to know how best to please her. She told him of her first orgasm at fifteen years of age and how she would always be grateful to Rob, the boy from school who had first shown her the possibility. She and Rob had never actually had intercourse and this was the first spoken clue to Katie's preferences that she'd ever revealed. It reinforced the discoveries that Graeme had already made over the previous months.

"How many men have you slept with?"

Katie thought about it, counting silently in her head.

"Fifteen," she said. "Is that a lot?" and she laughed.

"Fucking hell!" said Graeme. "Er… yes."

Then he laughed with her.

He didn't care about her past. He had his own skeletons buried away, he only wanted to know how best to bring their bodies and souls closer while making love, so that they could feel one another with every fibre of their being.

"Well, you know how it is," she said. "In your twenties, having fun, playing the field, experimenting with things like recreational drugs, poppers and toys".

"Do you have toys?"

"Of course I do."

Graeme had never been in a relationship involving sex toys but he was open-minded.

She lay in his arms with her back to him and he started fingering her gently. Then he whispered, "I don't have a toy with me but I can make the noise if you like and he proceeded to hum in her ear like a bee, "bzzz, bzzz, bzzz".

Katie was hysterical with laughter and Graeme joined in. Her smile, her laughter were enchanting to him and she had never known anyone like Graeme. After a few moments he continued his gentle exploration minus the sound effects, brought Katie gently to orgasm and she drifted off to sleep in his arms.

Very early the next morning Graeme woke Katie with his now customary kissing and fondling until she moaned with pleasure. Although the days were now getting shorter and Katie considered it to be the middle of the night, her body responded ensuring that the first few hours of their day began with delightful sensations.

Eventually, they rose, showered and left for work separately so as not to arouse suspicion. An important day beckoned. They were entertaining about forty guests at the office followed by a dinner back at the hotel. The day was stressful but went well and about 5pm they returned to the hotel where they now had separate rooms, a sensible precaution with so many people attending. Katie knocked on Graeme's door as soon as she arrived. He had been in the shower and was dressed in only a towel as he let her in. They lay on the bed and after a few moments, she began exploring.

"Oh look what I've found," she said.

"Don't worry, it's very small... although I've a feeling something's going to come between us very soon."

Katie removed his towel, continuing her explorations, teasing him until he could stand it no longer. He undressed her and they made love, by their benchmark it was something of a quickie. Still, Katie seemed pleased with herself as she got up to leave.

"I'll see you in the bar," she said.

Graeme got back in the shower and then dressed to meet their guests. As the evening progressed, they assembled for dinner. When Katie entered the room wearing a one-piece, skin-tight dress and thigh-length boots, without exception every man in the room turned to stare. When it came to flirting Katie knew that she had no rival. While everyone was distracted, he sent her a text that simply said, *Minx*. The effect that she had on the room only served to heighten his expectation as he fully expected to be with her later that evening.

After the pleasantries of dinner were complete and it was polite to do so, Graeme wanted to go to bed. He could see that Katie was in full swing and seeing the wine was going down at an alarming velocity, as he left he asked his colleagues to make sure the night ended sensibly.

They did their best, without much success.

Meanwhile, Graeme lay alone in Katie's bed. He sent her another text, *Come to bed babe*. After almost an hour, he could tell that she still hadn't read it and he knew where this was heading so he made his way across the hall, back to his own room.

In the early hours of the morning, he heard a commotion outside his door. He knew Katie was trying to get into his room, but she was blind drunk, being helped by at least one colleague plus a number of guests. He dared not open the door as he knew she would spill into the room, hold him and that there would be far-reaching consequences which would hurt them both, their families, colleagues and their employer.

They quickly figured out it was the wrong room so someone returned to reception to check the room number and get another key. Moments later, they returned opening the door to Katie's room. A female guest, with the help of Katie's colleagues, put her onto her bed, left the key in the room then closed the door behind them. Graeme looked through the spyhole, staring across the corridor at the plain brown door of room 144 whilst straining to hear the footsteps as they disappeared up the hall. He ached for her, but he knew she needed to sleep it off, besides he doubted that she would remember if he had been there.

Not long after, there was knock on his door. He looked through the spyhole where he saw one of the male guests standing in the hall. A flash bastard, Graeme recalled, with a Lamborghini who had been taking some other female guests 'out for a spin'. Instinctively knowing what was going on, as he opened the door the tall grey-haired man recoiled, knowing instantly he was rumbled. He had seen Katie on the floor outside the door earlier and assumed it was her room. He apologised sheepishly as he walked away but Graeme was going nowhere. He remained behind the door. A few moments later he heard the tapping on Katie's door as the guest had rectified his mistake over her room number.

Graeme opened the door.

"Why are you creeping around?" asked Graeme putting him on the spot.

"Er… she dropped her eyeliner, I wanted to return it."

"At 2am?"

A liar as well as someone in need of a penis extension, Graeme thought, as he closed the door, once more listening to the footsteps disappear up the hall.

Graeme doubted this was the end of it, so waited, listening and his patience was rewarded when a second male guest knocked on his door. He waited a moment, opened the door and got the same response as earlier.

"Erm… I'm looking for Katie."

"Well, she ain't in here."

Again he shut the door and listened to the steps disappear up the hall. Fifteen minutes later, the pantomime was played out again when a third male guest knocked on his door. He too was sent packing knowing he was rumbled. He could've given them the benefit of the doubt, assuming that they just wanted to check on her welfare, but he knew that they wanted to help themselves and he would've ended up reporting them for rape - or worse - because of the way he felt about her, he might have killed one of them.

A final episode came about half an hour later, when the female guest who had put Katie to bed arrived back with the night porter and two colleagues. Graeme opened the door and spoke to his colleagues who explained that the female guest had left her bag in Katie's room. The porter opened the door, she went in alone then came out with the bag.

About 3am, there was another gentle tapping on his door. Somehow this time he knew it was Katie. When he opened the door she grabbed him and, although he ached for her, he knew he couldn't let her in. She was still drunk, had no recollection of earlier events and became distressed when he insisted that she go back to her room. She couldn't take in what he was saying, the rejection cutting her to the quick. Back in her room she began texting him. He begged her to get some sleep, tried to reassure her that he still felt the same, asking her to trust him. Still Katie would not rest, soon she was back outside his door again.

This time Graeme got dressed. Suggesting she go for a walk with him, they wandered unsteadily down to reception where they sat talking quietly. He asked the night porter for some iced water, trying to persuade her to drink a little to bring her round. No matter how he tried, he couldn't get her to understand what he was saying and she was soon crying. He gave her a tissue to dry her eyes then blow her nose. He continued to try to explain whilst Katie continued not to listen.

Eventually, she asked him again to take her to bed and when he refused, she ran, stumbling, towards her room and he could hear her crying as she disappeared down the corridor. Watching her go, Graeme felt as if someone had put their hand into his chest and pulled out his heart. As he sat wondering what he'd done, Katie sent another text, again asking him to come to her room. *I need you, please, the door is open.*

Oh shit, thought Graeme as he had visions of another uninvited visitor stumbling on her open door incorrectly believing it to be for their benefit.

Close the door, he texted back. *Give me a moment,*

then come to me.

As he got back to his room she was waiting for him. This time he let her in, she smiled then held him tightly. He put her on the bed, took off her dress, stripped down to his underwear and cuddled her, never letting go for an instant. It was the first time they'd been in bed a together without making love. He kissed her gently on her cheek, her neck, her ears, whispered that he loved her then he held her close until, three hours later, he had no choice, he had to get up. He kissed her gently, all the way down her back, covered her over then jumped in the shower. He had a few things he needed to do for work, so that he could concentrate again on Katie and ask her to go home, where there were other - pressing family matters awaiting her.

Remembering none of this when she awoke, Katie felt like Graeme was ignoring her. She'd heard running water and knew that he was in the shower. She'd drifted back off to sleep and when she woke again half an hour later she saw him sitting fully clothed at the desk, staring at his computer. She didn't understand why he'd not come back to bed to wake her as he always did.

Foggily, some of the events of the early hours filtered into her consciousness and she thought that whatever had happened the night before had made him realise he was playing with fire and he wanted nothing more to do with her. She wasn't altogether sure what had happened, only that she couldn't remember going to bed. She knew that she'd been upset at some point in the night and remembered drinking water in the bar.

It must have been because he finished our relationship, she thought.

She couldn't quite process it, she knew that she must have done something bad, but couldn't remember what it was.

All Katie knew was that she was in pain. It hurt her so badly that she just wanted to run away. She wanted to get as far away as she could, not sure where, anywhere would do, as long as she could just curl up somewhere on her own until she could come to terms with it. She felt ill, sick. If she hadn't been sure she loved him before, she was certainly in no doubt now, but, in her confusion, she also thought it was over.

He pulled her onto his knee and tried to explain the events of the previous evening, but she still couldn't take it in.

THE MOON.

The Crown – Katie starts to wake up

Graeme had an important early meeting, but he managed to persuade Katie to go back to her room saying that he would return about 11 am and they could go somewhere to talk. A few hours later, as his meeting neared its end, he tried think of a good place to take her. He couldn't leave things as they were, Katie was devastated and he felt numb, unable to breath.

Despite Graeme's promise to return for her, Katie couldn't stay in that room. She packed her stuff and sat on the bed pondering whether she should go straight home, but she was concerned that if it was over, then just disappearing without a word would surely damage their friendship forever. In the end, there would be no choice, she had to face Graeme at some point. She would just be putting off the inevitable, so she decided to just drive somewhere, anywhere, to clear her head and to see if he would come to talk to her.

Heading back towards her room, Graeme's heart sank as he noticed that Katie's car was gone. He looked at his phone to see if she had messaged him and there was a note saying that she'd set off towards home and, if he wanted to, she'd meet him at the Crown Hotel in Peebles. He wasn't sure if it was coincidence or if they were truly connected as Katie had said all those months ago, but he'd been thinking of exactly the same place.

As soon as he got in the car, he called to see where and how she was. She seemed a little brighter. She was about half an hour ahead of him. He asked if she had an iTunes account.

Okay, he said. *Call me when you get there.*

He drove much faster than he should have.

Half an hour later, Katie called. *I'm here.*

He was having trouble getting through to her about his feelings, so he asked her to download a song called, *I believe in you.*

He didn't think she'd like the style, though the words said everything he wanted to convey. It could have been written for her.

Okay, she said. *See you when you get here.*

Katie reached the centre of town, parked and sat pondering. She re-read the messages from the night before as she remembered the feeling of rejection from that morning. She was terrified of what might be coming. Feeling dejected, she sat on a bench in the middle of the square looking up at the sky. What's it all about? she asked herself. Her stomach was in knots, and the fact that she couldn't get a signal or listen to the song was also bothering her. What was he going to say?

When Graeme arrived, he parked the car then made his way through the leisure centre at the back of the hotel to the bar at the front. He knew where she'd be. Katie was at the bar about to order a drink and he squeezed her tight. Katie wanted to cry. They stood for a few moments in each other's arms. "Let's a get a soft drink and order some food," said Graeme. "Neither of us has eaten much over the last few days."

They sat down to talk, in exactly the same place that they had five months earlier. Katie reflected on how different her feelings were now. Gone were thoughts of flirtatious fun, things had gotten serious. It had happened without trying, but it had happened nonetheless. Now the thought of losing him made her feel sick. When the food arrived she couldn't face it, she just wanted to sit as close to him a possible, holding him. Her heart beat faster as he told her of the events of the previous evening.

It was obvious that Katie had been reflecting on these too. She was ashamed and couldn't believe that random people had tried calling for God knows what in the early hours. Thank goodness that she'd passed out, although this didn't really give her the comfort that things would be okay between them. She'd let him down. Why hadn't she gone to bed when he had? Why hadn't she gone back to his room when he texted her shortly afterwards? Not for the first time, too much wine had clouded her judgment.

"I'm sorry, I have let you down," she said sheepishly.

While there was truth in her words, all he cared about was Katie. Somehow, instinctively he knew that it wasn't his forgiveness she needed. She had to forgive herself. Something deep inside Katie yearned to be heard and she was shutting it in.

"Come on," he said. "Eat something."

While Graeme ate a little, Katie struggled to eat anything. They cuddled and talked as he reassured her that things would be okay. He explained the possible consequences if they'd been caught together which she had not given any thought to. When the penny dropped she understood that he was only trying to protect her.

"Have you listened to the song?" he asked.

"I couldn't get a strong enough phone signal here" she said.

Graeme took out his laptop, plugged in his headphones for her. The lyrics hit home immediately, as he had hoped.

Although neither wanted to leave, soon they had no choice, they had to say goodbye. Katie packed the cheese sandwiches she had been unable to eat in a serviette, put them in her bag then they walked out to the car park together. They kissed passionately before Katie drove away, certain now that she loved him and hoping with all her heart that everything was going to be okay.

It was Thursday when they said goodbye, making it a little more bearable for both of them because they knew they would meet again in a few days.

"When you get home, have a laugh, watch a film," he said. "Above all, when you look in the mirror tonight and you see that little girl looking back at you who all those years ago had thought herself ugly, smile back at her. She is beautiful, have faith in her and give her a chance, she really is worth it."

Later that evening, Katie sent him a text to let him know that she had arrived home safely and at last he could relax.

The next day Graeme sent Katie a text. *Good morning beautiful.* Then he set off for work. It was early and the sunrise was a deep rose colour as Eos, the goddess of the dawn, spread her rosy fingers across the land. He could imagine the ancient god Hephaestus sitting in front of his burning forge, making the weapons and marvels of the Olympian gods. He was in a good mood, thinking of Katie as he drove; all he needed now was to hear her voice again.

The weekend was fraught for both of them, trying to make sense of their feelings for one another. Katie had been invited to meet with her ex-colleagues in Manchester on Friday night to celebrate Donna's birthday. Although she'd been tired and had things at home she needed to deal with, her husband encouraged her to go out. She caught the train into town and caught up with her friend. As the night wore on, they talked more and Donna made it clear that she was worried about Katie.

"We need to have a conversation," said Katie. "When we're both sober."

They'd already arranged a trip to New York for the following week with more mutual girlfriends, to continue the celebrations for Donna's 50th, so there would be time to talk then, but, in the meantime, something she hadn't expected stirred in Katie's heart.

She sent Graeme some flirty texts and selfies, saying that Donna wanted to know who she was texting. He replied to her in Spanish, deepening the mystery for Donna.

Katie didn't understand the reply so he sent another, which read, *Tell Donna, it says you're my dream. The queen of my heart. It's nice that she's worried for you. I'm sure you'll have a long conversation in New York, please let me know when you're home safely.*

Katie didn't stay late and, as she caught a train home, the texting with Graeme resumed. He had commented that he liked one of the photos she'd sent him.

I think I look like a doll, she replied.

Why do I want you to fancy me? Desire me? I think I know although it's only recently I've questioned why – startled face emoji.

I have NEVER known a guy like you, NOT EVER, sleep well gorgeous, can't wait to be with you on Monday in London.

Now when you get a text like that from a girl like Katie, you're going to go to bed a very happy man, thought Graeme.

Do me a favour, he replied, *on Monday, please answer your question.*

What?

Answer your question for me… please.

He sent her the address of the hotel with directions and finally, he added, *….and bring the toys.*

The Lord and The Berber Girl

When Richard Peak awoke from the blackness his head
swam as his sight slowly returned. He started to panic, it
was daylight and he knew he had to move if he wanted to
live, but as he moved a searing pain in his side made him
grimace with agony. He dared not cry out, the Spanish
troops could not be far away. If he gave away their
position it would mean certain death.

As he raised himself onto his elbows, a small hand
gently pushed him back down.

"We have to move," he said.

"No," replied the girl. "You are safe"

"No, we have to move. If they find us, they will kill
us."

But the girl was insistent

"You are safe," she repeated.

He was too weak to push her away and the pain was preventing him from moving, so gingerly he laid back down taking a very deep breath.

"How?" he asked.

"You have been asleep for two days, your men have been hunted and the Spanish have left."

He tried to struggle back up and this time she helped him rest against a large stone.

Gradually he became aware of his situation. It was early morning, the sunlight was streaming through the trees and there was a cool breeze blowing down through the valley from the North.

As he looked around, he saw that there was a small fire with what looked like a rabbit cooking on a simple skewer. Realising that he was hungry, having not eaten for almost three days he reached out for it but his side ached where the sword point had entered, narrowly missing his lung.

The girl handed him the skewer and he quickly devoured the food.

His leather battle corset had been removed so that his body could be bound in white cloth with a foul smelling concoction smeared over the wound.

"Be still!" said the girl. "Although the bleeding has stopped you still need to rest."

He slumped back against the hard rock.

"Why are you helping me?"

"Because you helped me, you saved me."

"Yes...I...I don't know why, but when I saw you, I

knew you were…important. Why didn't you run when you had the chance?"

The girl sat looking at him across the fire and her soulful brown eyes seemed to stare into his own soul as she absent mindedly toyed with a strange stone hanging around her neck.

A moment later she pulled back her gaze.

"We have met before," she said.

"Yes…" he replied, seeming somehow to understand yet knowing that was impossible, he asked "but how?"

"In your dreams perhaps. Who knows for sure, but the stone it never wrong."

"The stone?"

"It is more than a stone. It is the soul of my people."

"What do you mean? The soul of your people?"

"I am not Spanish. My people are Berbers, we come from the high Atlas mountains across the sea in North Africa. We were a happy people, not used to farming or living in houses. We were nomads, we made our camps under the stars according to the seasons that we needed to observe. I do not understand you people from the North, there is a rhythm to life that you do not seem to notice, even though it is what gives us life. We came to these lands centuries ago as slaves of the Muslim invaders and, although they are now defeated, still we are not free. The Spanish know our magic makes their land blossom leaving them afraid to allow us to return home."

Although he listened intently, he was confused by her story and, as he looked into her eyes, he felt himself falling, his head began to swim. He couldn't be sure if it was loss of blood but he did not resist the sensation.

"What is your name?" he asked

"The Spanish call me Maria, Maria Vasquez, but my real name is Maya. The elders tell me that I was named after my mother who was the spiritual guide of our people, it means the illusion. She died shortly after I was born and I was raised by my father, a Spanish farmer. The only thing I have left of my mother is this."

She held out the small stone necklace with strange circular markings on it.

"Somehow it guides and protects me."

"Why are you in Spain?" she asked. "I have seen the First Swords, the ones you call the conquistadors and I have seen your own nobles fight. You are different somehow, not like the others."

He winced with pain as he laughed. This strange girl was indeed a quick judge of men.

"You're right, I am not typical of the commanders who fight here because I'm not of noble birth."

"Then how is it that you can command so many men? When you forbad them to touch me, I saw the look in their eyes, that they feared you, yet you say that you are not their lord?"

"I am not of noble birth" he repeated. "It's true, I am their commander, that I enforce discipline when I must although they do not fight for me or obey me from fear, for I have fought by their side as their equal. The truth is, I don't know the family of my birth, I was orphaned at a young age, taken in by a kind family who gave me shelter then treated me as one of their own.

I live in a land far to the north. It's a beautiful island,

although life can be harsh in England. One soon has to make a living, so as soon as I was old enough, I took the king's shilling."

"You stole the king's shilling?"

He laughed again. "No, it's just an expression, it means I joined the king's army. When you join, you are given a shilling, a small silver coin to seal the bargain."

"Ah yes, a charm."

"A contract," he corrected. "If one is fortunate, it's possible to make a good life in royal service. It's unfortunate that sometimes that progression is at the expense of other men, but for me, my lord King Charles has been a generous benefactor."

"You must rest now," she said and, almost as soon as the words left her mouth, he fell back into a deep sleep, as though they had been a command he couldn't resist.

As he drifted off, he sensed her following him into his dream, as if guiding him safely to his rest.

Over the next few days his wound healed enough for him to stand and to walk and, as they made their way along the steep wooded paths of the gorge, accompanied by the sound of the water rushing below them, Richard learned more of the strange girl.

Her beauty entranced him. The sway of her hips as she walked in front of him, the sound of her voice, her voluptuous form, more visible now that she had shredded her clothes to bind his wounds, but most of all the depths of her eyes. He noticed every detail.

He noticed something else too, as his strength slowly returned, somehow the connection with Maria grew stronger, as though she were the source of his new-found health and he knew he had to take her back to England with him.

Long since tired of the war, Richard now yearned for home.

The Devil knows

The following Monday Graeme would start to unravel what the devil card from the tarot reading was telling them. They could not be complete together, not without understanding and that was going to come at a price.

He checked into the Cavalry Club in Gracechurch Street in the City, dropped his bag then crossed the road to Leadenhall Market to get a bottle of white wine. There was a delicatessen in the arcade so he thought about getting some cheese and crackers but decided to wait for Katie to arrive so that she could choose. They had arranged to meet in a bar near Monument underground, but it was a fine day, so he waited outside. If he was honest, he wanted to get Katie into bed as soon as possible as he ached for her. He had a few appointments later in the evening, which meant that was time he wouldn't be able to spend with her.

Katie meanwhile had spent her time thinking about what she was going to tell Graeme. After the episode in the Benjamin Franklin hotel, she couldn't wait to see him again. She hoped that things would be the same, yet riding down to London on the train she could not help going over the events of the previous week. Thoughts, feelings, hurt and shame all rolled around in her head. At the same time, she knew that she needed to answer the question she had asked herself.

Why do I want you to fancy me, desire me? I think I know, but I've only just started to question myself. Katie had texted a few nights earlier.

She thought back, there were things in her past that had happened in years gone by and much more recently on nights out with her husband that she really didn't want to think about. She was too ashamed to speak of them aloud so what would she tell Graeme?

From Euston, she took the tube to Bank. Exiting on to Gracechurch Street she soon spotted the bar that Graeme had told her to head for and then she saw him. He would have blushed if he'd realised that Katie thought he looked gorgeous in light pants and a blue shirt. She loved to see him wearing blue as she thought it brought out the colour of his beautiful blue eyes. Those eyes that now seemed to follow her around, looking down lovingly on her everywhere she went.

He was daydreaming when suddenly he saw her across the road, dressed in jeans, t-shirt and a brown jacket, pulling her suitcase. It seemed to Graeme that the smile on her face made the sun itself shine brighter and he too smiled. Katie crossed the road heading straight into his arms where he held her tight and kissed her passionately. Once again, Katie felt happy and safe.

Graeme wanted to make sure that Kate had something to eat, knowing that if he left her to her own devices while he was out later, she probably wouldn't bother. He held her hand as they crossed the road heading for the delicatessen, which Katie thought quaint. She chose a smelly blue cheese, Roquefort that was strong with a slightly salty finish, some chutney to take the edge off it and biscuits. When she mentioned wine, Graeme told her it was already on ice in the hotel.

She knew before agreeing to come to London that Graeme had appointments but that didn't bother her as he'd set her a task to ensure she wasn't bored. She had promised after their meeting in Peebles to tell him a little more about herself and she had her own questions to answer. He suggested that the best way for her to remember it all would be to write to it down. What did Katie think about the idea of staying in her hotel room whilst Graeme went out to dinner? If she'd been asked six months earlier she would have laughed at the idea, but things had changed a lot in that time. Now, as long as he was coming back to her, nothing else mattered.

The hotel room was surprisingly large and well equipped with a fridge, a microwave, a desk, a large inviting bed and importantly, air conditioning. Graeme jumped in the shower before climbing on to the bed with Katie where - ever so gently - he began making love to her.

Marvelling at his touch, so gentle, so considerate, she wondered why, in all her years, was she only now learning what making love was all about? She was so used to - putting it bluntly - the quick fuck where previous husbands and lovers took their pleasure leaving her to reach for a vibrator to satisfy herself. Never had she known such a tender loving touch and she let herself swim away with the sensations.

She was learning to let herself go; to not put on an act. It was hard for her because it wasn't what she'd been used to but, because she now knew she loved this man and she believed he loved her, loved her for who she was without her customary mask that she wore for everyone, she was finding it easier to let go. It was just amazing and afterwards they lay cuddling.

"I have to go" he said.

"That's fine", said Katie, and she meant it.

Before he left, he poured her another glass of wine; put out a plate of the cheese and chutney and then handed her his laptop saying, "Write."

She giggled.

She was so happy knowing she'd been forgiven for the events of the previous week. Katie turned towards him, kissed him and she smiled. While he was out, she read what he had written for her, laughing at some of the things he'd said then she got to work as she had promised, slowly, surely she started to slay her demons. Katie had decided that she would tell Graeme more about her life, just a little for now.

When he returned a few hours later she began. "I'll

tell you a few things that might explain why I'm so fucked up." Although to look at her, no one would ever know, Katie's first preoccupations were her confidence and her weight. This she put down to events in her teens compounded by a relationship with a boy called Wayne. A good-looking lad, he'd become controlling and abusive as the relationship developed.

His mother was a bitch, taking every opportunity to stick the knife into Katie, making her feel uncomfortable and unworthy of her son. She recalled how the weight had crept on and with it more hurtful comments until she was so desperate to lose weight that she resorted to slimming pills. Her sister had got her some from a so-called doctor and all she ate for a whole week was a couple of apples a day. It had the desired effect; losing nearly a stone she felt so good about herself she now looked forward to going back to Ellesmere Port for the weekend. She thought that Wayne would see her slim, that he would love her again. How different it all seemed from when they had first met at Barmouth. Had he ever really loved her she wondered?

She'd arrived feeling good about herself but it was short-lived, his mother revelled in telling her that she wouldn't keep it off and Katie couldn't stop the tears from rolling down her face. She didn't understand why this woman didn't like her; she'd always been polite, even respectful. For Katie, the worst part was that the witch had been right. Unable to sleep, she suffered from stomach cramps and fatigue. The weight came back on and she soon reverted to comfort eating. Needless to say, Wayne didn't want a fat girlfriend so his mother was only too happy to encourage him to dump her.

It hurt. Katie had cried for weeks, and she kept on eating.

Family gatherings only made things worse when her mum prepared dinner. They would all eat happily, with Katie's portion being as big as her older brother's. When mum asked, "Who wants apple pie?" Katie shouted up first, even before the first course was digested. She'd put a huge piece into a bowl, piling lots of ice cream on top.

Her brother would look on in astonishment. "No way Katie. You're never going to eat all that are you?"

"Yes!" she'd snap back. "Why not?"

"You can't possibly be hungry?"

She wasn't. Even as she shovelled it in her eyes stung as the tears began to roll.

Moments later, she'd go to the bathroom to make herself sick. Not always, only if she wanted to eat, she knew she could get rid of it and she would convince herself that maybe she could eat whatever she wanted and be happy. But she couldn't.

Although she didn't know the word for it then, bulimia would affect her life for many years. Acid reflux from constantly being sick and acidic white wine would affect her teeth resulting in the full set of veneers which she now had, well before her time, and her diet was to become another part of the mask she wore constantly.

Although they rarely ate when they were together, afterwards she often visited the toilet making Graeme wonder if she was still making herself sick on occasion. He didn't agree with it, but he understood that we live in a world where appearance, particularly for women, is seen as paramount.

Despite representing England at netball and touring Australia, a coach, called Barbara, had also ridiculed her for being overweight. With hindsight, Katie could now see that Barbara was probably trying to mask her own insecurities. At the time it just made the tour a lonely, miserable experience with one notable exception. At the end of the second week, she received a letter from her mum. It was just what she needed, the nicest, saddest letter. It told her that she loved her, that she missed her so much. She read the letter over and over and to this day it remains a precious reminder of her mother Elaine, of how TRUE love feels.

Soon after Katie got her first job she began to experiment. She had the cash to go clubbing with her friends. She was desperate to be slim, to be pretty and be liked by boys but she started drinking way too much. It gave her the confidence to be outgoing and chatty which resulted in her not being the last pick, because Katie had something to say for herself. Unfortunately the drinking was to become another defining characteristic of the woman she would become, another piece of the mask she felt that she always had to wear.

As her weight fluctuated she had several boyfriends of sorts. A few occasions ended up with sex in the back of a car, probably because she was grateful a decent looking guy liked her. It was only later that she began to realise that they didn't really. She thought they might, but really it was because she was easy. She hated herself which just made things worse until she met a nice guy called Pete. He was funny and liked Katie regardless of her weight. The relationship blossomed, at last she found comfort. Six months later, she embarked on a proper calorie counting diet, no more binges, no more being sick.

She found that fruit gums were her saviour when she wanted something sweet and still had a soft spot for them. It worked, her confidence grew as gradually she saw the old, pretty Katie re-emerge. She bought nice, sexy clothes, found men were again attracted to her and once more she couldn't help herself as the superficial world of appearances reasserted itself, fuelled of course by alcohol. She met a handsome guy in *Blaise*, a local nightclub, who had an RS 2000, the 1980s icon. Graeme would have called him something else, but Katie insisted his name was Colin. Suitably impressed she started dating him with Pete pushed to one side and told it was over.

She soon realised her mistake. She began to miss the security and love Pete had offered; she wanted him back so she called him. 'Yes,' he said, he would take her back, on the understanding that they would be married in the summer. It should have been the happiest time of her life, but Katie knew it was a mistake. Feeling like a guest at her own wedding she drank too much and deep in her heart she was unhappy. Her dad John had asked her months earlier if she was sure she was doing the right thing. She'd shrugged it off telling him that it was fine. As she now appreciated with the benefit of her years, parents have a feeling for things when it comes to the happiness of their children and it wasn't long before he was proved right.

Pete's mother had passed away when he was just eight and she found herself becoming a surrogate mother allowing her frustrations to surface. It seemed to Katie that he couldn't think for himself. He constantly relied on her to decide on everything, even choosing his clothes. When she'd agreed to marry him, it wasn't just the guilt she had felt. She had wanted him to look after her, to care for her and that just wasn't happening. He worked long hours too, so soon they were like ships passing in the night. Despite knowing he was a good man, kind and caring, it just wasn't working, so Katie started going out with her friends clubbing. It was not long before she was being unfaithful again.

The lessons she learned with the men she met were painful, including one encounter with an ex-teacher who, despite being handsome and something of a schoolgirl crush for her, proved to be abusive and only interested in sex. He had long since died young, of causes unknown. While she was saddened by the news, she couldn't forget his final, painful lesson and she shed no tears.

In due course, she attracted the attention of a guy who was to become her second husband. He had asked for her number as she jumped into her taxi home in the early hours of Saturday morning. She'd noticed him earlier and thought, okay, she gave him her work number, although she didn't expect him to call. At 4 pm the following Monday he did call and a new relationship began.

She had no idea then of the twists and turns that lay ahead.

Katie's view of herself had long since become fixed

which would affect her approach to men, to sex and her understanding of how it was to become her power over them. She had already told Graeme a little of her life wondering if he saw things the same way. From these early experiences, there would come times in her life when she would exercise that power ruthlessly. She would get hurt, and she would also leave hurt in her wake in pursuit of the love she craved.

Graeme shuddered, he wished he had known her all those years ago, but he knew, without a shadow of a doubt that she would have broken his heart and she still could. One ghost she finally laid to rest was her relationship with her sister Brenda. Katie had often been nasty to her sibling until she finally started to accept her as the true friend she would prove to be on many future occasions.

Roman Holiday

The stories of Katie's early years set the scene, but Graeme instinctively knew that this wasn't the source of the pain he had seen in her eyes.

"There's more, isn't there? Tell me what happened in Rome."

Katie hid her face, but he was persistent.

"I don't want you to get the wrong idea," she said. "It's not how it seems."

"It was your husband who threw you in the pool, wasn't it? That's why he had had nothing to say about it."

She was startled for a moment, she couldn't understand it, and it seemed to her that he could see into her soul. Tears formed in her eyes and she struggled to speak.

"Yes." she said.

"Tell me what really happened."

Katie said through her tears, "On the second night in Rome, we went to an amazing castle where opera singers sang on the lawn and the waiter brought canapés and far too much champagne. We had a fabulous five-course meal, again with lots of wine, a different one for every course. Later there was a show outside with fire-eaters accompanied by a fantastic firework display. I remember a big black soul singer and more alcohol.

"At the end of the evening, we got on the bus that would take us back to the hotel where the party continued for probably half the guests. There were lots more drinks and dancing on the patio. Before I knew it, we were around the indoor pool and the music had been brought inside. Suddenly I became aware that I was naked, fuzzy-brained and not understanding what was going on. I was picked up and tossed into the pool which brought me around. I could see there were probably about six men in the pool and a girl taking pictures.

"I swam to the far side, putting distance between us. My husband had a towel for me although he dropped it on the sunbed. I knew he wanted me to climb out in full view of everyone which I didn't want to do, so I doggy paddled about until people got tired and cleared off to bed. I got out, wrapped the towel around me then went to my bedroom where I ran a bath, much to my husband's annoyance, as he obviously thought it would make me want to have sex with him.

"The next morning I woke, remembering some of the evening so I asked him who had removed my dress and why.

"He laughed telling me that it was just a bit of fun and that I must have enjoyed it.

"I was embarrassed, this had been my invitation from one of my business contacts. When we went downstairs for breakfast I felt that people were talking about me. I was embarrassed so I went for a walk to the little local town."

"He has done this before hasn't he?"

"Not recently," she lied. "It only happened after he found out about the affair in 2008."

"There have been other times, more recently, haven't there?"

Pausing for a moment, she confessed, "Yes twice more since I met you. On New Year's Eve, the day after you came to see me in Manchester, he took me back to a house where there were just a few guys and us, acquaintances of his, two Irish guys, brothers called Callum and Sean, then again in August at a different party, when there ended up being just me and a girl called Linda being naked with a few guys."

She was upset now and would say no more. As she recalled events, she knew she would have to tell Graeme more eventually, but in her own mind, these more recent events had seemed tame in comparison to other occasions which she labelled 'the bad shit'. Her memory was fuzzy, even the bits she did remember, she dreaded telling him.

Katie would disagree, but Graeme felt that her

husband had been abusing her and he had no right.

"He adores me," she had said, "he just loves to show me off."

"No," said Graeme emphatically. "He's sexually abusing you, he's not making you feel good about yourself, is he? What's more he's putting you in some dangerous situations."

Katie knew he was right, even as she carried on making excuses for her husband.

"I've hurt him so many times," she said.

"Oh Katie. When are you going to forgive yourself? It's not your fault. He has no right, he's punishing you, he can't possibly love you, otherwise he would never do that to you. Please don't let him do that to you."

She was clearly embarrassed.

"I don't like myself very much," said Katie, tears welling in her eyes as Graeme held her tightly.

"I don't care about the past," he said. "We can't change it. Our pain is part of what makes us who we are, but we can't let it define us or drive us around the same vicious circle time and again, otherwise, we're never free of it. You have to find a way to free yourself Katie."

It remained unspoken, between them but one thing Graeme did know for sure was that men rarely lose interest in the company of naked women, particularly when they're as beautiful as Katie, until they've been satisfied in some way or other. In the situations Katie described, she couldn't remember how she got to that position and, although, she said she believed nothing had happened, she had clearly shut it out of her mind on each occasion. In the unlikely event that she'd not been violated already, she'd been very lucky, but Graeme knew in his heart that it would only be a matter of time if this continued.

Hiding it from Katie, he felt the anger rising within him. His veins were on fire at the thought of her being treated like this. He could have cried with her, but he had no right and he felt physically sick. There was something else too that he had not expected, he felt ashamed. He held her tight whispering in her ear, "I'm so sorry."

Katie didn't understand. "What have you got to be sorry for?"

"That first time I came to see you in Manchester, although it wasn't my intention, in the end, I treated you like all the rest didn't I? We got drunk then I took advantage of you."

Katie hadn't seen it that way. She didn't care about what had happened that first night she only cared about now, about the journey they were on together.

She laid in his arms, cuddling him, then after a while she said softly, "Make love to me… please."

He shut out the conversation they had just had and was as tender with her as he could be.

Afterwards, when they lay quietly, as she drifted off to sleep, Graeme looked into the darkness saying a silent prayer. He knew there was always someone listening as his thoughts turned to her parents John and Elaine, even though he never knew them, he asked them to help him reach her.

She was in a dark place, in need of a light to guide her.

Graeme had been to dark places in his life and he

considered all those he had lost as lights in the darkness for him when he needed them most. To make sure they could always find him, wherever he travelled, he always lit a candle in the local church to guide them to him. He made a mental note to tell Katie in the morning. For now, Graeme's world was changing beyond recognition, almost daily as he struggled to assimilate his mixed emotions. His feelings for Katie were off the scale, somehow he had to calm down because they were tearing him apart.

Throughout the night, Katie was aware of him holding her. He didn't seem to want to let go of her. If she turned over, he followed her and she loved it. Katie was so used to sleeping on the edge of a king-sized bed. She didn't like to be touched, or she thought she didn't, until now. As he lay beside her, Graeme knew that their journey was going to be difficult but he knew that they could get through it, that one day Katie would eventually be able to see herself the way he saw her, without her mask.

Her mask that was completed by her daily make-up routine, or 'slap' as he often referred it much to her amusement.

Life is much stranger than most people will admit and there were powers at work that Katie was just learning to sense.

The Magician

Realising that the night had been very painful for Katie, Graeme wanted the day to get off to a better start. He woke early as usual and started to nuzzle Katie gently on her neck. Katie stirred, opened an eye, thinking to herself it can't possibly be time to get up, it's still dark. He continued kissing her neck and this time she responded snuggling closer.

He then began to touch her, slowly working his way over her whole body. Every nerve ending sung. When he gently touched her clitoris, her head swam, she drifted into another world as the stroking became more intense and her body stood up as he brought her to the most mind-blowing orgasm. As her body jerked, he said, "I need to be inside you." They joined and once again their bodies shuddered before they held each other tight and Katie felt that neither of them wanted to let the other go, ever.

After a while, he said, "We forgot the toy. Where is it?"

"I don't need toys with you," Katie whispered, buttering him like a piece of bread then she giggled, but Graeme was curious.

She reached into her bag, pulled out a purple sex toy and handed it to him. His eyes widened in feigned astonishment. He looked at it, the toy, then down at his still erect manhood and back again.

"Oh thank God," he said. Katie giggled, knowing exactly what he was thinking. Apart from the strange shape, he was feeling good about himself.

"What do you do with it?" he asked.

"Well, it's not for internal use."

But it had clearly been well used.

"Is that why you carry such a big handbag around?"

This time she feigned a hurt look.

"Perhaps when I was taking the piss out of Bruce and Ciara in Dublin," he said, "I should have thought about this."

He rattled off another imaginary scenario to make Katie laugh. Putting on his best Irish accent, he pretended to be Ciara.

"Oh Brucie, my little stud muffin, I hope you have brought spare batteries for that big boy."

"No, I am afraid I haven't," replied Bruce. "That's my Thermos flask!"

Katie burst out laughing and a grin spread across his face.

"I think you have a secret obsession with Ciara." she teased.

Oh no, thought Graeme. That's what Bruce had told him in Dublin

"I haven't have I?"

They settled down again for a final cuddle and he said, "Thank you."

"For what?"

"The things you started to share last night. I think I'm starting to understand what the cards were trying to tell us in the Tower."

"I wonder what they would tell us now?"

"I have them with me if you really want to know."

Graeme leaned out of bed pulling the cards out of his day sack.

He picked out her chosen card, the Queen of Pentacles then passed the rest to Katie to shuffle. When she'd finished, she passed them back and he dealt out ten cards as before in the Celtic cross reading.

He dealt the cards;
The three of swords;
The six of pentacles;
The three of cups;
The Ace of Swords;
The five of swords;
The tower;
The three of wands;
The ten of cups;

The two of cups;

The Magician;

Katie was relieved to note that the Devil didn't appear anywhere in the reading, it had frightened her when she'd seen it previously. The prominence of cups and swords spoke of love and strife, but knowing what he now knew, how could they not? There were only two major arcana, which again signified the answer to Katie's silent question was once again in her own hands.

The three of swords; the general upheaval she was going through would work in her favour.

"Perhaps this change is what you need," said Graeme.

The six of pentacles; material things were working against her.

"Are you ready to give some of this up?" he asked.

The basis of her silent question; the three of cups was a quest for success in all its forms, most especially love and she recognised that it had been the card that had 'crowned' her reading some months earlier.

The five of swords indicated a passing away of defeat, failure and degradation.

Perhaps I could escape these influences and move forward, she thought.

The Ace of swords; the best that could be hoped for, was a triumph and the power to love strongly but the Tower showed the forces that were coming into play. If she really wanted this new life, there would be change, conflict, strife and her journey could be painful, but the disruption had the power to bring enlightenment in its wake.

The three of wands indicated that she was frightened to hope that this was real, only to be let down, yet the ten of cups indicated that her family and friends loved her so in the end, she would have their support.

The two of cups indicated her deepest hopes, the beginning of a love affair with a kindred soul.

However it was the final outcome, the Magician card that gave Graeme comfort. He knew intuitively that it was not a representation of him, as Katie had at first assumed. He knew that he didn't have the Magician's power to save her from her demons only she could do that. It was a symbol of herself which signified that she could do anything she wanted, if she chose.

This was a positive reading and he took comfort from the fact that the cards never lied. It was not always apparent what was meant until some of the future circumstances had come into play, but as with their earlier reading, in which the Devil - lack of understanding - was so prominent, Graeme knew they *could not* lie.

As with the Devil card some months earlier, the Magician as the final outcome would make its true significance known many months later, when Graeme would finally learn its true, deeper meaning.

When they got out of bed they showered together. Graeme held her tight washing her body all over as if washing away the pain and she reciprocated. Neither wanted to stop, but the day was upon them and they had too little time left together.

Afterwards he opened his laptop and put on iTunes

so that they could dance naked around the room, being careful only to choose slow songs so that he could hold her all of the time.

"I bet you would've been good at the ten to two slot," she said.

Graeme had no idea what she was talking about.

"In a night club," she explained. "At ten to two they put smooching songs on so that people can get together before they leave."

He smiled and held her tighter.

They packed, said good-bye to room 816 that had been their private oasis, checked out and made their way to Monument tube. They had intended to make their way to Kings Cross on the Circle Line but they had been so engrossed with each other that they boarded the wrong train and ended up heading towards the West End. Graeme noticed after a few stops. "It's okay," he said. "We can get off at Victoria then make our way to Euston instead. That way I can stay with you a little longer before your train leaves."

When they reached Euston, they checked the departure board for her train before making their way to the café where they ordered some coffee, water and a breakfast platter to share. They didn't talk a lot. Holding hands across the table, they looked into one another's eyes, it was as if they were both saying what they wanted to and the other knew.

After breakfast they said goodbye as Katie made her way back into Euston station. As she walked she kept looking back waving at him, wondering if his eyes were still following her. They were, so much so that Graeme was straining now to catch every last glimpse of her until she finally disappeared. He still had plenty of time before he needed to be at Kings Cross so being anxious to see her for even a moment longer he too went into the station. He saw her standing with her back to him, looking up at the departure boards and as he walked up behind her he cuddled her. She turned to greet him and he saw that she was crying. She had been on an emotional roller coaster over the last couple of weeks and opening up the previous evening had drained her emotionally. By the time her train arrived she felt a little better although they both knew that she had a long journey ahead of her in more ways than one.

On his train back to Scotland Graeme was pondering on how brave she'd been to trust him. Obviously, there was more to her story and he didn't know if she'd want to remember the bits she'd hidden away. Even if she did remember, how much would she want to share? He was, however, sure of one thing, Katie was on a dangerous path. She would never be free of her past until she dealt with it.

Non of this was lost on Katie. The following day she sent him a text, *I think our chat has opened up a can of worms for me. I drove to Chester remembering things I'd chosen to forget. I don't like what I've remembered and I need to deal with it. Thank you for understanding me, for not judging me, you have no idea what that means. You're the first person ever to know this stuff. You've helped me understand a bit as to why I might behave the way I do. xxx.*

Just get it all out then you can stand back and look

at it in the cold light of day,' replied Graeme. *'I know it won't be easy but it won't just help you. I am certain by what you told me that it is also the key to understanding and perhaps helping your son Tom too. I know you deserve much better but it can only come from you now.*

He knew that Katie wouldn't find this process easy but he promised to help her however he could. Knowing it would break his heart to see her hurt, he was happy at the thought that this was the first step towards getting Katie off that dangerous path she was on.

A moment later, another text arrived from Katie. *When I go to New York I am going to talk to Jenny. She knows the way my husband has been with me but even she doesn't know what I have told you.* Graeme's heart lifted again at the news, she needed a friend, he just prayed that Jenny would understand. Katie knew that there was more at stake here too, she needed to know what her son Tom had seen all those years ago that had disturbed him so much.

Tom was a clever, sensitive young man, although he had some unresolved issues. He was angry and jealous when his partner was out on her own, especially if he thought she was flirting, or even talking to another man, so much so that there was a dark undercurrent beginning to emerge in his attitude to her. His daughter Helen was just a few months old and Katie could see the same cycles starting to develop that would follow her all of her life if they couldn't be stopped. Katie had said that she just wanted to take Helen away from it all, and she could. All she had to do was understand what was behind it and deep inside she already knew the answer.

Over the past nine months, Katie had often talked about Tom and his relationship with his father, which was to say the least not good. At least that's how it seemed to Graeme. There seemed to be an underlying resentment, combined with his obvious desire to care for and protect his partner, albeit the way it manifested itself was often unpleasant. Graeme wondered if this was to do with the way he had seen his mother being treated.

Katie mentioned that he had 'seen things', though he had evaded the question as to what exactly. If she was being honest with herself, Katie was now wondering too, but it was too painful to go there right now.

Harvest Moon

The following day, as he drove to work, Graeme gazed at the western sky. It was a beautiful morning, the quiet tree lined roads giving no hint of the chaos that would ensue when he reached the outskirts of the city where the university traffic was again in full flow. But that was a minor inconvenience. The power of the harvest moon was starting to wane and he could feel the relief as if pressure were being allowed out of a sealed tube. Nothing would dampen his relief today. He looked up at the still large moon, bright in the clear blue sky as he headed to work thinking of Katie.

As he looked up, a plane flew right across the disc of the moon and he wondered what fate had in store for the next phase of their journey together. Katie was like a puzzle to him, a mystery he needed to understand as much for his sanity as she did for hers. The moon ahead of him nagged at his subconscious. The equinox was approaching when the world would pass a mid point on it's journey around the sun, tilt on its axis and the approaching nights would soon be much longer.

"As above, so below." They would also soon pass a point when Katie would read the outline for her story in which she had agreed to share her feelings to help him write it.

They loved their journey together, but if it was to mean anything it had to help her and he would soon have to tell her more of other worlds to guide her through her pain. He knew that people were complex by nature, that this complexity is built over many lifetimes, as both male and female, so trying to understand who we really are is truly like "looking through a glass darkly".

He had no idea how Katie would react if he shared this with her. Would she think he was mad, or would she have enough faith to continue on their journey together?

There were three things Katie needed to do and time was running out.

She had to confront her husband about his behaviour towards her if she was going to be truly safe. She had to reach out to her son Tom to understand why he behaved the way he did towards her and to women in general and perhaps most important, she needed to understand what her own demons were that drove her.

She was already beginning to question herself. What made her behave the way she did? Graeme wasn't sure what would happen next, but he didn't have to wait long for a clue. That morning Katie received a text from Carly. Tom was being abusive again. It was cry for help.

Hi Katie. It's taken a lot for me to say this so I hope you understand. Things are getting too much with Tom lately, I know he's not always at fault but I just don't know what to do anymore. I love him so much but our relationship may be coming to an end. The constant bickering is getting worse. I don't understand why he is so angry all the time, how he can snap so easily at the tiniest of things.

I don't want it anymore around Helen. I don't want to fight with him, I need your advice. I want to make our relationship work, to do everything I can to make things right. I'm saying this in confidence because he's your son. No one knows him better than you.

Katie called Graeme.

"I have to talk to Tom, you know I have been dreading it. Hopefully I can deal with a few things for me too."

"I'm very sorry to hear this," said Graeme. "You know I believe there is a right time for everything. Perhaps this is it, however don't be surprised if it takes a while. He needs your help to understand where his anger comes from and you won't find that a comfortable conversation. Just remember, no matter what Tom knows or thinks he knows, no matter what he saw or thinks he saw, yes you may both need to know *but* it doesn't make it your fault."

She doesn't deserve this, thought Graeme, but he knew that he couldn't help.

"What have you done to me?" Katie asked.

"Nothing, you're starting to believe in yourself, truly believe. You don't deserve this Katie, you deserve better."

He thought about her all day and they both wished their time away until they could be together the following day, but he also knew how important the conversation was going to be, so he texted her. *You know I am desperate to see you but if you need to spend time with your son I understand.*

Katie knew in her heart it was time, so resolved that she would speak with Tom when she returned from work. She felt sick all day, churned up at the thought of what she would say, then not knowing how he would respond. She knocked on the door of his apartment. Tom had been smoking pot all day and was in no mood to talk, he just laughed, breezed past her saying he was going out.

It wasn't lost on her husband that Katie was clearly stressed. He'd been questioning her more of late and while it was true that, as she said, she was worried about her son, this merely gave her a brief respite from his questioning. Katie was changing and there was a lot she hadn't yet come to terms with.

The timing couldn't have been worse. Katie was due to leave for New York soon and, although she was frightened as to what she may hear, she hated the thought of leaving this issue unresolved.

The Witch and the Amulet

Although he was tired of war and longed to return home, the journey back to England from Spain would take Richard Peak almost eighteen months.

After the defeat at Caceres, the few survivors who made their way back through the Tajo valley and back into Portugal had little appetite for further adventure.

While he was happy to be reunited with his men who also welcomed his return, they had been amazed to see him alive.

As he had approached the camp with Maria supporting him on one side and leaning on a roughly cut branch for support on the other, the guards raised the alarm. One of his own men, James Richardson, a page from the Ashton estate, ran to meet him at the camp's edge. He couldn't contain his joy as he hugged Richard like a long lost brother or father.

"James, it's good to see you, " said Richard .

"Likewise my lord." he replied.

After a few moments the page turned his attention to his master's new companion and when he saw Marie he recognised the camp girl taken during the attack on Aliseda.

"My lady," he said, "We are greatly in your debt."

He helped them back into the camp.

"Food for my lord!" he shouted. "And for our honoured guest."

James apologised for the food.

"It's not much, just some bread, cheese with a little wine, but rations have been low since we received re-enforcements from the Portuguese garrison at Castelo Branco. We provisioned as many as we could as we've been sending out patrols for the last few days back along the gorge looking for survivors. These are just the advanced detachment, their retinue of retainers with the supply wagons will be here in a few days."

Richard waved away his concerns. "After our recent adventures, that's of little consequence and, as always my friend, it's good to be back in your company."

After they'd eaten and while quarters were being made ready, he questioned James about the battle, his own survival, how he too had made his way back to the main garrison. Most of all, he was anxious for news of the rest of his men.

The rout that followed the battle had been complete

mayhem. There had been much confusion but James recounted what he knew. Their losses had been severe and, when Richard had failed to return with the stragglers, he too had been given up for dead. The sight of his wounds only served to compound their surprise and joy at his return. No one else who had suffered any major wounds had survived. They had all been put to death in the valley by the Spanish or had died of exposure.

Only fifty five men from a total of over three hundred had made it back across the border. Most had been fortunate to escape with nothing other than their lives, but not Richard.

Although he didn't yet know it yet, he had secured the greatest treasure of his life.

According to his wishes and on account of his wounds, he took no further active part on the front lines of the war. In truth, his wounds were completely healed, even though his work on behalf of his master was not complete, so the remaining time in Portugal was to be spent training further mercenaries for King Charles.

Even though they had lost many men, they had learned a great deal about the resourcing, strength and tactics of the Spanish forces leaving the King able to successfully press for concessions from his Hapsburg foe. The war was to last a further three years, but Richard Peak, his page James and his soulmate Maria set sail for home with the blessing of his king in the summer of 1627.

He arrived in Plymouth to the news that his wife Lady Eleanor had died a few months earlier. He had given her little thought while he was away on campaign. Although he was saddened by the news, it had in truth been nothing more than an advantageous marriage.

When Edward De Hulton, the previous lord of the manor of Ashton had passed away leaving no male heirs, his wife Lady Eleanor became a wealthy widow, a dowager. Unable to own land in her own right, she would hold the estate in trust, continuing to live in the manor until a successor was chosen by the king. That successor had been Richard Peak and, although Richard admired her fortitude and gracefulness, their marriage in 1625 was one of convenience, solely to achieve the transfer of the De Hulton estates along with the duties of lordship as was customary.

It was a small mercy that there was no pressing need to head north immediately, as now that he was back in England he would need to travel to London. He was carrying private messages for the King's family and the royal court was always hungry for fresh gossip.

By now Maria was inseparable from Richard, so much so that there would never be another who could turn his head, although, over the coming months many would try to attract a handsome, wealthy, powerful man in his physical prime. For the courtly ladies of England, Richard was now indeed an eligible man, a rich widower with close connections to the king. Even though he didn't welcome the courtly attention, there was little he could do about it. Maria was a catholic, a Spaniard as far as anyone knew, which, by definition, meant she was an enemy of the Crown so she couldn't be recognised as the wife of a nobleman for at least as long as the war raged... and there were more complications on the horizon.

In an effort to avoid further scrutiny, at the first

opportunity, Richard spent less and less time in London regaling the courtiers with tales of war and the glory of the king. Eventually he was free to set about tending his estates in the North, growing his fortune whilst introducing Maria to her new life in England.

She fell in love with Ashton, she would spend her time by the brook or in the forests on the estate, always with her amulet performing her strange rituals and, wherever she went, the land blossomed giving its riches freely.

Even the shadows that seemed to watch her from the tree line seemed lighter, drinking in the energy that flowed from her.

Although the manor house was a grand building with a great hall for entertaining guests, warm fires and soft beds, they would often spend nights sleeping under the stars. Maria would interpret the symbols she saw written in the sky above them and as the months went by he watched her intently, he knew that somehow she was in tune with nature. The energy of creation itself seemed to swirl around her, the sexual energy she exuded always excited him more than any battle he'd ever fought. As he lay in her arms by Hollins' brook, the border of his estate, he stared into the deep pools of her dark brown eyes and asked, "What did you do to me in the Tajo valley? I should have died along with most of the others."

She fingered the strange green stone she wore around her neck, looked into his eyes and said truthfully, "I love you and the amulet will not let you leave me in this world as long as I am alive. It will also ensure we are together in the next life if you are willing. Love is the most powerful force of all, but it is something that cannot be forced, it must be given freely."

Richard smiled. "You know I love you with all my heart, but no one has that power" he said, "yet, as I look into your eyes, I believe you completely."

Her expression changed momentarily. "I do," she said matter of factly "As long as I wield the stone."

New York

Katie woke early, dressed quickly in jeans and a white t-shirt, leaving while her husband still slept. She'd not given much thought to the holiday, telling herself that was because she'd been so busy with work. That wasn't strictly true; if she hadn't spent so much time with Graeme her work would have fitted comfortably into a normal day.

Arriving at Donna's house, she was greeted by five excited ladies drinking champagne. Knowing there was only one sensible one between them, Donna's daughter, Katie wondered how this holiday would play out. Despite having so much on her mind, she could already see that there was going to be a split in the group due to their personalities. They set off to the airport and she set a pattern for the rest of the holiday, checking her phone for messages from Graeme. The girls chatted about what they would do when they arrived but Katie's thoughts were elsewhere. Realising that she didn't seem as excited as the others, she couldn't decide if that was because she'd visited New York before, or was it because she felt that she was leaving something behind, something important?

As she thought of Graeme, of his eyes once again staring down at her, her phone vibrated. It was a text wishing her a lovely holiday, asking her to be careful and he had also included a picture of the two of them in bed with the message - *Take this with you.*. She thanked him, saying, *Oh I do love that picture.*

He recalled what she'd said at the time she took it, 'Look at how happy you make me.'

Drinks at the airport passed the time before her flight and, as she flew, Katie laughed at a Cameron Diaz movie, about a guy having an affair with several women at the same time. Katie didn't know it but Graeme also had a lot he needed to share with her when the time was right. He had told her that there were times he'd wished he was a better man, and he'd meant it.

He hardly slept and, whenever he woke, she was there looking at him. There were so many questions he wanted to ask her although he didn't know where to begin. He was afraid she wasn't ready to face the truth, afraid that he would hurt her. She had to face her past, to leave it behind if they were to have a future. She may not realise it, he thought, but she's in a battle for her very soul. He wanted her to have some space from everything, including him while she was away, so that she could think, perhaps take a step back, but they were in constant contact, sending one another photos with loving messages, both trying to stay as close as possible despite the distance. They didn't feel separated by three thousand miles, but an inch would have been too far.

Katie had asked him if he would take her to San Diego to watch the sun go down over the Pacific so he sent her the photos again, knowing she hadn't kept them.

'They are beautiful,' she replied, then he sent her another.

A picture of her, on that last morning he'd seen her in London when she'd just awoken. It was just her face looking over her shoulder at him. It was Katie with no mask and he wrote, 'this one is MUCH more beautiful.'

'With no slap on, hmm, I love that you love me with everything stripped bare.'

'Yes, even with no slap on, she's still more beautiful than the sun going down over the Pacific Ocean, how lucky is she?'

He loved that picture.

'I am lucky if I have you.'

Katie knew that no one had ever loved her the way Graeme did and, while she loved how it made her feel, not knowing how to deal with it she threw herself into her trip.

Graeme had to acknowledge how jealous he was feeling. She was driving him crazy, like an itch he just couldn't scratch. Katie couldn't yet control the urges within her and, at the end of the first night, she once again didn't remember going home.

She visited the usual tourist sights, drank too much, laughed with the girls and flirted with the men she met. She flirted for free drinks, charming the hotel staff to get recommendations for bars or more free drinks and again she found herself late at night in the bars, talking to strangers then not remembering how she got back to the hotel. She attracted men like a magnet. She smiled to herself, realising for the first time that, although she hid nothing from Graeme in their conversations, she found herself wondering why, when she sent him pictures, she was careful to miss out the pictures of Kielan, Peter, Aiden and all of the other 'randomers' she'd 'accidentally' charmed.

The following morning, still groggy, she grabbed her phone. She couldn't remember if she'd let Graeme know she was home safe as she'd promised she would. She lay back trying to remember returning to the hotel.

Jenny couldn't remember either, but at least Bel did. They'd apparently gone to another rooftop bar at some point and were chatting to 'randomers.' Katie still couldn't remember. Once again, she felt awful, hating herself for getting in such a state. Bel said that she'd seemed fine – drunk, although not totally wasted. Clearly, Bel had been wrong.

It was her birthday while she was in New York and Graeme had hoped this could represent a new start for Katie. In the morning he woke after dreaming of her and sent her a message so that when she woke she would know he was thinking about her. Then he had a strange urge and immediately started looking back through the photographs that she'd sent him some months before. This time, when he saw the one he was looking for, instantly he realised what had been bothering him.

Katie woke on her birthday, reached for her phone and there it was, the only message she was hoping for. Graeme hadn't let her down. She lay back down hugging her phone. Jenny was already up, she was sitting in the window seat watching a busy New York happening below.

As the sun shone, the time with her friends was a welcome diversion from the pressure at home. They shopped and, when she saw a beautiful bracelet in Tiffany's, Graeme wanted to buy it for her birthday although she politely refused. It was so expensive she'd thought he would choke on his coffee when he saw it but his reply had shocked her more. She received nice presents from her friends, laughed a lot and despite having had another fun day, Katie could feel that she was changing. She even surprised herself when she'd described Central Station as 'such a beautiful, impressive building; full of charm with whispering walls.' Whispering walls... what?

Later that afternoon, Katie received another message from Graeme. 'Have you spoken to anyone yet?' Yes, she had in fact spoken to Jenny and she got something of a shock. She sent Graeme a text saying that Jenny had told her some things that she found more appalling than she'd shared with him about her own experiences.

I wonder how that conversation went thought Graeme.

When they were alone for a few moments, Katie had managed to speak with Jenny telling her how she was feeling.

"I've fallen for him," she said. "I'm scared of where this is going. I love him, but I'm so scared of hurting everyone."

Jenny looked at her. "You can't help your feelings I suppose, just be careful this is what you want. If your husband finds out, it'll be over for you, he's surely not going to forgive you again."

Katie told Jenny what had been bothering her. "You know things have happened over the past few years that I'm not comfortable with. I've let it happen though, so I must be partly to blame, but I've always been so drunk that I've not been able to stop it."

"What do you mean?"

"Well, my husband likes to take my clothes off at every opportunity when we are with acquaintances."

Jenny smiled. "He just thinks you're beautiful, he wants to show you off."

"That might be true, but do you think it's right? Should your husband want to strip his wife naked showing everyone her most intimate parts?"

"Well, my husband is just the opposite, he stands as far away from me possible when we're out. It's like he doesn't want anyone to think we're together."

"What about allowing other guys to touch? Is that right?"

"No," said Jenny, "but all guys are perverts."

"No I don't think they are, but surely your husband should want to love you, keep you safe not subject you to these things? He promised to love honour and protect me, not love, honour, strip me naked then treat me like a plaything. That's not right, is it?"

"Have you talked to him?"

"Yes, it was a while back and it's happened again since."

"Well, you need to talk to him again and tell him in no uncertain terms. He loves you Katie, he puts you on a pedestal, he always has."

"Yes, you're right. I do need to talk to him. I shouldn't get that bloody drunk that I don't know what I'm doing. Why do we do it?"

Graeme could have told her the answer, but he was three thousand miles away and it was not his place, this was a question Katie would have to answer for herself.

Jenny took the opportunity to share a few burdens of her own. "Some strange things have happened to me while I've been drunk. My husband is always watching porn and I woke up one morning with a bottle of conditioner next to the bed"... she left the words hanging before adding, "it smarted a bit."

When the other girls caught up with them, Katie changed the subject, although they continued to ponder their respective situations as they walked.

Katie shared bits of the conversation with Graeme in texts later that evening and he tried to reassure her that it wasn't her fault. Clearly she wasn't alone.

I guess we all have our issues, he thought. At least Katie won't have to deal with hers alone, not if she doesn't want to.

He hoped that Jenny's revelations would help Katie realise that her circumstances could apply to many women.

His mind raced. Although he was worried for Katie he couldn't help smile at Jenny's story. Conditioner? He'd never thought of toiletries being a separate category of porn. He could only imagine that if it ended up anywhere too intimate, it would indeed 'smart a bit'. In fairness, she'd said that she was so drunk she hadn't remembered, so perhaps it was an innocent mistake. Perhaps they had been watching porn when she misheard him thinking he wanted her to give him a wash and blow-dry?

When he texted Katie his thoughts she had laughed, then he added, *I was wondering what they would be like with a salt and pepper cellar, are condiments another category of pornography these days?*.

Things had definitely got weird! He should probably have a look at the internet as he was clearly out of touch.

You're so funny, said Katie.

Me? They're your friends, they're hilarious. Just listening to the Rose; thinking of you. Just remember in the winter far beneath the bitter snow, lays the seed that with the suns love, in the spring becomes the rose… My Rose. We all have our demons but we don't have to give into them.

What's been niggling you?

What's niggling me? I've hardly slept since I saw you last. Last night I dreamt of you, then this morning I was drawn to a picture of you with Karen. Tell me about the night you had dinner with her, the weekend before we met at the Border Heifer. You didn't tell me that the evening was one of 'those' evenings.

Katie was startled. *How do you know these things?*

It was the Rolos that told me. Be happy. Be Katie, not

the person someone wants you to be.

Katie knew what he was referring to, that she'd have to tell him one day, but now was not the time. *I know what you mean, please don't be angry with me.*

I promise you Katie, I'm not angry. I don't care about the past. I know it'll be all right. How could it not be? I only feel the way I do because I love you.

You're tired. Just close those beautiful blue eyes, think of wrapping your arms around me and sleep.

And he did.

Later that evening, she sent him a picture of St Patrick's Cathedral with a note that read, *Just lit a candle.*

Although it was 2am for Graeme, he replied, *Did you feel it Katie? A light in the darkness; you are not alone.*

It was only afterwards, when she told Graeme about the experience, that she realised she had felt something, it was so subtle it hadn't struck her at the time. She'd gone into the cathedral to light a candle. For some reason she just couldn't seem to get one to take, so she walked out, but, once outside, she remembered what he'd told her and went back in and this time she managed.

The universe doesn't shout at us, it whispers to us if we open our hearts and are prepared to listen.

Tears ran down her face as her childhood memories surfaced.

My mum worried so much for me. Just before she died, she was forever telling me not to drink so much. You would have liked her and she would have loved you. I do believe now that things are going to be okay, I do hope my mum and dad are still looking out for me, they were the best parents ever. There's so much I want to ask you.

You have my heart in your hands Katie, ask me anything. Whatever it contains is yours to know. I'm guessing I'm the strangest guy you've ever known.

Yes, you're the most wonderfully intriguing person I've ever met. I honestly didn't think you would be as you are, BUT I so love you for it.

The following day Graeme drove to work in a trance and could remember none of the journey. He was still tired and he felt lost. If Katie was feeling the emotional turmoil of their affair, then she was not alone. The pieces of the jigsaw were starting to come together in his mind. As they did so, Graeme began to feel sick.

In New York, Katie awoke aware that, once again she hadn't texted Graeme to let him know she was home safe. Feeling dreadful, even the hangover food at the 'all you can eat diner' did nothing to lift her mood. They visited the Rockefeller Building and, at the top, she sent Graeme a picture. Sitting alone, looking out at the city under a bright blue sky, she wondered where her life was going. The alcohol from the night before had made her anxious. Instead of feeling happy, she was frightened for the road ahead.

Waiting at the airport for her return flight, Katie decided that she'd tell Graeme more. How would she remember it all? She boarded the plane, took her seat and, as they took off into the darkening sky, she took out her phone to make some notes. The flight raised bittersweet emotions; she was excited at the prospect of seeing Graeme again, but she could no longer put off her awkward conversations with her son and her husband. Her mind raced until eventually the sightseeing, dancing, drinking and flirting all started to make itself felt and tiredness finally overtook her. As she dozed off, she thought of Graeme once more and she giggled. Should she tell him about the guy she met from Didsbury who makes films in New York? Probably not, knowing he would just say he was 'probably a git'.

He would have been right.

Rendezvous

When she returned from New York on Wednesday morning, she was as anxious as Graeme to break their enforced abstinence from one another. They'd already arranged to be together the following week, but they both needed to hold one another again. They knew they couldn't spend the night together, but arranged to meet on Friday at a convenient location. Graeme suggested meeting towards lunchtime, knowing she'd still be jet lagged. In fact, he felt that way himself, due to the late night texting. He picked a hotel at random called Rendezvous where they could have lunch and talk.

"That's spooky," Katie had said when he suggested it. "I know that place."

She was starting to wonder about coincidences and to look at the world anew.

Graeme arrived first. He was early and his journey through the beautiful countryside on that rainy morning had been a blur although he did remember listening to *A world without you* and lyrics reverberated in his head. The hotel was busy, not a quiet place to meet as he'd hoped, and Katie was late so he began to worry.

When he saw her arrive, he walked to the door hugged her and they kissed passionately, oblivious to the people trying to pass through the doorway they were blocking. Eventually, he pulled her aside, as they continued hugging and kissing like excited teenagers.

They sat in the lobby on a sofa opposite five frumpy ladies who looked like they were engaged in a Women's Institute meeting. Graeme had never seen a WI meeting, he imagined a sort of 1940s affair with lots of tea, knitting, scandalous gossip and British stiff upper lips in the face of adversity. They dressed much older but were probably about the same age as Katie, although their attitudes were clearly decades apart. There was little doubt that they disapproved of their public show of affection which had resulted in much discussion. They sounded like clucking hens, especially when he accidentally took delivery of a coffee and a tea, which belonged to their party.

Katie looked fabulous in a tight top with skin-tight black jeans.

"I can just imagine what they are gossiping about," laughed Graeme.

"I don't care," said Katie snuggling into him on the

sofa.

She had been giving a lot of thought to the things she wanted to ask Graeme about his childhood. The tarot, ouija boards and his strange vision of the world. This took him by surprise, but he told her as much as he was able to about his relationship with his grandmother. It was from her that all those experiences came and, before long, his head was tucked into her neck and he was crying. Somehow she had taken him back through some of the most frightening, the most traumatic events in his life that no one, not even his closest family or friends knew.

Then it was Katie's turn.

"I've had a few dreams in my life that I'll never forget," she said. "One day, just after I moved into our house, I was aware that something was giving me an orgasm. It was so real, I'm not sure it was a dream. It was as if I wasn't allowed to wake until it was over. I didn't want to wake up because I was enjoying it so much."

She seemed deeply disturbed as she recalled the event as if her mind was reaching out, and there was something else, a feeling she was struggling to re-capture.

"Another was the night before last, when I found myself on a road with Jenny. I couldn't see far because there was a bend in it so I crossed over. When I returned Jenny had gone and I was being attacked by a dark entity, a shadow. I felt as if I was being pulled down. I was so scared then I broke away waking up, with my heart pounding. What do you think they mean?"

Graeme was sure he knew what the second dream meant straight away, it was Katie's subconscious telling her something.

"The road you're on is unfamiliar because it represents a path you've not chosen to take before. You're on the same path as Jenny because of the things she told you in New York. She disappears because she hasn't chosen to move forward as you have. The path isn't straight, it's unclear to you because you don't yet know which direction you'll take and the creature you're fighting represents a hostile situation or person in your waking life that you need to overcome, no matter how overpowering or intimidating the situation or person seems. It could even be something deep in your own subconscious. There is no need to be frightened, it cannot harm you unless you let it."

Katie thought about her husband. It could have been a reference to their rocky relationship. Graeme wasn't so sure, sometimes we are truly visited in our dreams but they are mostly about aspects of our own personalities. Could it be a representation of Katie and her own tendency to put herself in situations which she couldn't control? She had alluded to something much darker, something that she was not yet ready to share, so in the end, they left it at that.

The first dream was altogether different and Graeme felt a shiver run down his spine. There were several possibilities and unlike most 'normal' people, Graeme was prepared to consider them all. The first he shared with Katie, the others he kept to himself.

"Dreams about orgasms can just be symbols that you have sexual tension you need to release. Perhaps you're not getting enough sex, or it could simply represent an exciting end to something."

Katie thought back. She'd recently moved into her house, which she loved, and she was yet to embark on her affair with Andy, so yes, it could've been any of those things. She shrugged.

The other possibilities intrigued Graeme, one terrified him. People would laugh at the idea, but there exist entities, some call them shadows or daemons, that feed on the sexual energies in humans and he knew that these entities were very real because, as a child, he'd been taught how to see them.

Fate is unhindered by time, it sees across many lifetimes to guide all souls and there is no such thing as coincidence. In her own childhood, Graeme's grandmother had encountered a mystical group called the Theosophical Society. During her lifetime, there was an explosion of interest in mysticism, a desire to discover knowledge which had long been hidden from the public gaze. Foremost amongst these great New Age mystics was Mira Kirovsky, a strange woman from Belarus, who was herself on a journey of discovery. It was from her that his grandmother had learned to see new worlds and she, in turn, had taught Graeme to see the world in a way that few could ever master.

Few would ever want to if they understood the visions that would accompany them throughout their lives; it was part gift, part curse. Children are more plastic in their attitudes and learning than adults. As we grow older, we shut out the other worlds that exist alongside and interact with ours. We incorrectly rationalise things as personality traits or psychological problems. It's little wonder that they are so difficult to deal with when people don't understand the origins of their problems.

Most frightening of all, it's easier than people imagine attracting their attention then inviting them in whether by accident or design, all it needs is a strong emotional situation.

With human lovers, a woman takes a man's seed, but this seed is different. They impregnate the spirit with emotions that they then feed on. Fear and a feeling of worthlessness are common, because of the intensity of the emotion, a woman will struggle to find any equivalent in human relations that can snap her out of it.

Graeme knew, and Katie was learning, that sex without love isn't worth experiencing because it operates on far more than just the physical plane. The house and the date of this event were two of the keys to the journey that had brought Katie to where she was. They needed to understand this mystery, to make sense of it together.

A seed is easy to remove unless nurtured or allowed to grow, then it's much more difficult to remove. Fear, like all seeds, grows. Self-doubts are magnified over time and gradually people lose sight of their own divine nature, of their true value, as they give themselves over to their ghost riders. The tree needs to be pruned back, one branch at a time until it's weak enough to be uprooted.

The final possibility he considered was that the dream was an echo from a past life, some unresolved issue deep in her subconscious. Katie didn't believe in reincarnation. Graeme on the other hand knew with certainty that no one can escape from their actions, that you cannot leave without paying the bill. Sexual energy ran through Katie's core so powerfully that there had to be a reason, some emotional trigger she needed to understand. Katie had told him how she felt about his lovemaking, that he was the best lover she'd ever had, but he'd not known about her dream and one day he knew he must ask her, but not today.

Today they were unable to make love, yet they could both feel that the urge was as strong as ever. They sat so close that they could pass as conjoined, separating only briefly to move into the bar to order some food. As they talked, Katie relayed the events of the New York trip, her thoughts about her life and the direction she wanted to take.

"You know I spoke to Jenny in New York," she said.

"Yes."

"Well I tried to speak to Donna too although it was difficult with her daughter being with her all of the time. The night before my birthday, we had a chat but we were getting drunk so I don't know how much she'll remember. We're as bad as one another when we've had a drink."

"How did it go?"

"I showed her the picture of us together in bed. Seeing how happy I was, she asked me quietly what was happening. She thinks I am playing with fire. I told her it had gotten serious and now feelings were well in play. Like all my friends, Donna likes my husband, she is concerned about what it would do to him, especially with him being ill."

A few weeks earlier, Katie's husband had needed minor surgery yet, despite him being in hospital, Katie had chosen to be with Graeme.

"He's feeling very sorry for himself, talking about changing his lifestyle," she had said.

He's maybe regretting a few things too, Graeme thought.

"'How would he cope?' Donna had asked. What about Tom? What about your granddaughter? The dog?"

Graeme laughed. "The dog? That's no problem if he loves you like I do. He can come with us, as long as he stops eating my Rolos."

Katie beamed. "Yes, we come as a team. I told Donna I didn't think that you were prepared for any repercussions this could bring for you or your family. She asked about you, she could see that I've fallen for you, I could see the worry on her face. She'd been here before in her own life. 'I'm scared for you,' she had said. 'Just because you enjoy your time together and the sex is amazing you need to think carefully Katie'.

"None of them know what has really gone on in my marriage. I tried to tell her about my husband taking my clothes off when I'm incapable of stopping it and I don't think she quite believed what I was saying. She thinks I need to talk to him, to tell him there would be consequences if it were to happen again. I told her that I'd already had that conversation, that it had happened since, the last time after Karen's dinner party in August and also in Rome. I think she understands but we didn't get another chance to talk."

Donna was worried when Katie first told her that she was going to meet Graeme and it seems she was once again correct when she'd wondered if he knew what he was letting himself in for. He didn't, but he was slowly, too slowly, finding out.

Time had a different quality for them when they were together, each second seemed like a lifetime yet today they had talked for five hours, which passed as if in an instant. The day was emotionally draining for both of them, it was to lead them to a bridge they had to cross and Graeme didn't know if he could. He was certain he wanted to be with Katie but he still didn't know which Katie he was talking to. That was to become apparent to him the following evening but, for now they kissed, saying goodbye as he handed her a packet of fruit gums.

She laughed. "I'm not on a diet now."

They drove away in opposite directions and half an hour later Graeme's phone rang. It was Katie.

"I'm going the wrong way," she said.

At first, he misunderstood thinking she was lost. How could she be? She knew where she was going, she had sat nav.

She repeated, "I'm going the wrong way. I was driving and suddenly thought what the fuck am I doing, I should be going with Graeme."

Katie never swore. She'd once put profanity in a text but he'd never heard her actually swear before. It had been an emotional day and again they talked again about how they were feeling. By this time he was driving past a military electronic warfare listening station.

"You do realise there's probably some poor kid sat listening to this strange conversation?"

He'd been drained by the day in a way he hadn't expected. He didn't like being apart from Katie so in an effort to lighten the mood he couldn't resist having some fun, all the more so just in case anyone was really listening.

"Could you imagine what the Women's Institute lot would have been saying if we had met the way we wanted to?" he said as he rattled off another imagined scenario.

"Katie walked purposefully into the reception when Graeme grabbed her and kissed her passionately. Oblivious to all around her, she fell to her knees, unzipped his flies letting his now erect manhood loose for all to see. Slowly she licked him and took him in her mouth in full view of everyone…".

He could hear Katie giggling on the other end of the phone and he continued.

"Mavis and Dorothy had been the only two of their party facing Katie. Dorothy couldn't believe her luck; she'd read about things like this in *Women's Weekly* and had wanted her husband Seth to try it. Mavis was not so lucky, she clutched her chest, was struggling for breath as she slumped to the floor, her last thought was that she was glad they had had that cake baking fundraiser to install defibrillators near the canal."

Katie was by now laughing hysterically, practically wetting herself so Graeme stopped. He didn't want to distract her from her driving, but he always wanted to leave her with a smile on her face. They said goodbye and continued their journey home, both in a much lighter mood.

Hedonism

Catching the train north Katie was pensive. She resolved that tonight she would tell Graeme everything even though she was unsure how he'd react.

He picked her up at the station, dropped her at the small hotel she had chosen, away from prying eyes where they could make love, then talk while sharing some wine, cheese, crackers, grapes and sandwiches. He couldn't wait to hold her again but, needing to go back to the office, promised to return as soon as possible.

At 4.30 pm she came to the door to meet him. It had been almost three weeks since they'd been intimate and they made hasty love, a needy, animalistic affair both seeking again to mark their territories reclaiming what was theirs.

Afterwards, Katie told Graeme more of her story. The more she did, the more it disturbed him.

"After my husband found out about the affair with Andy, I really believed that it was over between us, but, as I guess most married couples with a family would, we talked about what, if anything, could be done to repair the damage, perhaps even see if we could rekindle some of the passion and fun we'd once felt. My husband pushed for us to go to an adult resort he'd heard of in the Caribbean. We did a bit of research and I was in the bad books so agreed to book a holiday there later in 2008."

Graeme reeled struggling to keep his imagination in check, he had heard of these places, they had been the subject of more than one pornographic documentary.

Sensing his discomfort, she continued, "I know their reputation, but looking into it, it appeared that you could be naked if you wanted, but there were compulsory clothing areas if you didn't. There were lots of themed party nights, like schoolgirl, fetish, toga and you could join in if you wanted to, or not, as the case might be.

"We were trying to repair our marriage and it was much as we had suspected. Although there was a lot I didn't want to get involved in, nothing was pushed in our faces, so it was very relaxed. We had a relatively fun week, spent time naked on the beach, drank at the swim-up bar, danced in the nightclub in pyjamas but never got involved in anything and, to be honest, we were probably viewed as a bit prudish. The only thing that marred it were the arguments over Andy, which I suppose I should've expected.

"On the back of the good time we'd had, the following

year we agreed to up the stakes a little booking a week at another adult resort. The people there appeared more outgoing, louder. As well as couples, there were groups of guys and girls, and there were the rubber people, a strange lot who dressed in latex despite the blistering heat. They were bizarre, yet at the same time quite intriguing, they tied each other to beams. They weren't interested at all in normal people.

"I loved the music they played. It was a constant feature, I wore nice, sexy clothes and danced my socks off. There were rooms where people went if they wanted to have sex, but I thought myself far too good to have sex with any randomers, although if I'm honest, I did love the attention. People of both sexes approached my husband to ask if we would like to join in, but I always refused.

"One night, in the club I did find a guy quite attractive, then unbeknown to me he arranged with my husband that we would go back to this couple's room later. On arriving at the door, I asked what on earth we were doing, basically turned and walked away. My husband apologised to the couple accepting it wasn't what I wanted. Despite the pressure to go further than I wanted to, it was a fun week. Being constantly naked seems to make everyone far friendlier."

"Yep, you are incredibly friendly when you're naked - or drunk, or both," Graeme teased.

Katie gave him a withering look then continued her story.

"In 2011 we went back to the first adult resort we'd tried. The fun party side was far better than most

Caribbean hotels, but I had preferred the quieter side and we managed to get a cheap last-minute deal. It was a bit of a disappointment though, as it seemed to be closing down with relatively few people staying there, so the atmosphere wasn't as good as the first time we'd been. I didn't see anything outlandish or offensive - you could have been in any hotel anywhere.

"Our final visit was in 2013. My husband had heard of an event organised by a group called Love Voodoo. They shipped out their own DJ's and he persuaded me to go on the basis it would be a great party atmosphere. When we arrived, although it was clean enough, I couldn't believe how scruffy the place had become. It seemed to have gotten older, seedier and I felt that lecherous old men were ogling me everywhere I went. More than once I asked myself, what are we doing in this dump?

"Alongside the nudity, daft things were going on, like goat racing, bouncy boxing on the beach, lots of fun games and again the music was great. There was one real bright spot too. One night in the bar, a lovely black lady approached me, telling me I was beautiful, in a full-on American accent. I'm broad-minded but not attracted to other women. Thinking she was gay, I backed off. Marsha, as I later found out she was called, seeing the expression on my face, started laughing, explaining that she saw beauty in everyone and she liked to tell them.

"She was an ex-cheerleader, a swinger from Detroit along with her husband Ian. He was a nice guy, probably about ten years older, they had met when he had played American football professionally. She was lovely and she became a real friend. Ian asked me if we might have a little fun, but I told him that it would damage the relationship I'd formed with Marsha, although that didn't stop us spending time with them. We spent several days sitting on the beach, drinking tequila, while Marsha entertained us with her outlandish stories. She was fun to be around, I'd like to introduce you one day."

Graeme must have visibly shrunk; Katie just laughed.

She hadn't found it easy to talk about her visits to the Caribbean, about how she had seen more and more. These experiences along with the constant pressure to push the boundaries further were starting to be mirrored at home, leaving scars in their wake. The constant theme emerging was her husband's desire to see Katie involved in group sex.

Graeme listened, as slowly yet surely she lifted her mask a little higher, he could see her mind working, it was if the memories were so deeply hidden that she was physically pulling them into her conscious mind.

"Let's leave it there until tomorrow," he said.

Again Katie defended her husband who, she continued to insist, loved her. Maybe he did, Graeme was in no position to agree or disagree. Maybe he'd sought out the excitement believing that she needed more and perhaps this had been the reason behind the affairs. Irrespective, the more she told him, the more it seemed to Graeme that Katie's sexuality was far stronger than either of them imagined and the paths it was leading down were getting worrying.

Katie got up to ran a bath. Graeme joined her and held her tight. The revelations she had shared had clearly been painful yet he knew there would be still more to come as she had made veiled references to earlier events as 'the bad shit' then skated over them. The events of the last twelve months had bothered her for sure, but not nearly as much, still he'd wondered how could they be tame by comparison?

The affair with Andy had been rekindled briefly in 2010. When her husband found out, he sent him photographs asking him if he knew what he was getting himself into. Graeme had a vivid imagination but, based on what she'd told him, he really didn't need it in order to guess the what content of those photographs might be. This in turn led to continuing visits to the Caribbean. Katie had booked them knowing her husband liked the place, it was her way of trying to make up for the guilt she felt for hurting him again.

Graeme knew it was hard for her, that it would take time to come to terms with, so he pressed no further. He took some comfort that she was on the right path and was cutting down the tree, one branch at a time. One day she'd be strong enough to uproot it. He didn't judge her, he was simply worried about her safety. She assured him that she'd tell him more when she was ready. Much of it was hazy to her and, although she didn't want to, she knew she had to remember it and share it for her own sake.

As painful as it was for Katie to share these things, it also hurt Graeme to hear them. "No secrets," he said. "I need to know the Katie behind the mask."

"No secrets. When my husband finds out he'll do the same to you; send you pictures, so I want you to know everything. Please, believe me, I don't want these things.

I'm sorry, I don't want to hurt you and you have no idea of the pain to come."

As he squeezed her tightly, with tears in her eyes, she turned to kiss him.

After they'd bathed, they went back to bed to make love again. He held her as she drifted off to sleep and was attentive to her every movement throughout the night.

For Graeme sleep would not come, he was trying to make sense of something he'd no experience of. With no frame of reference to guide him he silently called out in the darkness, again asking for help.

The following morning, he woke Katie early in the manner to which she'd become accustomed. They made love, showered then went down for breakfast. Graeme needed to leave early and Katie followed about an hour later.

Once in the office, the pretence began again. Graeme said hello, kissed her on the cheek and they settled down to their respective tasks. At various points during the day, she had to walk behind his chair and struggled to stop herself reaching out and stroking his neck. They were both wondering the same thing, how long could they keep this up before they gave themselves away with careless words or gestures?

Although they were both going to Manchester that evening, Katie travelled from Edinburgh, but Graeme drove to Berwick station where he could leave his car for his return the following day. When he boarded the train, it was packed. Fortunately, he had reserved a seat. Instead of sitting down, he spoke to the lady next to

Katie.

"Excuse me, I've a reserved seat just there," pointing to a nearby table. "I wonder, if I give you the reservation, would you mind swapping places so that I can sit next to my wife?"

She kindly agreed and Katie cuddled into his arm as he settled down beside her. Knowing that he'd not slept much the night before, she encouraged him to sleep. As he dozed, Katie made some notes on his laptop trying to remember the events, the hidden memories and to draw out some of the missing details of the things she wanted to tell him.

Arriving in Manchester at about 7.30pm, they made their way to the hotel. Graeme had found it difficult to book somewhere at short notice and there'd been little choice. The reason became clear when they exited Victoria Station to find touts selling tickets for a Justin Beiber concert.

"Oh, he's cute," said Katie.

Graeme laughed. "Oh Lord! You're not on the lookout for a younger model already, are you?"

Holding his arm tighter, she gave him a sour look. Graeme didn't know Manchester well and, as he stepped over the beggars, drug addicts and rough sleepers on the streets near the hotel, he thought, hmm, doesn't look much like the website.

Sensing his discomfort, Katie said, "I know this place, I've stayed here before, it's fine."

Graeme silently marvelled at her strength of character. He didn't like the thought of her walking through the streets late at night, even though he knew she'd done it a thousand times. As he walked to the check-in, he signalled to Katie to phone her husband.

I can't believe I do that, he thought, he really doesn't deserve it, but him worrying would only make matters worse for Katie if she didn't call.

"He thinks I am still in Edinburgh," she said.

"In that case, take your location tracking off your phone, it's close enough for him to come into town to find you if he realises you're here."

The room on the ninth floor was small, but it served their purpose, another haven in which to lie together. Katie had been out for lunch with clients, but Graeme was hungry. Once inside, they took out the remaining wine, cheese, crackers and grapes that Graeme had bought the day before. Oblivious to everything except one another, they laid on the bed with a meal which could have not been better had it been a banquet and it wasn't long before they were again wrapped in one another's arms.

As they listened to the busy streets of Manchester below, Katie was surprised that, even though it was still early, she'd no thoughts of going out. She was happy to snuggle into Graeme continuing her story from the previous evening, recounting some of the episodes which she had found too difficult to talk about.

"About six years ago," she said, "a destination club called The Lounge opened on the outskirts of Wilmslow. It became the place to be seen. A group of regulars would meet there to listen to bands, drink and dance until about 2am. My husband and I often accompanied a group of people, many of whom had quite a lot of money. One of the regulars there was an acquaintance called Tony."

Graeme recalled Katie previously mentioning Tony, alluding to his leading role in events whilst never being specific.

She continued. "When The Lounge eventually closed, the party scene started to move to bars in Wilmslow like the Ensign, or Jo Farnley's, where Tony's crowd hung out.

"Often at closing time, we'd be invited back to someone's house for a party, or sometimes we hosted them. Tony was heavily into coke and at one of the parties, we went to I was already drunk when he persuaded me to try it, saying 'just have a little of this'. Before I knew it, I was walking around in my bra and knickers, among a room full of ten or so men. Who took my clothes off? My husband or Tony, I wasn't sure, but when I came around fully, I realised I was completely naked. I asked my husband to give me back my clothes and we left."

"What else happened?"

"I don't know," she said, with tears in her eyes. "I remember one guy looking at me, not in a sexual way, more with concern on his face. It was as if he was asking me what I was doing?' I'll never forget the look on his face. I guess Jenny was wrong, not all guys are perverts. On the usual pub crawl through Wilmslow I was so embarrassed in case I bumped into him I avoided Jo Farnley's for months, because he was a regular there."

Graeme struggled with his feelings again. He could see that she was in pain from the reaction the memory had provoked, the guy feeling pity for her then avoiding him for months because of her perceived shame. There had to be more. Had she been forced to participate in group sex? If she had been drunk then drugged, it was highly likely that she had in fact been gang-raped. No doubt Tony and Katie's husband would have called it `a consensual gang bang, a bit of fun… only to please her', but they were a pack of bastards and she did not deserve the treatment she had met at their hands.

"What did your son Tom see?" Graeme asked.

Fresh tears welled up as she struggled with her thoughts. "I think I remember the night in question. After the usual pub crawl, we invited people back to our house. There were lots of guys and just two girls, me and a girl called Julie. We played music, danced and had a lot more drinks. Julie wanted to dress up. She knew I was into that so she asked me what spare dressing up clothes I had? I told her a nurse's outfit?

"Julie asked if she could put it on then we found a skimpy maid's outfit for me. When we came down in our costumes, the guys cheered encouraging us to dance.

"Somewhere during the course of the night we both ended up naked and, at the end, there was just me, my husband and two guys called Callum and Sean. Do you remember I told you that on New Year's Eve the night after we met in Manchester, my husband took me to a party?"

"Yes."

"Well, when we got there, there was just my husband, Callum and Sean. When we got home, I told him never to put me in that situation again. I think it all harks back to that night that Tom had spoken about."

"What else happened that night? "

"At the end of the night I came to my senses, as if I'd been drugged and I was waking up from a dream. I realised I had my head on my husband's lap, Sean was between my legs licking me and Callum was fondling my breasts.

"In shock at what was happening to me, I got up, grabbed my clothes and walked to the bedroom, where I got dressed. My husband followed me asking what was wrong. I was so pissed off with him, I felt I'd been violated. If I hadn't woken up when I did, I don't know what might have happened."

Katie felt sick, she couldn't bring herself to admit it to Graeme, but in her heart, she knew exactly what would have happened. Worse, in her drunken state, how could she be sure it hadn't happened?

He asked her again, "The things you've told me about, did you seek them out?"

She again assured him that she hadn't.

"In that case, you're being abused. He and his acquaintances should be in prison. What's the difference between what's happened to you and a Rochdale taxi driver plying a young girl with alcohol or drugs then passing her around, other than the fact it's your husband doing it to you?"

Katie reeled in horror, she seemed genuinely startled.

"I never thought of it like that."

They were both tired now and Katie could take no more questions, so they cuddled closer. "I feel so safe with you, I love you." She said.

"I love you too Katie, we'll find a way to leave all of this shit behind."

The following morning they were once again too busy making love to have breakfast. Immediately afterwards they showered, dressed and headed out to their appointment. Walking side by side, Katie shifted her bags in her hands, freeing up the one closest to Graeme. Absent-mindedly she stroked his bum.

"Don't touch me," he laughed. "There's a reason I'm walking with my hands in my pockets, precisely so that I don't do that to you. This is your town. I'm worried about your reputation here." She laughed and, as they entered the building they'd been seeking, she started walking up the stairs in front of him sashaying her perfect behind, because she knew he couldn't help himself. And he couldn't.

After their appointments followed by a pleasant lunch, Katie pointed Graeme in the direction of his final appointment of the day. She knew who he was meeting and didn't want any awkwardness, so she kissed him goodbye then made her way home. Graeme had a few drinks with an old friend then he too headed for the station. As his train arrived, he looked at the departure boards. Upon seeing the train to Wilmslow, deep in his soul he couldn't help feel that was boarding the wrong train. Finding his seat as the train headed out towards a darkening sky, he closed his eyes and reached out to Katie.

THE EMPEROR.

Ashton Rising

Although Richard Peak tired easily of court preferring to spend his time tending his estates, Maria's presence in Ashton hadn't gone unnoticed in courtly circles. In every sense of the word, she had a captivating presence. Although only five feet tall, she was a beautiful woman. She attracted the admiring attention of the neighbouring noblemen, who coveted her, and the jealousy of their ladies in equal measure.

For the men who came into contact with her, she was the epitome of womanhood, she could charm any man with ease. Her warm smile that lit up the room only accentuated her beauty and her soft lilting voice was a soothing balm to any who heard her speak. For the women who accompanied them however, Maria magnified their own imagined insecurities. Although none would dare to be openly rude to her, their haughty manner betrayed their feelings all too easily.

During their visits to his home, his guests would often express their admiration for the estates noticing how strangely serene, rich and balanced the land seemed to be. Ashton was like an oasis of peace in a turbulent, troubled world. Richard played it down, saying it was due to the new farming methods he was employing, something he had learned on his travels across Europe with the king, but they always suspected he was holding something back. There was an almost palpable thirst in the air for new knowledge. England was creating a maritime empire built on the piracy of the Elizabethans, Sir Walter Raleigh and Sir Francis Drake just a few decades earlier and the world of ideas was opening up in cultured circles. This was not without risk as the church still held mighty sway in both England and across the continent. Wherever these conversations were held, whether in grand halls or quiet rooms, the shadows seemed to dance in the candlelight, revelling in the mixture of excitement and fear generated in equal measure.

It was rumoured that an Italian called Galileo had invented a looking glass, something to help him view the moon, even the distant stars claiming that the secrets of heaven itself would soon be discovered.

There was no distinction made between alchemists and scientists, the Church was equally suspicious of both. Anything that represented a challenge to its authority was to be rooted out, to be dealt with by any means necessary. Even the great schism in the Church, that fateful split that gave rise to the Protestant movement, was still not strong enough to guarantee safety from persecution.

Across Europe, the Catholic Church slaughtered Protestants bold enough even to print or distribute anything that disagreed with the Pope's views and the reaction of the Puritans in England was equally violent. John Pym called in Parliament for all Catholics to be forced to wear special clothing to mark them out.

It was only because the king had a Catholic wife that he used his influence in Parliament to quash the move, but it only served to sow the seeds of his own downfall and inevitably of those who followed him loyally.

Although it bored him, as lord of the manor, a certain amount of entertaining was required for the great and the good, the noblemen, churchmen, minor dignitaries, circuit judges or visiting courtiers. Richard would share the responsibilities with his neighbour, Henry De Bernier who was lord of the manor of Renwick.

Henry De Bernier was a little younger than Richard, a slightly built man, clean-shaven, he was studious in his approach to life. He was married, but as yet had no children and, although he had never seen war first hand, he liked to hear the tales Richard told him, naturally embellished in the telling to add a dash of excitement.

The De Bernier family was amongst the richest in England, they had arrived with William the Conquerer and, along with the Percy Family, the Stanleys and Zetlands, they owned much of the land stretching all the way from Scotland to Derby.

As custom demanded, during the dinners they would host, Maria was always treated as an honoured guest rather than as the Lady of Ashton. She was constantly questioned about her background and the nature of life in her family's ancestral homelands of North Africa.

Although she explained that she'd never visited the Berber lands herself, she knew plenty of stories passed down through an oral tradition among her people. She would regale their guests with tales of noble savages, of the majesty of nature and of great magical power wielded by a powerful shamanic caste who, it was said, could walk through men's dreams. To the incredulous guests they seemed almost comical, like Indian chiefs with their feathered head dresses.

Even as she listened to them laughing, Maria was slowly casting her own magical spells.

Many reciprocal invitations would follow. Maria in particular would become a sought after guest and teacher, as all who met her fell under her spell.

He could deny her nothing but he had to warn her.

"Maria," said Richard, "if you must teach them about your magic, you cannot do it openly. You will put not just them, but all of us at risk. You must have noticed how some of the ladies already resent your presence."

Maria laughed. "Yes, I have noticed. While she is courteous, our neighbour Lady De Bernier can barely contain her jealousy. I see her across the brook sometimes on their estate and I can see the bitterness riding alongside her like a shadow, enjoying a life of its own as she canters with her horses. Perhaps it is because her husband and his friends, more than most, are captivated by the stone."

"They are dangerous, Maria, the Church is at war with itself and even a rumour whispered into the wrong ears could be fatal. Please promise me you will take more care."

"I will my love," said Maria.

"You English are a strange people with so many repressed feelings. In my culture, these things are for everyone, not just for a few. If it makes you feel better, I will teach only a few, always behind closed doors."

"Thank you my love."

As the summer turned to autumn and the crops were harvested, it would soon be time for the Lord of Ashton to hold a festival to give thanks. Every year a great ball was held, but this year it was to be different. The ball would be held at the time of the full moon, the harvest moon, and the invitations were sent with instructions that all who attended were to wear masks.

The evening was a great success with music, dancing; a sumptuous banquet with the wine flowing freely. Then as the full moon rose over the horizon, a small group, twelve in number, all male, were selected to follow Maria into the adjoining library. Although she wore a blood-red mask with black lace around the edges and around the eyes, her presence still radiated throughout the room.

For these twelve men, their education was about to begin in earnest.

For the next six years, the same group would meet monthly at the time of the full moon, sometimes at

Ashton, but over time Renwick Hall was to become their main meeting place. The De Berniers were more interested in the things Maria and her guests explored. They were also more accommodating when it came to supplying the young servant girls who also participated from time to time. He could not be sure, but he doubted that the illiterate servants understood the significance of the meetings or were aware of the true identities of the masked guests in their midst.

Although he was aware of the things that Maria was teaching them as she discussed it openly with him, Richard was a practical man, rooted in what he regarded as the real world so he was happy to distance himself from the group, except for one of her young followers, Adam Bright. He was a regular visitor to the estate and Maria took him under her wing, like a mother hen. Over time even Richard came to think of him as a family member, as the son he didn't have.

She would spend hours with Adam, who was in every sense to become her spiritual successor.

In time he would carry the knowledge to continue the work Maria had begun, but it would only be through their daughter Grace that the power of the amulet could eventually flow.

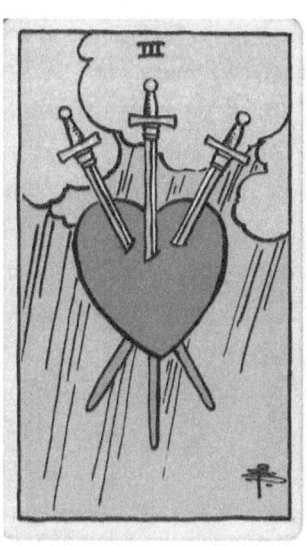

Hunter's Moon

The coming weekend was hunter's moon, the first full moon after the harvest.

For most people it goes unnoticed, but not for Graeme. For him, it was full of symbolism and he could feel the changes coming.

He saw many worlds intersecting with the physical world, some benign, others frightening, and there were times such as this, when they briefly touched one another in a way that created crossroads for the souls of men, crossroads where we're forced to make choices, consciously or otherwise. It's an intense time, when the veil between the worlds starts to weaken gradually, culminating on Halloween, in the run-up to All Souls' Day on Nov 2nd.

All Souls' Day is traditionally held to be when the book of the dead is opened and forgiveness may be asked for poor choices we have made. We have a brief opportunity to change our paths before they become fixed again and the intersections between worlds diverge once more. In the run-up to it on this day in particular it is not unusual for the dead to make their presence felt in this world and his grandmother was making her presence known to Graeme. This didn't disturb him at all, she'd always appeared to him when he needed her, and he needed her now. As he looked for her, he suddenly realised that the first day he had travelled to Manchester to see Katie had been his grandmother's birthday. Her name was also Helen, her symbol too was the moon, the great celestial mirror.

Graeme looked out of the window, staring up at the moon. He texted Katie. *Can you see the moon?* He was surprised when the response came straight back.

Yes, I am standing in the back garden looking out over the trees, it's magnificent yet very strange.

What is?

It's like the sky isn't real. It looks like a picture, as though I am looking at a set painted in as the background, like those you see in the movies. There's something else too, my vision is blurred on the very edge of my right side, it's almost as if I can't see in that direction.

Is that west?

Yes.

Don't worry. You are waking up.

Although Katie didn't realise it yet, her parents were also calling to her too in answer to the candle she had lit for them in the cathedral in New York. Like Graeme, She'd also come to a crossroads and when the time came when she needed them most, she wouldn't be alone.

For Katie, this date had more significance than she yet understood and it would be another full year before she did. This is the day when it is not only possible to take a different path but also to atone for our sins, the pain we have caused others. People don't realise that their personal salvation is tied up with the salvation of others, even those we think of as having 'gone.' When we shine a light in the darkness for them, then, like a reflection on a still pond, they *always* reciprocate for us.

As Graeme lay in bed his mind wandered, he wondered about the complex webs we weave in our lives. Fate is nothing if not thorough. It covers all aspects of a man's life. The three sisters of destiny; Clotho who spins the thread of life; Lachesis who draws lots determining how long a life will be; and Atropos who decides how a life should end when she cuts the thread with her dreadful shears. Yet even fate is not all-powerful. No force in the universe is more powerful than love, although love is a fickle thing, at turns both delightful and painful.

Graeme meanwhile was approaching his own crossroad. His birthday was just a few days away and he knew he would be in London on the date, so he arranged to go out with his wife for a meal when he returned. It was an enjoyable meal, a pleasant evening with much reminiscing and talk about the children. They'd been together for many years, but, like most married couples, their relationship had changed over the years.

It had changed a lot. Unusually on this occasion, the conversation turned to their lack of intimacy. Things had not been good between them for a long time, although they shared a bed, in many ways they had become worse than strangers. Nothing had changed in this regard for almost a decade yet they had both just accepted the situation for what it was. This time, for some unknown reason she asked him if he'd been unfaithful. Tired of the deception, he said, yes, he had been. He felt the percussion of the bombshell exploding silently across the table, even though her expression didn't change.

After a brief silence, she pressed him for details. He gave a little, but he didn't mention Katie. He didn't want to hurt his wife any more than he already had and, besides, he knew he couldn't speak for Katie.

"Does it matter?" he said. "Who it was, when it was, how many times. The point is surely that things have got so bad between us that it had happened at all. I guess I'm not as strong as I thought I was, the distance between us became too great and I can only take so much rejection."

"I'm sorry," she said, to his surprise. "I don't blame you."

"You need to talk to someone," he said. "There's a lot to think about."

They travelled home in silence then, as usual, his wife went to bed alone. Graeme made himself comfortable on the couch but he couldn't sleep, he knew the consequences of his confession and he was now wondering how they'd unfold. He lay in the darkness, calmly examining the situation until the dawn came.

Katie was worried when she woke on Sunday morning because there was no good morning text from Graeme. Realising that she'd sent him a strangely worded text before she retired to bed, now she was worried that he'd misunderstood it. She started texting him and, even though she knew he'd not read them, she was wracked with doubt so she sent even more. Eventually, when he replied, updating her on the development, she said, *Oh my God! I had no idea.* She wanted to reach through the phone to hug him.

His wife needed some time to take things in herself so it would be some days before they would speak more on the subject. As expected, the following days proved quiet with little passing between them as the depth of their situation started to sink in. Katie had told Graeme he wouldn't believe the shit that would follow and the hurt. Now he knew he'd find out soon enough. For now, his emotions were raw, his mind wandered as his thoughts were scattered on the wind, yet still he wasn't sorry he'd told his wife, for both their sakes.

Katie had been through this before and she'd warned Graeme that his wife would become obsessed with finding out more. He didn't want to hurt her with further revelations, although he knew that he would over the coming weeks and he felt sick. Sure enough, Katie had been correct, a few days later the questions started again. He knew in his heart where the discussions would go. Could they make a go of it? Was it beyond redemption? How did it come to this? Would it be too little too late?

Whatever conclusion his wife would come to, he owed it to them both to give her the time she needed.

He knew it would be difficult and he didn't want to cause her any further problems at home, but he was due to be in London again a few days later so he asked Katie if she could join him. Katie reflecting on her own experiences thought of the pyramids of playing cards that they would build as children. She knew that Graeme had just removed one of the bottom cards and when the structure started to fall, it was anyone's guess where the cards would end up.

Knowing how he would be feeling she simply said, 'You need me, I am coming.'

As he boarded the 5.30am train, he looked around the old Victorian station. Even though he knew he'd be back the following day, this time he felt as if he was leaving the past behind. He took his seat, put on his headphones and let the crowded carriage fade into a haze as he listened to his music. As Bette Midler started, his thoughts turned to Katie. *It's the heart afraid of breaking that never learns to dance, it's the dream afraid of waking that never takes a chance,* she sang.

Well, he thought. We're certainly taking chances now.

As his train sped towards Katie, through the early morning mist, he could see a beautiful red ball of fire slowly rising in the eastern sky. As it rose with the promise of nourishment for the world below, it reminded him of her smile which lit up his heart, warming his soul and, as he did so a wave of guilt washed over him again.

It would be late afternoon before he could see Katie. First, he had a speaking engagement in the city, so he headed for Liverpool Street station. Although the conference was supposed to last all day, he couldn't wait that long to see her, so he stayed only as long as necessary to network, passing the time until her train would arrive into Euston. He called by the hotel on the way to the station to drop his bag then made his way to the station cafe.

Katie meanwhile had pondered on what he was about to tell her, although she knew he'd be needing her, if only to hold him. On arriving in London, she headed for the cafe too. As she walked through the door saw Graeme, head in his hands, looking full of woe.

Oh God, she thought. He wants to let me down in the nicest possible way.

She fought through the crowd and they hugged and kissed. Graeme wanted to leave and Katie was happy to follow, although that fear in the bottom of her stomach swilled around. She understood why the conversation felt awkward as they walked to the hotel, buying some cheese along the way. Graeme was trying to put into words alien feelings that he'd never experienced before. Katie wondered again what was coming? She knew he loved her, she also knew that when the shit hit the fan it wasn't uncommon for the adulterer to want to mend the broken pieces or to sellotape over the cracks, as she had done on more than one occasion.

Taking with them a couple of glasses of wine from the bar downstairs, they made their way to their room. It was small, clean and, once they were inside they had everything they needed. As soon as they'd dropped their bags, Graeme grabbed Katie hugging her so tightly, she knew instantly it wasn't bad news. They kissed, then chatted and Graeme told her a little of the events that had transpired at home. He told her that he wanted her, that he had told his wife. Although he hadn't mentioned Katie directly, he had declared his infidelity, his unhappiness, so the die was cast.

Katie was relieved, but there were other feelings too. As she listened to Graeme's confession, she felt the hairs on the back of her neck stand up. Why hadn't he mentioned Katie? Was there someone else? She didn't like competition, especially where Graeme was concerned. Thinking he was about to tell her there was another romance still going on, she felt sick. That bombshell didn't come, but her mind raced nonetheless. Was her imagined competition younger, prettier? She focused; brushing her thoughts to one side. With all the shit he now knew about her, she knew it would be hypocritical for her to feel jealous, yet she was and that was an unusual feeling for her, something she hadn't felt in many years. She was certain he loved her; she felt it with every touch; with every tender look of love he gave every time their eyes met.

She didn't want to cause him pain. He had enough to deal with and she knew from experience that the weeks to come would take their toll.

They made love as usual and perhaps it was the intensity of what was occurring, with so many things going on in the background, that, although she was revelling in their intimacy, Katie's mind continued to race. Even though Graeme was always patient and gentle with her, she was unable to reach a climax.

"What's wrong?" he asked, "Something's stopping

you."

To his surprise, she replied, "I don't deserve it."

He could see that deep inside, she really believed that to be true and he couldn't help wondering why. They lay in one another's arms for a while until eventually, he asked her if she wanted to explore her own self a little deeper.

She did and so he told her to close her eyes.

"Do you remember, I told you about the light in the darkness?" he said. "Well it's behind our eyes all the time, can you see it?"

"Yes," said Katie, almost surprising herself. "I can."

She was concentrating hard, letting her mind drift into the light.

"And there's something else, I can sense there's someone behind the light but I don't know who it is."

"It's you Katie, your eyes are the windows to your soul, didn't you know? Everyone you've ever known throughout all of your lives is there with you too. Keep practising and, as you learn to go deeper, you'll begin to sense how much more connected you are than you would ever have believed possible."

They lay together on the bed talking for hours, drinking wine, eating cheese and grapes and later they made the most exquisite love.

Katie could feel it now too. Every time it got better and felt more intense.

The next morning, after Graeme woke Katie in his most fabulous way, they lay wrapped in each other's arms. Knowing the pressure from home would be intense and he might end up feeling that the right thing to do would be to give things another try Katie wanted to let him know that it was okay if he needed space from her.

She lay thinking, oh my God! What on earth am I saying?

She understood the pull of family having been in the same position herself. He didn't need her to start saying what she wanted, he just needed to know she was there for him.

She said, "I know you'll come back to me. I know how you feel about me. Do what you have to do, I'm not going anywhere."

He held her close, looked into her eyes "I'm not giving you up."

God, Katie said silently to herself, please let me have this man.

As always, they squeezed every moment they could out of their time together. When they could wait no longer, they rose, showered then headed out for breakfast. He had meetings to attend and she needed to get back to Cheshire. He walked her to the station, they kissed each other passionately then, as Katie headed off she couldn't resist looking back three times to see him standing there, watching her. The fourth time she looked, knowing he had a meeting to go she had to fight the urge to run back to him, she turned and walked away.

Ouch, she thought, as tears pricked at her eyes.

Ten minutes later she was sitting on the train thinking about their time together. Wow, how fab is he?

She ardently hoped that the coming weeks wouldn't be too draining for him, that he'd manage to stay strong, for both their sakes.

Thank you for being you, she texted.

Your welcome, I've got plenty of that, he replied. *You have shown me things in my own heart I never thought I would see. Calm your mind Katie, listen quietly, there's a distant voice trying to reach you.*

Thank you for opening my eyes to a bigger world than I ever thought possible xx.

You do realise that if people knew me like you do most of them would consider me mad. Are you sure you know what you're letting yourself in for?

Tom

Fate, it seems, is both thorough and has a sense of humour. As if to underline the meaningless nature of our daily routines, after weeks of Katie trying to find an opportunity to speak to Tom, it finally came in the form of an argument with a neighbour over, of all things, a dustbin.

Katie was in her garden when two ladies appeared around the side of the house, looking at her bins. As she wandered up to them, she realised that it was her next-door neighbour with a friend. "You have my bin," said her neighbour.

"Have I?"

"Yes but it's full and it's not my rubbish."

"Well, they must have been mixed up previously. It

shouldn't be too difficult to sort out."

For some reason the other lady, then spoke rather harshly; in fact she was decidedly rude. Tom, overhearing Katie saying there was no need to speak to her that way jumped out of the window of his apartment to his mother's defence. He, in turn, was aggressive, in his posture telling them, in no uncertain terms not to speak to his mother like that. Katie, not wishing to escalate the conflict, pulled him away then sent him back inside. The women took the bin away, muttering under their breath and Katie went into the house to speak to Tom, who was now sulking, believing, incorrectly that Katie was chastising him.

"Tom, can I talk to you?"

"No. Just go away."

Katie texted Graeme who suggested she give him a little space before going back to talk to him later. *Seems to suggest what I have suspected all along,* said Graeme. *It's the way you have been treated that is the root of his anger. I hope you can talk. He clearly wants to protect you, why wouldn't he? When he was younger, he couldn't. I am willing to bet he blames himself even though it's not his fault. He seems to be a soft hearted kid who loves his mum. There is always a way back.*

Katie tried to work for an hour or so, but, finding it difficult to concentrate, she soon found herself back at Tom's door. She found him smoking outside, still in no mood to talk.

"I was trying to defend you mum, and you totally showed me up."

"Look, I'm sorry if it felt like that, I just didn't want

the situation to get out of hand."

She was worried about his reaction to the situation, his aggression toward the ladies was frightening, even so Katie knew she had to be the one to say sorry, knowing he needed help. Eventually, they went inside and sat on the couch.

"Where is all this anger coming from?" Katie asked.

He didn't reply.

"Is it me? Is it about what's happened in the past? My affair?

Tom seemed to soften for a moment, he smiled. "No mum it's not that."

"Well, it appears to have started about the same time. Can I ask you something Tom? That night you spoke about when we last argued, what exactly did you see?"

"I came down for a drink and, when I was in the kitchen, a guy went past into the loo in his boxer shorts."

"What else did you see? Tell me. I need to know."

"I saw you in your bra and knickers and..." His voice trailed off and at that moment she was horrified because she knew in her heart that he'd seen everything. "It just wasn't right," he added.

"I'm so sorry Tom. I can't change the past. I'm just trying to understand. I can hardly remember the night, but I don't like what I do remember. There's something else isn't there? Please tell me what it is."

Tom was now visibly shaken and upset, "Johno - a so-called friend - keeps saying he's slept with you."

Katie recoiled. "Who? I don't know him, Tom."

She handed him her phone so he could look through

her contacts, texts and Facebook links.

"I can't stop him saying what he has, but I can assure you that it's not true. He's trying to wind you up. Next time we see him, point him out and I'd like to speak to him with you there.

"Are you angry at your dad?" Tom shrugged, but the smoulder behind his eyes told Katie it was time to leave it there.

She felt frustrated that she'd not really got to the bottom of things with Tom, but this conversation was the start of turning their relationship around. Deep down, he recognised that his mother was trying to reconcile things and they both started to get a growing sense that what he needed now was space between them, something which would come a few months later when Tom's feelings would resurface.

Following her return from New York, relations with her husband had been frosty. He sensed the growing tension between them, yet still craved the physical contact she was now withholding for as long as she was able. When Katie had been drinking, her insecurities would rise due to alcohol withdrawal. She had used the tension with Tom to keep the peace, telling him she was worried, but eventually, she confronted him about the events she had recalled to Graeme, confessing these memories were painful and she was hurt.

After the conversation with Tom, Katie was now more determined than ever to get to the bottom of the things that had happened to her. The next time she saw Graeme, she was ready to talk again. She had sent him a couple of pictures from the night she'd found herself naked again at the end of August. One was at the dinner party and the other was the following morning laid in bed feeling sorry for herself, cuddling her granddaughter. She couldn't understand how it had happened, as well as the worst hangover she could remember, she also had bruises on her head.

"There has to be more to this," said Graeme and they looked back through her phone. "What's this?" he asked, pointing to a picture of her sitting on a kitchen worktop at Barry's party shortly after arriving. At first glance, it looked innocent, but, on closer inspection, it was clear that she was being held tightly by Linda, her dress was already unzipped and she looked totally drugged up. Katie was horrified.

"Oh my God!" she said. "Look at my eyes, the lights are on but nobody is home."

"It seems a bit strange that someone has taken a photo of you on your phone and it stops there."

Katie had already spoken to her husband about it, but she had to know if he was lying, if there were any more photos from the occasions where she'd been undressed. He had assured her there weren't any, going on to excuse himself by saying he had been drunk too.

Katie knew that, although she often drank to the point where she couldn't remember, her husband didn't. She resolved to get hold of his phone at the first opportunity to check it eventually managing it while he slept.

She texted Graeme. *I can't understand it. There are lots of photos of me, yet there isn't a single one from any of those occasions. Could he have erased them, or have them somewhere else?*

Graeme wasn't sure but something didn't seem right and he said so. *Photos... hmm. Well, they could be on an SD card I suppose, or on the desktop computer? Maybe there aren't any more, although someone took some, otherwise you wouldn't have them on your phone. How well do you know Linda? I only ask because she looks to be in a better state than you, so she might remember. How far back does the camera roll go?*

I'm going to ask him about the photos. I guess I wanted proof but it really doesn't matter. Up to a point, I know what happened. I don't like what I remember even if there is nothing else. I don't know Linda at all really. Do you know how I feel about you? I so love you.

Although Katie was worried she felt better having confronted her husband about the things that had happened and this would be just another step. She knew in her heart that, even though it was a painful process, that one conversation was never going to be enough. The tension between them was palpable and she found herself wishing her life away for the days she could spend with Graeme or her beloved Helen.

Her husband had promised it would never happen again, but only time would tell.

Two hundred and fifty miles away, Graeme could feel Katie's anxiety so he sent her a long good night text.

Find a quiet place, close your eyes, clear your mind. Imagine a bright light in your heart, a shining love. That's where I will be. Then feel it radiate out until your whole body is bathed in it. Let it continue to radiate out, as far your imagination can carry it. if you keep practising you'll find a few surprises. It has no beginning, no end, it cannot be exhausted no matter how far your mind carries it. Do not be afraid Katie, things have a way of working out.

I don't understand how you know these things, she said and tears welled in her eyes when she saw his reply.

It is a privilege sharing life's journey with you again Katie. You are more special than you know.

Graeme tried to drift off to sleep, but sleep wouldn't come. He tossed and turned as visions of Katie haunted him.

ACE of CUPS.

Jersey Boys

Despite behaving more like excited teenagers, they were keen to spend time together like any normal adult couple, which they were unable to do for the most part, so the prospect of a few days away would offer a welcome break from prying eyes.

As she walked through Waterloo station wondering which way to go Katie's phone rang, it was Graeme. He'd just arrived at Waterloo too so told her to stay put, he'd find her. She soon saw him walking towards her with a big beautiful smile and his eyes shining bright. She melted as he walked towards her and they embraced, neither caring who might be looking on, only that they were together once more.

They walked arm-in-arm to the hotel. It had only

been a few days since they'd last seen one another but it felt like weeks had gone by. Asking for rooms close together, they checked in separately to the Hotel where the industry gala dinner was being hosted that night. Feeling comfortable, Katie never saw her own room, settling very nicely into Graeme's room instead.

She was wearing a corduroy dress with snap-shut buttons down the front. Inevitably it wasn't long before Graeme decided to torture himself by pulling the dress apart leaving Katie standing there in her bra and a tiny G-string. "Oh God!" he said, "I've got to dial into a conference call at 2 pm. How can I do that with a hard-on?"

Kate laughed. "It will keep... well just until after the call." she teased.

An hour later, they opened a bottle of wine and she ran a bath for them. As she sat between Graeme's legs, resting her back against him, she felt so at ease, so loved, as he gently cupped his hands pouring water over her breasts to keep her warm.

They couldn't relax for long though - too soon - Katie sensed time catching up with them. Jumping out of the bath, she said, "Come on, let's get ready. You're meeting people in the bar in half an hour."

As she set about putting on her makeup, Graeme lay for a few moments longer, watching her, but soon he too had to get out. Once dressed, Katie thought that he looked handsome in his dinner suit and pink bow tie.

As always, he had to leave first, then half an hour later, Katie, fashionably late, would follow. She wore a long, low cut evening dress that hugged her body, showing off her fabulous figure and she wondered if he'd approve. It was black with shimmering gold glitter all over so she knew she'd stand out, attracting male admiration and attention as she intended, but she told herself that she only wanted Graeme to be impressed and want to be the one taking her home later.

The evening proved eventful with Graeme seated at the top table, while Katie shared a table with a couple of their colleagues and guests. She had set off with good intentions sipping the wine slowly, but, as the night wore on the drinks flowed faster. Looking around on several occasions for Graeme, yet unable to see him, she wondered if he was enjoying the night. She knew that he'd rather have been seated next to her, even though she probably wouldn't have been able to keep her hands off him, so it was probably for the best that they were separated.

Graeme meanwhile most definitely was not enjoying dinner, neither was the lady sitting opposite when he accidentally knocked a bottle of red wine all over her. She was hysterical, her husband was embarrassed and Graeme was horrified at what he'd done to the honoured guest and he couldn't wait to leave. As soon as the speeches had finished, he made his excuses then went looking for Katie in the bar, where she was up to her old tricks, thinking it a good idea to have shots with her colleagues that tipped her over the edge. Once again she didn't remember Graeme taking her up to bed.

Fortunately, it hadn't raised too many eyebrows as Graeme didn't usually stay up late anyway. As a precaution he'd already suggested to Bruce earlier that he'd make sure she got to bed safely after what had happened in The Benjamin Franklin Hotel.

During that night as they slept, once again, Katie was aware of Graeme being close, holding onto her at every opportunity. They slept with their bodies wrapped around each other, until Graeme thought it early enough to arouse Katie gently and, as she started to wake, she thought, boy, is he getting good at this.

Neither were eager to get out of bed but they decided it was necessary, if for only a couple of hours. Although it was raining, even that didn't dampen their spirits.

"I want to buy you something", said Graeme. "Something that you'll wear all of the time."

"You don't need to spend money on me. I don't need anything."

"I'd like you to have something. I would've bought you that bracelet if I thought you would've worn it all the time."

Katie thought about the six thousand dollar bracelet she'd sent him a picture of from New York.

"I know you would've, but I really was only joking. I'd never expect you to buy something so expensive."

"Come on. Let's head to Oxford Street where all the shops are."

Travelling on the escalators in the underground they were playful. Katie always stood on the step higher to Graeme, making them the same height so they could kiss each other easily as they moved. Aware that people were looking at them, neither cared, they were totally lost in one another and cared only for the time they had together.

Along Bond Street, they ventured into a couple of jewellers but nothing took their eye. "Come on," said Graeme. "This is just cheap costume jewellery, let's go look somewhere else."

Walking down the street in the rain, they bobbed into a couple of more upmarket jewellers.

"What do you like?" asked Graeme. "What will you wear?"

He examined some beautiful diamond pendant necklaces.

"They are beautiful!" exclaimed Kate. "They're too expensive though. Come on, let's go find a pub."

A few minutes later, they fell upon a quaint, old-fashioned boozer, found a space at the busy bar and ordered drinks. Eventually, they managed to get a table, sat gazing into each other's eyes and chatted.

"I'm not really your type am I?" he said.

"No, you're not really."

"What is your type?" he asked, although he really wasn't sure he needed to know.

A moment later, he was absolutely certain he hadn't needed to know.

"Well," teased Katie. "I tend to attract blokes between the ages of eighteen and seventy so you've just about sneaked in - only just. I like tall, handsome, very good looking, muscular, fit blokes, with more money than you have."

Graeme pondered this and she laughed when she saw his look of horror on his face.

Oh shit, he was thinking. One out of seven and I've only just scraped into that category.

Katie, realising what she had said, continued with a few extra attributes, unfortunately for Graeme, he didn't have any of these either.

He didn't look happy now.

"For fuck sake!" he joked. "It's a good job I'm bigger than your vibrator or you wouldn't take me anywhere."

Katie laughed, leaned over, squeezed his arm and kissed him. As the afternoon wore on, the rain started to clear and they made their way back to the hotel.

Graeme's hopes of getting any lunch faded rapidly as Katie immediately stripped off in the bedroom and ran a bath. Needless to say, he wasn't far behind her. When they emerged, she revealed her next surprise, a black tasselled dress with pop-open studs that showed off her ample assets to best advantage, complimented with black thigh length boots. Graeme's eyes nearly popped out. "Are you sure you want to go out?" he asked hopefully. But she did. They'd booked tickets to see Jersey Boys so they headed out to the West End where they went into a bar, shared a single meal and soon it was showtime.

Katie had convinced herself that she didn't really like the theatre. She had only seen some of the more serious, dramatic productions which had left her bored. Jersey Boys, however, allowed them to re-live their' youth, singing along to familiar love songs whilst staring into each other's eyes. The evening was only punctuated at the half time interval with ice cream. By the time the show had finished, they only had one thing on their minds, getting back to the hotel as quickly as they could.

Not wanting to go to for a drink as she usually did,

Katie wondered what was wrong with her. What has he done to me? she asked herself. She only wanted to be with him and she was so looking forward to making love again.

They undressed, which for Katie didn't take much due to the pop open buttons all down the front of her dress.

There's a bit of a theme going on here with the pop-open dresses, thought Graeme.

Katie washed her make up off before they lay down on the bed and started to stroke and touch one another gently.

Graeme then playfully said that he wanted to see what Katie's vibrator could do so she fetched it from the bathroom. This was a new one, leading Graeme to wonder just how many she had, why did she need so many? Did she wear them out or was it just the novelty angle... hmm?"

He pressed the button and it started to buzz noisily. He tried to turn it off, which resulted in it pulsating in a different way, much faster now and he had a panicked look in his eyes as was getting really noisy and he couldn't turn it off. What would the neighbours think? Katie was in stitches, but she knew that he was really saying to himself, that he could do much better than that thing.

He soon resumed his explorations and, as Katie's body responded, she began to relax. His touch was gentle and the pleasure was wonderful. He turned her over so that she was laying on her front whilst gently pushed his fingers between her legs, moving them backwards and forwards, applying just a little more pressure with every stroke. Katie had never felt intensity like it, not ever. Her head swam, the sensations were amazing leaving her feeling as though she was leaving her body, floating above herself and, when it came, it was the most mind-blowing orgasm she'd ever experienced. The waves of absolute pleasure rushed over her as her body convulsed again and again. It just went on and on and Graeme held her tightly, while still applying a gentle, intimate pressure.

"I've got you babe."

Yes, she thought. He really did have her. He had her completely, body, mind and soul.

The following morning was very relaxed. After a repeat performance, time eventually caught up leaving them no choice but to go down for breakfast before making their way to the station. She alighted the underground train first at Euston, saying "goodbye" on the train. As the doors opened, she stepped out and she didn't look back, not wanting him to see her crying.

Graeme felt as though she had ripped his heart out and that she was taking it with her. She had put the black dress with the pop open buttons on to travel home which once again, served to highlight her fabulous figure. She had promised to let him know when she was home safe, but her train journey was disrupted and she ended up once again the centre of attention in a carriage full of pissed up lads from Grimsby on their way to a football match.

Kids who have too much bravado, she had texted to

Graeme.

He replied, *are they singing, you're fit and you know you are?*

Although all she could think of was Graeme, she smiled to herself because it was the truth, she was fit and she did know it.

Katie was feeling brighter, planning on going out around the town with Jenny that evening, but Graeme was going home to his wife. His mood was subdued and he wasn't anxious to repeat the awkwardness of their situation, which was still raw for them both.

The Crucible

The next venue on their tour of Britain's hotels took them to Sheffield in early November. Although it had only been a couple of days since they were last together, as always the anticipation added to the excitement

The night before, Katie was laid in bed thinking of Graeme and wondering why she felt so lost, so consumed.

"You are not lost," he had told her. "You are finding your way home."

Graeme meanwhile had just seen Thunderbirds start on the TV and it reminded him of something else on Katie's list that he didn't have.

'Virgil was handsome for a puppet, wasn't he?' she had said.

He had to attend a dinner in Sheffield and Katie made

an excuse to be in the city so that she could spend the night with him. He checked into the hotel at 4 pm and she arrived shortly afterwards.

A nice hotel, Graeme thought, as he walked down to the bar for a bottle of wine and a couple of glasses.

Back in the room, they talked for a while then made love and, as he dressed to go out for dinner, she unpacked the grapes, cheese and crackers she had brought to snack on.

"Do you have a CD player in the car?" Graeme asked.

"Yes."

"I've bought you a present," he said, handing over a CD of Frankie Valli's greatest hits.

"Fab," she said and her smile was like the beam of a torch. She had loved the show Jersey Boys, especially the songs, so now she'd be able to play it in the car everywhere she went, allowing her to take a little of Graeme with her too.

He hated to leave, but his clients were waiting for him at the Crucible. It was a tame affair and he sent her a couple of pictures of the dinner. She replied: "It doesn't look very exciting, you could be having much more fun naked with me.' Graeme didn't doubt it for a minute and sat nursing a semi for most of the evening while he ate his meal, contemplating the promise of what awaited him.

As soon as he could, he returned to the hotel where once again they lay in one another's arms. Katie loved their time together for the physical experience but also because she could open up to Graeme in a way she never had to anyone, even her best friends. Gradually her life seemed to be coming into focus and, as she drifted off to sleep, she said, "I thought I liked rough sex."

Graeme was horrified. "Why?"

"Well, I thought it was normal," she said closing her eyes before drifting off to sleep in his arms.

Graeme lay awake, stunned, staring into the darkness, holding her tight.

Less than a week later away they would meet again, this time in Carlisle where they had arranged to meet an old colleague and some business contacts for an early supper. This would be followed by a long evening in bed in the Castle Hotel.

As they climbed the stairs to their room, Katie egged him on.

"Behave," he said, laughing. "It's a very grand staircase, but we can't make love here, we'd be a health and safety hazard."

"I'd do you anywhere,"

Oh Lord! thought Graeme still giggling.

Although sensual, the night also proved to be restless for both of them. Graeme dreamt of being swept away on a restless sea and, even though he knew it was a metaphor for the emotions he was drowning in, it was unpleasant all the same. Only reaching out to Katie and holding her gave him any respite.

Katie too was disturbed. Her husband had been at work all night and Tom,once again 'high,' had threatened Carly with a knife. Her fear of Tom was also rising. He was too unpredictable and living in the adjacent apartment he was becoming a threat to not just to himself but to his whole family. Even his father was afraid of where it could go next, from threatening behaviour to lighting fires, it wouldn't take much for someone to end up badly injured, or worse.

The next day Graeme would have to drive back to his home in the Borders, leave his car and jump straight on a train for London, but, as dawn broke, he held onto Katie as if their lives depended upon it. Eventually, they had to get up. They skipped breakfast and, after dropping Katie at the train station, he headed off into the sunrise across the North Pennines. It was a surreal journey, peaceful and stunningly beautiful, almost as if the scene had been created as a soothing balm for the raging torrent inside him.

It was mid-November and 'The Donald' had recently become President-Elect of the USA and defacto leader of the free world. The next few days are going to be very strange, he mused, as he drove to work in the rain, but at least he'd be heading back to see Katie tonight.

He finished his day at the office then drove south-west into the setting sun, through the beautiful Border Country to a charming country pub, the String of Horses. Savouring the beauty he saw around him; the countryside, the ambers, yellows, browns, copper and golden leaves swirling on the roadside as the cars passed, even as he admired it, he knew it was all an illusion. *Oasis* were playing on the radio. He smiled at the lyrics, '*Some might say that we should never ponder on our thoughts today 'cos they hold sway over time.*'

Did they understand how close to the truth they were?

Katie had booked the room this time and when he arrived the magnificent sight of her draped across a four-poster bed, greeted him. If he had been wowed by the sights on his journey, this topped everything, heralding the next few hours which were a hedonistic haze of pure pleasure.

Whilst outwardly it may seem that Katie and Graeme only ever spent time with one another, they were also diligent when it came to work. After a soak in the large bath, they dressed in their finest clothes to network with the great and the good of the Border Country at the local Conservative Party dinner.

Although Graeme looked handsome in his black tie dinner suit, it was Katie who stole the show. Dressed in a shimmering silver skin-tight dress, she was the centre of attention with lots of potential suitors queuing up to buy her drinks, and chat her up. Graeme was relaxed though. This wasn't a raucous night out dancing at the local nightclub with her friends. John Major was no Luther Vandross, although he did seem surprisingly youthful among the general crowd of illustrious attendees.

At the end of the night, Katie happily walked to the door with Graeme where their taxi was waiting. So it seemed, was Noah's second deluge and, by the time they got to the car they were soaked, but once again wrapped in each other's arms in the back of the cab heading back to their four-poster bed, nothing dampened their spirits.

Mid-November also brought with it a supermoon, the biggest since 1948 and the pressure for Graeme would be unbearable. The full moon was always the time that the visions came and he never knew whether they would be good or bad. The dreams had started a few nights ago and he knew they would last a few more days. What messages would they dredge up from his subconscious this time?

In the modern world, we look at other cultures as somehow backward, when the truth is that we have not moved that far forward since the Middle Ages when anyone considered different could be burnt at the stake. We know that people have incredible abilities, but we only acknowledge those things that are comfortable to assimilate and what lowly, dull-witted creatures we have become as a result, filling our lives with a plethora of worthless things, wasting time in pursuit of the material, weaving complex webs of... nothing.

Is it any wonder that our lives feel so empty? Working time regulations, employment law, conduct codes, tax returns, investment decisions, compliance reports, TV listings, newspapers full of drivel, business conferences, traffic jams, rules of the road, on and on it goes until a man's soul is buried up to its neck, while the rules solidify around his throat choking the true life from him. Why have we become so afraid to stop, to listen to that still tiny voice inside us? This is the ever-tightening web of the material world. Yet this is not the only world our souls partake of. Man was never created to walk in this world.

Graeme could always sense the approach of the full moon, even when he couldn't see it. Like a tidal rush inside him, making him toss and turn in the night, disturbing his dreams. Whilst sometimes the messages were comforting, whispers from the beyond, or symbols he could interpret using the tarot cards as his guide, equally, they could be nightmares when the shadows would become visible again.

Although he was no longer a child, the shadows still frightened him. He would always avoid their direct gaze whenever he sensed their presence. At least now, he knew what he was dealing with. He knew he could control the raging tempest within him, even though it required a huge effort which always left him drained. Then the headaches would come, they were painful, lasting for a week at a time. He wondered what Katie would think if she knew of the things he had seen.

Occasionally, at the time of the full moon, the pull was so strong that he could loosen the girders of his soul, leave his physical body and his spirit would sail the astral plane looking down on the world. From this place, it wasn't just the world he looked down on. He could look down on time. Most people see time as sequential when in reality, the past, present and future along with every possible permutation are all happening together all at once.

Graeme knew that nothing was fixed, the universe is continually coming into being, ever changing. If you turn right instead of left, you don't just change what is about to happen, you change it all; past, present and future. They are all happening together at the same time; every permutation is being written and re-written. New histories are constantly becoming visible in the Akashic record, that great universal compendium of all human events, thoughts, words, emotions and intent that is encoded on the etheric plane.

You can tell yourself in the past everything will be all right because you, the future you, already knows. Déjà vu is nothing of the kind. We're not experiencing something we have experienced before, we're always experiencing everything at the same time, but we just can't process it, that's why we live in a metaphorical cave. Our minds are so closed off, our thoughts really do hold sway over time in a very literal sense. Sometimes, it overwhelmed him, making him feel physically sick. One day he would have to tell Katie about the cave and Plato's allegory. Would she understand, or would it just frighten her? He didn't know.

High in the sky, looking milky through the clouds, the moon looked down on him, like a giant eye, which, in a way it was, a visible symbol of the hidden worlds which rule over us. Mars and Jupiter fought for supremacy in the night sky which reflected the battle of wills going on inside his soul as it was being torn apart between his love of his family and his love for Katie.

Grace

During the few golden years, he had enjoyed with his beloved Maria on his estate, the Lord of Ashton did as much as he could to discretely distance himself from the courtly life in London.

After Maria's death in 1633, Richard Peak became increasingly withdrawn. He mourned her passing daily and there was little joy in him, save for the time he spent with their beautiful daughter Grace.

Every day she seemed to change, to become more and more like her mother and, except for her piercing blue eyes, he could have been with Maria.

Over the next nine years, he would spend every morning with Grace, riding through his estates. Each afternoon he would attend to the matters of the estate whilst she would be schooled by her tutors.

Sewing, weaving and cooking were normal pass times for young girls, although it was unusual for them to learn to read or write unless they were of noble birth Just like her mother, Grace was a quick learner with her interests ranging far and wide.

The Lord of Ashton had always harboured suspicions about the motives of the people that Maria had tutored at their masked gatherings. Maria was, in his eyes, the purest soul he had ever known. She had always shared her knowledge freely and she truly believed that her lessons were to be for the good of all. Richard however was more sceptical, believing that most of her pupils sought only power, money or influence which, once gained would rarely be used for the benefit of others.

As a soldier, he had fought across Europe and seen first hand the fate of those who opposed the powerful elite, not just kings but also the Catholic Church. Kings would come and go, yet the Church was eternal and the sins of the mothers and fathers, whether real or imagined, would often be visited upon the children, sometimes even grandchildren.

In an effort to protect Grace, on the day of her birth he had forbidden any in his household to speak of her mother or to tell her that she was his daughter.

Grace herself was told that her mother was the old maid Catherine, head of his household who, by the grace of God, had received the gift of a child late in life. Catherine herself died in 1637, aged 46 when Grace was just four years old.

From that day forward, Richard formerly adopted her

as his ward, maintaining to all who asked that it was his promise of the reward for loyal service, just as he had been rewarded for his service to King Charles.

There were many occasions when he longed to tell her that he was her father, of his love for Maria her mother. Perhaps she suspected, he did not know for sure, her safety was his sole concern so their secret, whether their hearts knew the truth or not, would remain unspoken.

For the most part, his ruse was successful. His tenants were completely loyal to him, even the few who liked to gossip, dared not question him. As his courtly visitors became fewer, his life became more private and he became ever more absorbed with Grace.

Whilst teaching her to ride they would often find themselves wandering down to the brook to let the horses rest or to drink from the stream.

On occasion, he would find himself calling her Maria.

"Who is Maria?" Grace would ask.

His answer was always the same. "Oh I am sorry. " he would say, "my mind was wandering to someone I once knew."

"You seem to mistake me for her often." Grace would observe.

"Well, she saved my life when I was a soldier. She was a friend of your mother."

In his heart, he knew that he could not protect Grace from her fate. He had allowed the stone amulet to be given to her before the maid Catherine's passing. She too had come to realise that the stone was to protect both him and the child so she had implored him on her death bed not to keep it from her.

Grace had been instantly attracted to it somehow and now it always hung around her neck. As she grew, she would play with the stone, reciting strange words she could not possibly have known the meaning of.

She grew more like her mother every day, stronger, more confident, her mannerisms, even the way she would absent-mindedly play with the stone, were the same. Everyone could see that she too was destined to be beautiful.

There was something else too.

By the time she was nine years old, she already had strange dreams. She would walk through the house, asleep yet talking as if engaged in conversation with disembodied souls. She was never disturbed by anything she saw. She could live in the dream world and in this world and, where she walked, the land blossomed, just as it had for Maria.

Despite his loneliness, his constant ache for the loss of Maria, these nine years were the happiest of his life. He lived in a cocoon of peace and harmony, whilst in the world outside of the lands of Ashton, chaos reigned.

In London, meanwhile his master King Charles had continued to create enemies at every turn.

Many of those close to him in the royal court whispered in his ear of royal privilege, of divine right.

'King by the will of God'.

'Kings were not meant to be subject to the rules of other, lesser men...'

They did not truly believe that kings ruled by the will of God alone. Fear and suspicion reigned supreme so they were merely trying to ingratiate themselves into his royal favour or, if they were Catholic, trying to avoid an untimely demise for themselves and their families at the hands of the executioner.

In the end, these whispering serpents served to fuel the royal ego, sense of entitlement and paranoia.

A few trusted courtiers, aware of the rising anger that some of his decisions had engendered, tried to defuse the coming confrontation, but his refusal to listen to his most loyal advisers or to parliament, in the end, had only one outcome. By 1642 the kingdom was again at war, this time with itself.

No stranger to war, Richard was a brave man, always willing to fight, but he knew that civil wars are the worst of all. They turn fathers against sons and brothers against brothers. Before long it is hard to know the difference between friend or foe. These wars do not begin with hard declarations, they would begin with argument, entrenched positions then grow, spreading like an insidious black shadow until, at last, they took on a life of their own. 1642 was no different. The early part of the year began with minor skirmishes but by August, there was all-out war, it was a dreadful situation. Careless gossip could result in a father, a brother or a cousin being tried for treason then summarily executed at the gallows by the constable of the local castle.

Although he was no longer the fearless young warrior he had once been, the Lord of Ashton was still a fearsome sight astride his heavy horse wearing his battle tunic. Now in his forties, his hair was grey and his girth clearly reflected the privileged life he had enjoyed on his estates, but he was a skilled strategist, a wily commander of men. He was summoned to court to pledge his allegiance once again to the king before reporting to the supreme commander of the royalist forces, Prince Rupert, to receive his orders.

His skills were invaluable so he was given command of a regiment, three thousand men in all and, in the name of the king, they fought bravely at Edgehill, Aylesbury, Brentford and Turnham Green. Foremost in his mind was trying to keep the war away from his own doorstep so he had supported the Banbury initiative to keep Cheshire neutral but, by Christmas, the agreement had failed and the war was indeed coming home.

As his loyalty to the king had led Richard Peak to his riches, so his loyalty would ultimately be his undoing. Neglecting his estates, stripping them of his men for battle, the coffers were drained to pay for armaments and the farms were untended. To stave off starvation for the families he governed, he was forced to turn to his neighbours for financial support. His lands were rich and this was an opportunity too good for the neighbouring Lord of Renwick Manor to pass up.

As the New Year dawned, Richard's young illegitimate daughter, who believed herself to be his ward, stood by his side gripping his hand tightly. Although he had no choice but to hand her over to his neighbour as security for his debts, his heart writhed and he felt like he would explode. He felt Maria by his side and, remembered her words when she had visited him in his dream a decade earlier, "I will never leave you. Our daughter will be a great comfort to you, but you must remember her purpose. I am for you always but she is here for another."

The young girl cried, writhing to stay with him and, even as she did so, he knelt down looking into her tearful, blue eyes. Smiling, he whispered, "Everything will be alright, you will be an honoured guest in their house as you have been in mine. I love you." The little girl fidgeted, playing with the strange green stone that hung around her neck and a strange calm descended over her. She returned his smile, turned and was led away to the servant's quarters.

Power and Sex

A week later, back in London at their West End hotel, Katie arrived first and checked in. When Graeme arrived, he texted her and she came down to meet him. He waited by the lifts and as she stepped out in her blue t-shirt and jeans, he grabbed her, answered her first questioning kiss and immediately she relaxed.

"Come on, let's get a drink at the bar before we go up," he said.

As they talked, they tried to peel another onion layer from Katie's story, to truly understand what she'd experienced in order to help her make sense of it.

"Have you ever been hypnotised?" Graeme asked.

"No, I don't think so. Why do you ask?"

"Well, there comes a point when you drink enough,

that one extra drink seems to push you over the edge and you become very compliant. You seem okay, but you're not. It's like someone else takes over. It reminds me of the shows where someone from the audience is hypnotised and think they can't let go of a chair. You know the kind of thing I mean? I've seen it on a few occasions, in Dublin and The Benjamin Franklin Hotel, for example. Just like the picture of you on the counter with Linda at Barry's house."

Katie was confused.

"Do you really have any idea how many guys you've slept with?"

"I don't sleep around!" she protested, clearly annoyed. " I like to be flirty, but I'm not interested in sleeping around."

"How do you know, if you can't remember?"

Katie was horrified. She didn't want Graeme to think of her being like that, but she knew that, to a point at least, he was right and the photos from the evening of Karen's party in August had created doubt in her own mind.

She looked again at the three pictures she had of that evening. In the first, she was bright and happy, posing with Karen, waiting for dinner to be served. In the second, she was clearly drugged up to the eyeballs, partially undressed, sitting on the kitchen counter, and, in the third, she was laid in bed with her granddaughter, nursing a hangover along with a bruised head. Had she been subjected to violence too? When she'd asked her husband about what had happened that night, he'd told her that she'd fallen on the steps getting into the house.

She needn't have worried about what Graeme thought. He loved her, all he cared about was her safety. Now that she'd started to broach the subject with her husband, she was in less danger so perhaps she could start to deal with the deeper questions. She was starting to understand her sexual nature. He knew he couldn't change it nor did he want to, but he could help her explore it. Perhaps in this would lay the key to much of what had happened to her. They finished their drinks and made their way up to the room with a fresh bottle of wine.

Katie was quiet, thinking about the things they had discussed and what she should tell him next. She poured two glasses of wine and they continued their conversation in bed. "Sex is my power," she confessed.

Graeme already knew this, but it almost seemed to surprise Katie as she acknowledged it to herself and, even when she did, she wasn't fully conscious of how deeply this ran through her. She believed that she could control it, but not understanding the true nature of the power within her, she was mistaken. Few can awaken it consciously, almost none can control it.

"I guess I've always known it," she said. "It seemed quite natural to be able to get men to do the things I wanted. You should be able to do it in your twenties or thirties but in your forties?"

Katie was still adept at it in her mid-fifties. It wasn't just men either, women were equally attracted to her and the power within her was primordial, almost animalistic. She was propositioned constantly on social media. Some were clearly lost souls caught in her web of power, others were much coarser, wanting her husband to watch as they offered to act out their fantasies with her. They would send pictures of their penises in the hope of turning her on.

Worse still, some were work colleagues, others were friends of her son.

She had a look approaching sadness in her eyes, when she recalled how she had used her sex appeal in a calculating manner on her husband.

"I guess it was a combination of knowing I could do it and my competitive spirit."

"What do you mean?"

"Well, when things were bad, I was having the affair with Andy so my husband started seeing a girl called Diane. I guess he felt he had the right because of what I had done, but I wasn't going to put up with that. Even though I didn't want him, there was no way I was going to let her have him. I knew I was better than her, so I became a real vamp, bought sexy underwear and made sure he knew it too. Sure enough, it worked.

"I guess I'd used it on Andy too when I met him in Cyprus. It was getting late. He was the best looking guy in the place, the other girls were a bit intimidated but Jenny encouraged me so I flirted with him and, in the end, I had him, because I could. I thought I loved him and he loved to walk into a pub or a club with me on his arm, but I guess you need to be on the same intellectual level too for a relationship to really work. Don't get me wrong, Andy was lovely, although he wasn't too bright. I told you, he spent a year in the gym to impress me."

I guess a lack of self-esteem isn't a gender thing, thought Graeme. He couldn't figure out whether she was confessing or buttering him up. He wasn't "fit", but she'd always said he was clever, even though he didn't feel it.

"Have you brought the cards with you?" she asked.

He handed over the tarot deck and she browsed through them, looking intently at the pictures, asking about each in turn.

"Oh my God!" she exclaimed. "I think I'm using the wrong queen. I think I'm the Queen of Swords".

Graeme smiled, pulling her closer and they lay in one another's arms until he had to leave, making his way across London for a business meeting.

As he sat on the underground, his mind raced and he remembered Katie's recent confrontation with Tom, specifically the revelation that he believed that his friend had slept with her. A big event was on the horizon, a friend's fiftieth birthday and Graeme wondered what an explosive mixture that might be. Katie was determined to confront the person Tom had spoken about, should he be there. To complicate matters further, her friend Alison - Mad Ali, as she called her - would be there too which inevitably would mean it wouldn't just be alcohol in the mix, there'd be drugs too. Did she have the strength yet? he wondered.

By the time of their next rendezvous in Manchester, Graeme was relieved to learn that the party had gone off without a hitch. He needed to know she was safe and at the moment, she was.

The Mondragon hotel was an old converted warehouse. It was close to the town but quiet and they felt comfortable there. The intensity of their relationship continued to build and, even by their standards, the lovemaking was a marathon. After they'd made love three times, they lay in each other's arms as Katie resumed her revelations.

There wasn't much she hadn't experimented with, from anal sex to threesomes and, when Graeme had observed in London a few weeks earlier that he wasn't really her type, she'd promised to bring a picture of someone who was. A fireman, yes the type you see on girlie calendars, complete with the six-pack and long hosepipe.

She showed him.

"That's nothing," he joked. "I've got a twelve pack." He had, the result of lack of exercise, present company excepted, and a pie or two more than he should have had.

Katie laughed.

"Hmm, who is that?" he asked.

"That's Steve, My husband and I got friendly with him and his wife Susan on holiday in Dubai then we went to visit them when we got home. We drank a lot, one thing led to another, Susan went to bed then the three of us carried on the party and we had a threesome."

"Was this all about the same time as your move to your new house?"

"Yes. Almost everything harks back to that time. Obviously, when I was in my early twenties I experimented, learning I suppose. You know the sort of thing, any thing... in any hole, but things really started happening around that time. Do you think there's a connection with the house? I'm sure I have some of the original documents for the house going back to the eighteenth century. I'll look for them when I get a chance. I think the house was built for an old Scottish family called Seers."

Graeme lay holding her. Words are powerful he said, Names don't come to us by accident. Hmm, he'd have to look into that.

From Bad to Worse

Christmas was going to be a real test for them both. They'd managed to spend a couple of nights together in mid-December but they would now be apart for almost three weeks and their enforced abstinence cut them both to the quick.

With problems to deal with at home, Katie was feeling particularly anxious. She'd never admit it, but she was jealous of Graeme, who seemed to be having a lovely time, out walking in the forests, on the beaches and across the hills with his wife, as they tried to come to terms with their relationship.

She couldn't have been more wrong. Even though their lifestyles couldn't have been more different, his feelings mirrored her own.

There would be no shortage of electronic contact, but, to make matters worse, this too was briefly interrupted when Katie bought a new phone. She texted Graeme telling him, her husband was going to try to set up her new phone tonight because it was driving her mad. *I want to hear from you but wait until I text you later otherwise I'll be moving out before Christmas.*

Graeme used the time to look again at Katie's dream-like experience. He started exploring the history of the area, looking for any obvious links. There were several historical things that - in his philosophy, where all things are connected - could be in play.

Whilst he dismissed some more recent news reports of sexual impropriety locally, his attention was drawn to a local legend several hundred years old.

Renwick Hall, the ancestral home of the De Bernier family, was quite near Katie's house. Centuries ago, they were engaged in some sort of feud with the lord of the neighbouring Manor of Ashton. Legend had it that they tricked him out of his land and estate after he failed to pay some kind of debt on the due date. They foreclosed and, as a result, some sort of curse was called down upon them. From that day, the De Bernier's horses, it was said, wouldn't cross the stream which marked the boundary between the two manors. As he wasn't familiar with the area, he made a mental note to ask Katie if there was a stream nearby.

His interest piqued, Graeme's dug deeper into the strange family history of the local landowners. The De Berniers had powerful allies in the Stanley family and it seems that they were fortunate not to have been executed. The Stanley's had been de-facto rulers in Lancashire and Cheshire since the Norman Conquest. Long credited with stories of intrigue at court, it was they who had conveniently reaffirmed their family loyalty to Parliament by uncovering the gunpowder plot in 1605.

The De Berniers were also clearly skilled at matters of court, they had lost and regained their title and lands on more than one occasion. Strongly Catholic in what was then a puritanical Protestant country, it was rumoured that they had supplied information to the Hapsburg Spanish King Philip IV during the war with King Charles.

Catholics and Protestants were still vying for supremacy in England so publicly refusing to submit to the religious authority of the day was dangerous. There were also other, quiet, whispered stories of strange guests, some of whom were said to worship older gods. There were also tales of sexual debauchery, of demonic forces. The manor itself, or rather the Tower, which was all that was left of it, was still believed to be haunted.

For the next few nights, Katie had trouble sleeping. Although it was almost certainly due to the alcohol withdrawal, she would wake in the middle of the night anxious, worried and frightened. The more she did, the more she looked forward to seeing Graeme again, as when he held her she felt safe and reassured.

Even though they were both papering over the cracks in their respective relationships and neither was happy, once again, their attentions were diverted by the needs of others. As Christmas approached, Katie got into party mode. Out with contacts, out with the girls or her husband, she was always dressed to kill and would send pictures.

Oh no, thought Graeme. The dress... the boots...

December had been a bad month for Tom too, but ultimately it would be the beginning of his rehabilitation. He was spending long days in bed and Katie knew it wasn't good for him. Worried about his state of mind, she suspected drugs were a factor once again. His mood improved when Helen was present but Carly was unsettled, returning to her mother's house and taking Helen with her.

Katie had texted Graeme. *Looks like they can't sort things out this time. I'll try to talk to him as soon as I know he's awake. What a bloody mess.*

On discovering that Carly was pregnant again, Tom's controlling instincts had taken over. As Katie had suspected, combined with the accessibility of drugs, it didn't take long for the situation to approach boiling point again and Carly considered an abortion. Katie had cried at the thought of it and was grateful that nothing had been decided, although that could change and she couldn't blame Carly for leaving.

Relationships aren't plain sailing; she had put up with a lot from Tom, they both had, but recently things seemed to have calmed a little, at least in Tom's attitude towards his mother.

Katie had chatted more openly with him now that he'd decided that he did want help to get off the 'coke' merry go round after all.

As Carly came and went the days were punctuated with minor episodes such as Tom threatening to leave with Helen, which in turn resulted in Carly threatening to call the police, then blocking the driveway with her car. Katie played peacemaker and, as usual, Tom just couldn't see that he was always going to come off worst as he risked losing the things most precious to him.

It was becoming a pattern, so much so that when Katie returned home from a party in the early hours of Christmas Eve, she couldn't help texting Graeme, *Tom's car is on the drive, he's in bed... no police here... result!*

Her joy had lasted until about midday when she rose with a hangover and realised that Tom hadn't been in that night after all. The drama was far from over.

Katie tried to unravel the trail of events. Yes, his car was outside but he had been to see Carly and they had again ended up arguing. Carly was already fragile and Tom was upset when the subject of abortion was discussed. He didn't react well to the news, defaulting to his petulant, abusive style. He had verbally abused her, so being fearful of what could happen next she had called the police. Tom was arrested for assault then cautioned to stay away from her.

When he returned home, Tom's mood was once again dark, he was shaking with anger but eventually, Katie managed to calm him down and talk to him.

With the threat of abortion of his unborn child still fresh in his mind, he broke down. Again Katie was left to sort out the mess, trying to reason with Carly, imploring her not do something in anger that might haunt her for the rest of her life.

Graeme, as usual, tried to cheer her up. *Your favourite film is on the telly, Jason and the Argonauts.*

I might just watch it. Due to be out again tonight, although I am not feeling any motivation. Think I need to sleep more.

Well, if you change your mind, Jason has just had his little run-in with Talos.

Is that the big iron man where he unscrews the thing on his ankle? I like the sea god best where he holds the rocks apart. Memories... wish I was sat on your lap.

You have a very good memory. You need a break. I worry about you, but you already knew that. I hope it goes okay, I will text later but will understand if you can't reply. Enjoy the rest of your day. I hope Santa calls.

Christmas Day was a family affair, but Helen being absent hurt Katie deeply. She tried to take her mind off the situation, dressing up. Graeme meanwhile dressed as he always did. His imagination doesn't extend too far in that direction, thought Katie laughing to herself, but the stress and tensions were still all too evident even though she was surrounded by her extended family. The day consisted of drinks - lots of drinks - followed by dinner after the visit to the pub, then more drinks. She couldn't remember quite why exactly, somehow it had become a family tradition.

The partying continued into Boxing Day and, by this time, Katie was feeling the pressure.

Fuck this, she had thought. I'm going out to get pissed.

Pressing the self-destruct button once again, she did.

The next morning, she read Graeme's customary

good morning greeting asking if she'd had a good time at the party. She had. At least, up to the point where she could remember, now she was feeling rough, very rough.

A duvet day was called for.

Her mood was up and down. She'd wake in the early hours, sit and fret before going back to bed exhausted. When she did, she would dream, something she noticed she was beginning to do more freely these days.

'Your dreams have meaning,' Graeme had told her. 'Your dream on the rock face means that you're feeling low or emotionally drained. Your goals are in sight, but there's something in your subconscious holding you back.'

She knew he was right, the question she'd asked herself about why she acted the way she did arose again in her mind. Christmas hasn't been what I wanted or expected. Anyway, it's done now, so I can move on. Alcohol is a depressant, highs to hide the pain and then the lows. Her reaction to anything she didn't like or felt hurt by was to put it in a box then move on, yet deep down, she knew she had to confront things sooner or later.

As December 30th approached, Graeme couldn't let their anniversary pass without seeing her, so he texted to ask if she could join him for lunch at a hotel in North Lancashire.

Katie quickly agreed. *It feels like so long, we have lots to talk about.*

Graeme teased her with a note in Spanish, which he sometimes whispered in her ears as they made love.

No puedo esperar para abrazarte y besarte Reina de mi Corazon. You know what it says, read it with your heart not your eyes.

I think so. I have to check the translator because I need to know how close I am.'

You are funny.

I was just thinking about how I was feeling twelve months ago

Me too funnily enough. Tomorrow will be lovely, quite strange too, won't it?

Guess so, I am just hoping we pick up where we left off.

Why? Are you nervous?

Well, just a little. It feels like I've not seen you for so long, you may have gone off me.'

Graeme wondered if Katie had been at the sherry again. He knew she would be laughing now.

You're funny. Sherry! Now you're showing your age.

Then we will get to know one another afresh, starting it all again tomorrow. A wonderful journey I would very much like to take with you again.

To make her laugh, he added his predictions for 2017. *Sherry will be the new vodka. There will be lots of alcoholic old ladies raiding Aldis, hunting in packs. Grown men won't be safe and trifle will be reclassified as a class B narcotic.*

Katie kissed her phone and went to sleep with a smile.

Graeme arrived first around 11 o'clock and, on impulse, asked if he could book a room for early check-in. He must have had a desperate look about him because the manageress, taking pity, on him said she had a room ready.

When Katie arrived in the car park, he texted her.

I'm upstairs in the bar.

They spent a wonderful afternoon together and, to an outside observer, the second year of their relationship would appear to have begun as the first had, but they both knew that was just in appearance, that they had somehow accessed a much deeper level and experienced an intensity new to both of them.

After making love, they settled down to talk.

"What have you turned up about the history of the house?"

"Not much about the house specifically."

He relayed the story of the De Bernier feud with the Lord of Ashton and asked, "Is there a stream near your house?"

"Yes, there is. It's called Hollins' Brook. It marks the boundary of my land and also the boundary between Renwick and Ashton. There's a gravestone of some sort on the opposite side."

"When you get home, send me a picture of it."

Katie knew she'd be in trouble when she got home. She'd made an excuse that she was going out for lunch yet she didn't leave Graeme until around 6pm but she didn't care. They tore themselves away from one another, said goodbye and a couple of hours later she texted Graeme. *I'm home safe. Thank you for such a wonderful afternoon. It was just FAB. I love you.*

Happy anniversary mi sueno. I am looking forward to sharing the next twelve months with you and doing it all again.

Later that evening, after Katie had gone to bed, he sent her a note.

Katie era la mujer más hermosa que Graeme había conocido.

It would be waiting for her when she woke to start the next phase of their journey together.

The next morning, when Katie awoke, she translated the message. It was so beautiful she began to cry.

When she got out of bed, she wandered outside to send Graeme the pictures she'd promised him of the gravestone opposite her land. When Graeme saw the photos, he shuddered as the hairs stood up on the back of his neck. The stone simply said, 'Division' and underneath the words 'Renwick and Ashton,' but there was something else that had almost been eroded away. Graeme instantly knew what it was. He sent Katie a photo of a daisy wheel asking her if she'd seen this design either on the stone nearby or particularly in her house.

They would usually be near doorways or windows, he told her. *Perhaps you have painted over it or taken them out when you have been renovating.*

That looks familiar. I can't think where I have seen it. What is it?

Well, said Graeme, unsure how Katie would take this.

It's a magical charm, designed to protect against witchcraft, curses or evil spirits. They are a bit like an American Indian dream catcher, the design is sometimes quite similar. They would have been quite common in old houses, particularly for your area because whoever built the house would have been aware of the Ashton curse.

You know I don't believe in that kind of fairytale.

Perhaps not, but the people who built your house certainly did. You said the Seers family may have had the house built for them.

Yes.

Well, names are not accidental. Seers is an English translation descended from the Picts in Aberdeenshire. They would most likely have been the royal advisors, or literally the prophets of their time for the Pictish kings. If that is the case, then they were almost certainly sensitive to this sort of thing.

Graeme did some more research and made the best of his enforced separation from Katie, travelling the country to events and to give talks. Katie had done her best to wind him up, ordering sexy outfits and teasing him.

Hmm, she had wondered, *how short should I make this dress?*

If it stops just above your ankles that would be fine. Graeme knew too well that all the men would be drooling over her once she was out partying again over New Year.

Katie continued to tease him, wondering if he had missed the long black boots.

Go on then, she thought, she'd maybe wear them just in the bedroom.

Graeme wasn't laughing. He wondered what had Katie found so funny about the long dress? *The boots wouldn't go with the big knickers that start just under your chest and go down to your knees that I am going to buy you.*

Do I really have to have such huge knickers? They'd take far too long to prise off, you're not that patient when it comes to getting naked, she teased.

It wasn't unusual for her to try to make Graeme jealous.

She needn't have bothered, he was always jealous and it ate away at him. Katie felt the same, when Graeme was away with his wife for a couple of days she was fretful. He had been in touch constantly though. Almost without fail, somehow she would find little reminders of him when she needed some comfort. He had often hidden sweets in her clothes when they'd been together and she was building up quite a collection of fruit gums.

Graeme had Franki Valli songs going round in his head constantly. He saw pictures that reminded him of Katie everywhere and sent them to her. One picture, a little boy and girl playing in the street decades ago and obviously poor, really struck a chord. It spoke of what they had missed and of what their lives may have been had they met as children.

Darkness Before the Dawn

It was New Years Eve 2016, As Graeme's text had made her cry when she woke, before her day was over, Katie would be crying again, for altogether different reasons. As the tears ran down her face, she reviewed the events of the last few weeks in her mind; much of which seemed to have seen various members of the family at loggerheads.

She had tried to get a referral for Tom to see a psychiatrist, but initially, he'd refused to attend the first evaluation. He eventually agreed to go to the hospital, but not with Katie. So his cousin "Edward, to whom Tom was close, went instead. They managed to secure a psychiatric referral for early in the New Year, in the meantime, the drama had continued to build.

"He really needs to find someone he can talk to and also listen to, to help him work through it," Graeme had observed. "If he doesn't, he will lose Helen and she seems to be the one thing that brings out the best in him. Don't let him kick off at you. You shouldn't be taking the brunt of his anger."

Graeme, meanwhile, had continued researching the area Katie lived in for clues. He didn't believe in coincidences. Everything had meaning, names, symbols, dates - everything. The more he looked into it, the more the legend of Renwick Hall piqued his interest.

How far is Renwick Hall from your house? he asked Katie.

She didn't know the place, so looked for it on a map then replied, *It's about half a mile away, just the other side of the golf club.*

I'd like to go there in the New Year to see it for myself.

Katie readily agreed.

One more thing, can you look at a few names to see if they have any significance for you or your close family. Most people historically were employed or connected to the local manor in some way or other, coopers, fletchers, painters etc. Do you recognise any family connections?

Katie wasn't from that area originally, so she promised to make discreet enquiries. She didn't understand what he was looking for but had long since realised his way of looking at the world was unlike anyone she had ever met.

It's funny, I was just thinking about how I was feeling twelve months ago. I was excited, inquisitive and nervous - a bit like I feel tonight. God! I miss you.

It was uncanny, like a mirror being held up to Graeme's own feelings.

Apart from her day with Graeme on their anniversary, Katie's festive season had been a roller coaster of partying, sobering up and family quarrels, interspersed with welcome breaks when she corresponded with Graeme to take her mind off things until tonight - New Years Eve, when she was to host a fancy dress party at her house.

She knew she looked incredibly sexy in her beer wench outfit. Her hair made up into pigtails with red ribbons, a tight, red and white corset to accentuate her full bosom and her petit waist. The hemline was high with just a little of her thighs visible, the rest covered by high heeled, long black boots. She was gorgeous, all that was needed was alcohol, men, music and Tom - and she had the perfect recipe for disaster.

Soon the guests started to arrive, dressed as ninjas, matadors, flamenco dancers and more. As Katie started partying, Graeme was waiting to exchange New Year messages then he would go to bed. His new year wouldn't start until he saw her again, fortunately that was now only a few days away.

Two kisses, one for the last day of this year, one for the first day of next year. If you have a hangover in the morning and start to worry they will cheer you up. You will know I am thinking about you, that I love you, he said. *It has been my privilege to be by your side Reina de mi Corazon.*

Happy new year gorgeous. Sad to say goodbye to

2016 because I fell in love with the most amazing guy who is kind, generous, loving, gentle, clever and makes me feel like I am his queen. I am very privileged to have been able to share so many fantastic evenings with you. Thank you for putting up with my insecurities, for holding me while I slept. You are simply the BEST. I am looking forward to sharing much more in 2017, although if I only get half of what we had in 2016, I'd still be very happy. On the stroke of midnight, I am yours, I love you.

It was late on New Years Day when Katie surfaced and Graeme texted to ask if she had enjoyed the party she had hosted to see in the New Year.

Not really,' she said. 'Even you couldn't write this one.

What happened? No, let me guess, we're having twins?

Jenny, who had arrived as a ninja, realised she wasn't a ninja after all and was upset when her husband threw the large German sausage-shaped thing away because he said he just couldn't get it to lather up like it promised in the Timote advert?

Your husband's lover Diane turned up... dressed as a fireman?

Katie laughed but it was short-lived.

No, it's Tom. I'm at the end of my tether with him, he's disappeared. Last night, with the party in full swing, he went off on one. He started throwing people out.

Who and why? Presumably, in his mind at least, he had a reason.

He decided that he didn't like certain people. I didn't

know anything about it until Stephen had blood all over him then the police turned up.

Who's Stephen? Should I know?

Just a nice guy, he's just a friend from the pub. He came with two mates. They were just having a good time, dancing with everyone until Tom decided it was time for them to leave.

Graeme suspected immediately what was going through Tom's mind.

Dancing with you? he asked

Not just me, everyone was dancing. Tom also hit his cousin Edward who was sticking up for me.

How many men and how many women? I wouldn't mind betting that's what Tom thought he was doing too, sticking up for you.

Katie thought about it for a moment. *Possibly, but he spoke to me this morning like something on the bottom of his shoe. I've had it. I'm so sad. I can't let him continue to treat us all this way. Whatever issues he's got, it's not fair that we're all scared of him and what he might do next.*

Graeme persisted, while events were fresh in Katie's mind.

How many men? how many women? who were Stephen's mates? Had they been to your house before?

Yes, they all have because they're just friends. Stephen is a bit full of himself, but he's okay, he didn't deserve being punched.

You've had some adventures Katie. Tom knows, or thinks he knows more than he's telling you if it's sending him over the edge. How many men and how many women were left when it kicked off?

I honestly don't know. More men than women. I can't remember who was left.

Then how do you know Tom was wrong?

I guess I don't, I wasn't there when it kicked off. I was in the kitchen. Yes, I understand, you're right - far too many adventures.

If you can calm him down, you need to ask him. It all keeps coming back to the same thing doesn't it? He may be acting like a prick but one thing I've never doubted is that he worships you. He doesn't know how to deal with it when he sees how attracted men are to you. What has your husband to say about it all?

He's scared of him. Tom is really unstable. He told me this morning that he was going to burn the house down with us all in it. He really isn't a nice person, his dad's on edge, wondering what he'll do next. I'm sure it's all talk, but Tom with a night of drink, drugs and no sleep makes for a scary young man. The police only came because it was New Year's Eve, although no one wanted any trouble so no one 'saw anything'.

Graeme went out for a walk in the hailstones to blow the cobwebs off. The events described by Katie ran over and over in his mind. He never understood what Katie saw in him, he was lost in her and he was just greedy for more. Her life was a raging torrent, but she was a drug to him, there was no cure, he just couldn't get enough of her.

For the next couple of nights, emotionally exhausted, Katie slept well. She, at last, knew what she had to do to help Tom. In his anger and torment, lashing out he had wrecked the apartment. The police turned up several times, in the end, Katie was called to the hospital at 3 am where the only respite would be to have Tom temporarily sectioned. It proved a turning point and the coming days would be calmer. In spite of their fight, Edward continued to act as a go-between, encouraging Tom to attend his counselling sessions. Combined with a prescription of anti depressants it provided a temporary relief until a more permanent solution could be found.

Counterintuitively, Katie knew that she needed to get him out of the house so she looked for a nearby rental property she could help him and Carly afford. She couldn't lose the connection with Helen at any cost.

For Graeme, New Year began in earnest on January 4th when he met Katie at a hotel in Coventry where they could relax and again spend the night in each other's arms. He had continued to send her pictures of his walks in the hills, enjoying the solitude they afforded, but he always craved Katie's company. They had dinner with a client to attend first, but most of their time would be their own and they had a lot of catching up to do.

The following morning he said, "I've been reading through the notes you made about your house. How long did Karen own the house?"

"Why?" asked Katie.

"Just curious."

A clearer picture of Renwick Hall was emerging. It had once been a magnificent house, a half-timbered building with four overhanging gables dating back to Elizabethan times. Although not originally built for them it had been renovated and extended by the De Bernier family in the 1600's. Above the entrance were initials, representing Edward and his new wife Eleanor Beauchamp De Bernier. They were evidently a very powerful family. Graeme surmised from the name that their roots were much older.

Most of the rooms would have been wainscoted or paneled, although they were long-since destroyed by fire. Only the gatehouse now remains, built up with a doorway that would have originally been open, large enough to ride horses through.

Katie needed time to take it all in. When it was time to leave, Graeme dropped her at the train station and within minutes they were messaging one another.

I feel a bit better now I have seen you, he said. *Just a bit.*

I miss you as soon as I walk away. I would have given anything for a few more hours in bed.

Graeme was worried that he was turning into a bit of a trollop because he would have given anything to hold Katie close.

It's amazing waking up with you... then waking you up.

He didn't want Katie to think he was easy, so he played it cool.

Oh shit! he thought. *'I said that out loud didn't I?'*

Katie was laughing. Too late, she already thought Graeme was easy.

He knew he was anything but cool with Katie. She pushed every button he had and she was going away skiing soon, so it would be at least two weeks before he would see her again.

I know it's strange, I'm not bonkers. People put those magical charms into your house for a reason. We think of people who came before us as simple, superstitious peasants, but they weren't. Also, I sense that Hollins' Brook has some significance for both you and Tom.

The next night, exhausted, Graeme slept well. He woke with a smile, having dreamt about Katie's spectacular behind as he drifted into consciousness, then he texted Katie but she couldn't talk.

A few hours later, the reply came. *Sorry, just had social services here to get some guidance. Social housing could be an option for Tom. By threatening to evict them, they would jump up the queue. He was okay last night. At last, he seems to want to sort himself out. He helped repair the damage he had done, so that was good, all that remains is to wait for a call from the hospital to see what they propose following their assessment.*

The next few days, Katie spent as much time with Helen as she could, whilst daydreaming about Graeme until it was time to go skiing. She took every opportunity to ski and party, so for her, the early months of the year were always busy and action-filled. Her first stop was the airport at Innsbruck en route to St Anton in the French Alps.

Graeme felt lost for the better part of a fortnight. To make it worse, he spent most of it ill with man-flu feeling sorry for himself. Katie texted every day, updating him on the weather, her adventures skiing, the après ski, memory loss and the hangovers that would follow. The sexy pictures of the parties, the lap dancers, the inevitable crowds of men cut Graeme to the quick but he knew that she was in her element and that she was happy.

He also knew from the garbled late-night texts that he was constantly in her thoughts, even when she was close to passing out. She truly did carry him with her in her heart. This was an annual fixture with friends in Katie's social calendar so, despite the torment, he also knew that her husband wouldn't put her in any of those situations she'd come to dread.

Towards the end of the week, the weather made skiing difficult so to compensate the drinking became more intense. So much so that Katie broke her collarbone falling from a table while dancing on it drunk. A brief return to England beckoned for some specialist medical treatment before she could fly out again, this time to Bormio in the Italian Alps, where she'd ski with her nephew Edward and his wife.

There was little Graeme could do, other than look forward to their next meeting and make arrangements to see her in early February, at a prestigious wine tasting event that he looked forward to every year.

Katie continued to tease him, even from a thousand miles away, when he texted her late in the evening to confirm arrangements.

Oh you want me to be there all day. Here's me thinking I was just your 'afters'. Go on then - I'll be that as well. Are you feeling any better?

Cheeky! After lunch and all the wine, you may not be up to 'afters'. Yes, I am feeling a bit better, thank you.

Before signing off for the night, Katie's mood suddenly changed, turning serious. *Just sat pondering.*

What you pondering sweetheart?

Pondering on what you said to me before I left, that life gives you what you sometimes need rather than what you want. Just something that's been playing on my mind. I love you so much.

It's true... there is a lot that's hidden from us. I don't know why, we keep being brought back to the same challenges again and again. Our lives take us in funny directions, sometimes unexpected ones. It's a rich tapestry for all of us, perhaps we don't appreciate just how rich it is, but there are lessons we need to understand. Do you want to know the secret?

Do you have it? Life sometimes seems simple and other times feels ever so complicated. Yes, who knows what's in store for us all. You're constantly on my mind.

I wish I did, but I believe that what we struggle with is getting to know who we are. One thing keeps coming back time after time; Know thyself.

It's not as easy as it sounds. On our very deepest levels, it means admitting things we don't find pleasant or are not proud of, and finding what really makes us happy, not superficially. That isn't easy either. What touches your soul? God knows you touch mine in a way very few ever have.

I know what makes me truly happy, spending time with just you. No masks, just us.

Sweet dreams.

Paulee

A couple of weeks later, Katie found a place in Ashton about four miles away from her own home in Renwick for Tom and Carly. Fortunately, they loved it, although they wouldn't be able to move in for a few weeks. Although Katie wouldn't have believed it, Graeme sensed a ripple through time and, by being on opposite sides, it would be Hollins' Brook again that would provide the protection both Katie and Tom needed.

Graeme was intrigued by Renwick Hall, he wanted to arrange a visit at the next opportunity. "Okay," said Katie. "Next time you're over here, we'll arrange a detour to Wilmslow. I've never been to the Hall, so it may be interesting."

Something kept drawing Katie back to the strange

house in her dreams. She'd stand in her own garden, throwing a ball for the dog, with her mind recalling fragments of dreams. Always the same house, the grand dining room, the staircase along with the uneasy feelings of tension that they triggered in her. Katie was indeed oblivious to hidden worlds on a conscious level, but she was certainly feeling their effects.

She he was feeling better though and, as she put it, "for now all is calm on the Western Front. Helen is so lovely, she's such a smiley child for all she's had to live with, she makes me very happy." Her mood was lightened again when Jenny confirmed the arrangements for the annual girls' trip to Ayia Napa in May. There would be ten of them going this time.

Oh Lord! thought Graeme. It won't know what's hit it.

Riding her luck, she texted him. *Hiya, how's your day been? Only one week to go before I get to put my grubby little mitts all over you. What wine shall I bring?*

Graeme wasn't in good shape. He was on his way back from a dinner with friends and he pondered the forthcoming event through an alcoholic haze. The dinner would be great but personally, he found it hard to beat a bit of cheese and a glass of wine locked away with a nymphomaniac!

Just bring your dirty little mitts, he replied. *I will sort the rest.*

Are you drunk?

Er... yes.

Katie was about to get a taste of how confusing her own text messages were late at night when somehow all the words seemed to merge into one and your thumbs seem too large for your hands, or at least the letters on your phone screen.

I am going to buy a boat, would you like to go sailing? My mate Jonathan is a keen sailor, he will teach me, but every captain needs a crew. I can't think of a more beautiful crew than... well... you really.

She smiled. *A boat? Okay, I'll be the captain's mate, can we go somewhere warm, please? Not the Firth of Forth or the North Sea.*

Well, I will have to start somewhere, but the Med or the Caribbean sound appealing. I will look after you babe, you know I will.

I know, just like a queen.

You know you're my queen, you always have been.

I've never been anyone's queen, I like it though, when you've been drinking, you're funny, you have lovely dreams.

There was a few minutes' pause before Graeme replied.

I am still here. I was thinking about you all the way here. I came in the bus... don't worry, I managed to disguise it as an asthma attack... I hope you are laughing.

Katie was, indeed giggling. *Good night gorgeous.*

The following day, nursing a hangover and trying to shake off the residual flu he'd been carrying for the last few weeks, Graeme spent £320 ordering four bottles of wine to take to the Paulee at the Melrose Abbey estate. Two bottles of Eden Roc 2010 and two bottles of Nuit St George Premier Cru. He then called the venue to make sure they'd booked two rooms. They wouldn't need them, but this was a special event with some influential people so he needed them close together to avoid either being seen on the inevitable walk of shame the following morning.

He would be dressed in a boring suit. Katie, as always, would be dressed to kill. High heels complementing a stunning, skin-tight, light blue dress.

They met in the car park and kissed furtively before going into the dining room where the wine was laid out on the central table. Despite her love of wine, it was Katie's first Paulee and she drank in the magnificent sight, some eighty or so bottles of some of the finest wines she would ever sample.

"I hope you have had your porridge for breakfast," said Graeme. "This isn't the day to skip on food. Don't forget to spit it out."

He smiled when he saw the pained look she gave him.

The dinner was superb, a leisurely seven-course affair with endless wine sampling, red wine, white wine, dessert wine followed by port. In a beautiful setting overlooking the garden and the Cheviot Hills in the distance, the hotel, The Caithness Arms, was one of Graeme's favourites, even though there could sometimes be a whiff of snobbery exuded by the hunting, shooting and fishing set. Not today, the conversation was good and the guests were interesting people, brought together by their love of food and wine. This was a business lunch for Graeme and Katie so they sat at separate tables entertaining. Although there were a few ladies in attendance, the event was male-dominated. Katie wowed everyone, as she always did, holding court over dinner and later as the afternoon drew to a close when they all retired to the bar.

The common practice was to regroup about 7.30pm for a steak supper, but, once they'd checked in and Katie had made her way to Graeme's room, they wouldn't be venturing out again that night. As they lay down together, Graeme teased her about the afternoon, her drinking and the effect she had on everyone.

"You're really not funny," said Katie. "I only drank half of them! But you're just perfect for me, I know you can handle me just fine."

"No," said Graeme. "No man can handle you just fine Katie and never without your permission."

"You have my permission," she said softly. "You're my pleasure."

Graeme pulled her closer. It was definitely the best Paulee he had ever been to.

A few days later, Katie was delighted that her weekend would start by looking after Helen. This was something she cherished anyway, but she'd offer more and more over time, as she continued to distance herself from her husband's behaviour. She continued making excuses to avoid sex, saying it was her age, being post-menopausal she had no interest in it. He was, in fairness, giving her more space, although the comments would continue when he saw her undressed… 'the boys would love to see her naked.'

Katie simply brushed it off. She would be with Graeme soon then, once in his arms again, she knew that all would be forgotten.

It was as if they were living many lives simultaneously, a home life, a work-life then their true life when they were together and all masks were removed.

I prefer us both without our slap, Graeme had often said.

Me too, thought Katie. You have no idea how good you make me feel.

As she meandered around the bathroom, musing about Graeme, she smiled as she found another packet of fruit gums in her wash bag.

The following morning he texted Katie. *I woke up early today, thinking about you, about the Paulee and wanting to do it all over again.*

For some reason, I woke at about 4.30 am too. The birds were singing but you weren't there.

What were you doing awake at that ungodly hour?

Thinking about going out to Bradbury Hall with Jenny and the girls tomorrow night.

Oh no! he thought.

I remember you telling me about that place, that's your cop off joint isn't it?

Katie laughed. *I'm minding Helen in the morning. We're going to head off about 2pm. We'll have a few drinks in the afternoon then put our party frocks on for the night. We've got a meal booked at 9pm. Looking forward to it but wish you were coming. I would gladly swap it to be with you, some cheese and a bottle of wine.*

My day is suddenly getting worse... much worse,' he replied. In his head he could hear Katie singing to herself. *I am fit and I know I am.* 'Well, have fun, just *remember it's better to be safe than sorry... except with me... so dress appropriately, go prepared, none of that sexy stuff you usually wear.*

Mr Not-so-funny-man. You'd have me wearing knickers up to my armpits. How could I wear such a figure-hugging dress and them not show? Probably best not to wear any.

Graeme cringed. *There are occasions when the idea of a visible panty line doesn't really bother me if I'm honest. Tomorrow night might be one of them. I wish I could come with you.*

The invitation's open, she teased.

Don't worry about me. I have plans too. I'm hoping to get an early night and cry myself to sleep with a glass of milk.

Katie laughed.

As it turned out, Katie spent much of the night at Bradbury Hall texting Graeme.

She sent him a picture of her and Jenny getting ready to go out. She looked beautiful. Surveying all the cleavage on display, he said he'd suddenly remembered they needed a new bike rack at work.

Katie giggled. *I wish you were joining us. Next time I'll give you plenty of notice. You will have a good time.*

Will I have to dance?

Oh yes.

Well, we'd better get some time for you to teach me then. Better bring your hula hoop, or isn't it that kind of dancing?

You're making me laugh and the girls are asking why.

Good night beautiful, enjoy.

The next morning, tucking into black pudding and poached eggs on toast, Graeme realised his get fit training routine was taking a little set back. Better not tell Katie, he thought then he texted her to see how the inevitable hangover was.

Not too bad. I am going to go home and sleep it off. There was an act on but we didn't see it, we went to prop up the bar instead. Then at 2 am when they were shutting, Jenny, Bel and me went back to the club bar. It was 4.15 am when we fell into bed. Even though it got a bit messy we were all good girls.

Did you tell them why you were laughing last night?

'No, They knew I was up to no good and obviously talking to someone though. Jenny knew who. I've only got eyes for one guy.

Can we go and see another show when we go to London next? I thought I didn't like them after seeing Phantom of the Opera, but Jersey Boys was fabulous.

What show would you like to see?

Well you picked a good one last time, so you decide. I haven't seen many.

There's an excellent show called Wicked. It's the story of The Wizard of Oz from the perspective of the Wicked Witch. You'll feel sorry for Ciara by the time it's finished.

Mama Mia - is good if you like Abba songs or Thriller, Michael Jackson. I would gladly go back to see Jersey Boys and sing them all to you all over again.

I like Michael Jackson, the Wizard of Oz sound good too.

OK, I will sort something.

A present for Jenny

At the beginning of March Katie visited Edinburgh again, offering a welcome but unexpected opportunity to spend another night together. When she checked into the Radisson she was horrified to find that the room contained two single beds. Although Graeme was busy preparing a speech at the university he laughed when she texted him.

We'll just sleep in one, we're never further away than that anyway he replied

True, thought Katie, but she asked room service to put the beds together before Graeme arrived.

When he did he was surprised to find that there wasn't much wine or cheese. Katie loved wine and cheese and he was starving. Even though she was indeed his joy, he needed to keep his strength up.

Perhaps it was the unexpected timing, but Katie's mood was strange, she was arsey.

"What's wrong?" he asked.

After saying 'nothing' once or twice, Katie couldn't hold it in any longer, she was having doubts about how he felt. She tended to tell Jenny everything and, when she'd said to her that Graeme had confessed to having an affair, Jenny wasn't convinced that it wasn't merely a ruse to cover his tracks ahead of his wife finding out about them.

Graeme was in turmoil. He assured Katie that Jenny couldn't have been more wrong. He had confessed anyway; in the full expectation that his marriage would be over. Consequences would have to be faced. What benefit would it have added to talk of Katie? She had a family too, besides he didn't want her dragged into this. He knew of her past and that any repercussions for her would be final. He had no right to make that decision for her.

She listened as they held one another.

"I love you," he said. "Can't you feel it?"

Katie's emotions were running wild, but, yes, she could feel it, she could always feel it and it wasn't long before their animal passions took over once more.

They made love twice before settling down for the night, but each time she struggled to climax.

"You have not to be frightened of hurting me," she said.

She wanted him to be rough with her, but he simply couldn't, it wasn't in his nature.

"Shall I tie you up instead?" he joked. "I seem to recall you said you were quite partial to that. Should I buy you a rope for your birthday, tie you to the bed then leave you until room service comes, or worse, one of those rubber people you told me about from Jamaica?"

She laughed as she snuggled into his chest. "You are funny," then she drifted off to sleep.

In the early hours, he woke her gently with the approaching dawn to continue their mutual explorations.

"What time is it?" she asked.

Graeme looked at his phone and saw that it was 3.45am.

"Quarter to six," he lied.

They rose early and went to work separately. Katie was entertaining a new colleague, initially by driving him to the office in her Porsche, frightening the life out of him in the process. Graeme had lots of meetings so the day passed quickly and as Katie was travelling home that evening, they had agreed to leave early so that the could meet again at the Crown Hotel in Peebles.

Graeme was napping when she arrived, but, as always, was delighted to see her. They sat in their usual spot, ordered food and drinks then Katie asked if he'd do a tarot reading for her friend Jenny. She acted as a surrogate, picked a card she was now familiar with to represent Jenny and they began with a silent question. Katie shuffled the deck then Graeme dealt out the cards. Once completed, he paused to photograph the formation. "I'll write up the reading later and email it to you," he said. "Our time together is too precious to waste." Again they became absorbed in one another until it was time to leave.

The following day Graeme sent Katie the reading, written out card by card.

Hi babe,

I have sent the picture of the cards for Jenny – a Celtic Cross reading which you have seen before. As agreed, you picked the card to represent her and haven't yet told me the nature of the question. So here is the reading.

*Querant – You chose the **Queen of Cups** to represent Jenny.*

*What covers her – factors working in her favour. The general aspects relating to the question. **The empress***

Material things, often related to marriage. Tends to suggest she is financially secure/settled with her husband? This is something she is conscious of.

*What crosses her – factors which may be working against her. **The moon**_*

It can relate to intuition an awakening to the more spiritual aspects of her question, but in this context and position, I would suggest that it is indicative of something hidden. She does not yet know everything she needs to know about the circumstances surrounding her question and desired outcome. She should make sure she knows as much as possible.

*What is beneath her? **Five of wands**_*

Wands are symbols of change, this is the basis of her question. It relates to a change that may have occurred recently or that she is considering making. She may feel as if she is in a battle, strife, at odds with someone or (perhaps edging towards violence?) a situation that she wants to change for the better. There may need to be legal involvement.

*What is behind her. The recent past – influences which are passing away. **Ace of Cups_***

Cups refer to love. The things passing away may relate to a loved one? Perhaps feelings for a loved one, end of a relationship. One thing that seems incongruous here is that Aces are generally associated with beginnings so this would suggest something that is not very long-standing but brought great joy and beauty.

*What crowns her? Something that may happen in the future – perhaps the best that can be hoped for. **Knight of Cups***

Again, Cups refer to love. Perhaps she dreams of sensual pleasure and an invitation, proposition or message related to love?

*What is before her – something that will come to pass. **The world***

One of the most positive cards in the whole deck. Liberation and freedom and perhaps a change of residence.

What she fears – the negatives feelings she has about

her question. **King of swords_**

Swords often signify strife. She fears conflict with someone. Someone she sees as strong, in a position of some authority in relation to her. The law is aspected again and this concerns her perhaps?

The view of friends and family who she has discussed the matter with. **Four of cups_**

This card suggests she has love and support from friends or family. They see she is dissatisfied with solely material things or perhaps attachment to material things which is resulting in her not being able to move forward.

Her hopes and ideals. **The Devil_**

This isn't necessarily a negative card. It can refer to strong physical passion without understanding. Perhaps she has some strong, passionate urge, she needs to understand whoever or whatever the situation is that results in this strong desire or attachment to things. The chains around the neck of the lovers depicted in the card are loose and can easily be taken off if they so choose. She has a choice. It could also mean that she hopes to force an issue to a conclusion and fears hurting someone as a result.

The final outcome **Ten of swords_**

Disruption of home life with the potential for tears. Trouble may come in spite of money or riches.

Summary

Where a high degree of major arcana are present in

a reading, as in this case, it suggests that the answer to whatever decision she is seeking to make does not rest solely with her, there is another party or parties involved. She should look at it from every angle because not everything is clear to her yet.

There is a real focus on the material aspects of life, on raw passion and emotions - sexuality rather than spirituality. Interestingly there are no pentacles in the reading, which often refer to intrigue so her choice, in the end, may be very black or white with little, if any room for compromise meaning the decision may be a painful one.

Should she worry about material considerations in her decision? She seems to be quite lucky in that regard as symbolised by the first card drawn, the Empress which covers her; it is a card that can represent material comfort often concerning partnerships. 'The World' suggests a very material change could come to pass. I think her question is not a minor one; it relates to a difficult decision with far-reaching consequences.

Maybe when you have discussed it with Jenny, she may let you tell me what her question was?

Renwick Hall

In April, Graeme arranged to visit Chester to spend the day with Katie allowing him at last to take the opportunity to visit Renwick Hall. He'd been to a business dinner the night before and, being tired, he fell asleep on the train.

Katie was waiting as the train pulled in. He kissed her and as they drove away, he admired her silently. She was gorgeously dressed in her favourite colour, a bright blue jacket, blue jeans with matching blue nail varnish. Although she'd lived nearby for many years, she'd no idea where Renwick Hall was.

She turned into Hall Lane, saying, "This must be it." But, as they traversed the rough lane, it got worse. The area was mainly industrial estates, but over a wire fence, they could see what remained of the Hall. If only they could figure out how to get to it. She turned the car around trying two other nearby lanes without success. Eventually, she retraced her route then turned into a small housing development. Although a sign said it was a dead-end, she continued and eventually came to a small lane behind the golf club, to a cattle grid that her low slung sports car couldn't cross.

They parked the car then walked towards the Hall. There was a small pond to their left. As if protesting at their sleep being disturbed, ducks quacked loudly on the bank as Graeme and Katie walked along the gravel path, which crackled like lightning beneath their feet.

Approaching the metal gates, Katie was apprehensive. "I had no idea this was here."

"It can't be far from your house," said Graeme.

He thought the Hall, which was only the gatehouse of the original building, was an attractive home and clearly it was occupied. There was a sturdy gate and CCTV. While he took a few photos, Katie took in the scene.

It was a yellow sandstone building, weathered with age, green in places, presumably from several centuries of water ingress before the guttering had been repaired. The cost of the upkeep of such a building would be substantial.

It had three floors with mullioned stone windows to the front, a decorative parapet on the roof with a large oak door in the centre of the building. There were two sets of double sandstone columns down either side of the door. The design of the building, the symbolism of the pillars, the number of windows and the crest, which could not be made out easily, were masonic in style. Whoever built or commissioned this building, must have been immersed in both Masonic and deeper esoteric doctrine.

To the rear, part of it had been converted into a separate gated dwelling. This may have been a later addition, a conversion, or perhaps it was originally a coach house. As he studied the building, he noticed that Katie was unusually quiet. He stood behind her, holding her and waited for her to speak. Although Katie didn't realise it, until Graeme told her later, she stared at the building for almost twenty minutes as if mesmerised.

"What do you feel?" he asked.

"I don't like it. I've never been here before, but I feel drawn to it. I've seen this house many times in my dreams, that side window on the second floor frightens me."

"Tell me."

Katie trembled as he held her. "It's always the same house in my dream. It's where I live. I live downstairs and there's something frightening on the second floor. I've been on the second floor. There's a large hallway, which runs in a square of large doors. I've been in one of the rooms, but I feel as if I was forced to go in and I can't remember what happened. There are secret passages in the house that run from the attic to the basement which I would often use."

Although not yet sure how, he knew that Katie was connected to this place. Her feelings were palpable, so he suggested they head into town for the meetings they'd arranged. He also knew that dreams aren't always fragments of past lives. Sometimes they're the subconscious seeking to bring things to light in waking life and Katie's life was complicated, so in this case, he felt all options worthy of investigation.

He could feel the magical currents flowing around them, crackling in the air, mirroring the gravel crackling under their feet, as they made their way to her car.

"Please don't come back here without me," said Graeme.

After the intensity of the visit to Renwick Hall, they both felt they could use a drink although Graeme wanted to eat first. Katie was having none of it. They headed into Chester on the train and went straight to The Ape and Apple pub.

"I often send you photos from here," said Katie.

He could picture her where she was sitting.

"Can we eat?" he pleaded again. "A snack?"

"Don't forget we have an appointment, let's meet the contact then eat."

Katie had warned that this meeting was going to be a longshot. The business contact they were meeting had some great clients but Graeme knew a little of the background; and the kindest things he could think to say about him weren't repeatable.

When, an hour or so later, they met him in another bar he realised that his earlier harsh assessment had probably been, if anything, too kind.

The world of finance is strange, it seems that everyone is, or can be, an expert. Tyler had worked with Katie some years earlier. He was, in fairness, a good looking guy in his early forties, but could pass for someone around thirty years old. His appearance was particularly striking. He was of Afro-Caribbean descent but had bleached blond hair complemented by piercing blue contact lenses that made him look as though he would burst into tears at any moment. He was tall, wore the latest fashions, was in good shape and made sure he had the tightest possible clothes.

Despite him being gay, their ex-boss, Joanne, had fancied him something rotten. Clearly, the chemistry was too much, so much so that Tyler could do no wrong and, although Katie was easily the best performer in the team, this seemed to be forgotten in the mutual love-in leaving Katie's star somehow shining a little less brightly for a while.

He'd left to set up on his own with a female friend who was also clearly fashion conscious. She too was blonde, wore blue contact lenses and her teeth were so white that when she smiled, she resembled a squirrel. As the team expanded, they had added an estate agent who, by her own admission, had something of a shady past. She didn't seem to be going for the full corporate look and merely had blonde highlights. Finally, they were joined by an ex-football coach from a small town in rural Wales. He had brown eyes and hair, although he did seem to be on message with the very tight clothing.

In short, the perfect team for a wealth management company thought Graeme sarcastically, though he had to admit that they had tapped into something that resonated with the Instagram age and their Cheshire based clients seemed to like them.

They met in Bogart's on Watergate Street. Tyler shook hands and said hello. As well as the striking appearance there was something else - he sniffed a lot. He was also twitchy and kept touching Graeme, not in an aggressive way. Still, his idea of personal space and Graeme's were not in accord, so much so, that he was having to resist the urge to give Tyler a Glasgow kiss, despite years of experience having taught him that the meeting probably wouldn't end well if he did.

Tyler, sounding like a comic book version of Liam Gallagher – and, to Graeme's Scottish ears, any Mancunian based dialect sounded like a parody of Liam Gallagher - proceeded to tell Graeme how great he was. His colleagues recounted how little experience they had, clearly, in the hope that he would be impressed and allow them to work with his business.

It was after Tyler had disappeared every few minutes that Graeme, being sheltered in his outlook, realised that he was actually off his head on cocaine and not, as Katie had suggested, a little nervous at meeting him. He must have voiced a desire to nut Tyler in the face as he was disappearing for another fix because Katie gave Graeme an alarmed look to say, I can't believe you just said that! When Tyler returned, he seemed to have missed his nose, the giveaway white powder marks were all over his otherwise spotless blue jacket.

In short, Graeme thought that the meeting was a car crash but it was only a few months later that he would come to realise that he was surprising even himself with his prophetic abilities.

Making their excuses, Katie made sure they left as soon as they could to continue their crawl around Chester pubs and, as he had suspected, Graeme didn't get anything to eat after all. After five pints plus a cocktail so acidic that it made him look like he was gurning, things started to weigh heavily on him. These days he was a lightweight when it came to drinking. Katie knew this, laughing all the way, she walked him to the station to make sure he caught his train before she headed home.

As Graeme boarded the last train, he could smell the diesel fumes, he felt sick. He took a seat at a table next to a fat lady then promptly passed out, so his day ended as it had begun, asleep on the train. Katie meanwhile was laughing at the thought of a tipsy Graeme making his way home to Edinburgh. She managed not only to put him onto the train but had returned to her place, then visited her local haunts in Renwick village followed by a trip into Wilmslow with her friends where she got bladdered and fell into bed in the early hours of Saturday.

When morning came, Katie woke and started to think about her house, back to her experience with her unearthly morning visitor in 2002. When the house went on the market, she had introduced herself to the then owner Karen. She remembered that at the time she wanted the house, no matter what. She fought three other buyers to secure it and took out a lot of risky debt to fund the purchase, which could easily have ruined her financially. To this day she didn't know why.

There was something else too that she couldn't put her finger on. Shortly after moving into the house, she'd felt compelled to buy a mirror for the hallway. An antique one had been advertised in the local rag. As soon as she saw it, she'd purchased it on the spot. The mirror had a wooden frame with a shelf along the bottom and she habitually placed a red vase on either side of the mirror then placed white lilies in the centre. She had no idea why, it just seemed the right thing to do.

When she told Graeme, he remembered his tarot cards, The Magician, the final outcome of the last reading he'd done for her when she'd asked what drove her.

What were the cards trying to tell them?

"What made you think of that?" asked Katie.

"The Magician is always shown in a white tunic, surrounded by a red robe. Everything in the cards is symbolic of course; the white tunic symbolises the pure intention of the will surrounded by the red passion of the emotions that make the magic work. Emotions or desires are much more potent than you would believe. When combined with a strong will, their power is unlimited.

"Often, they are so intense that they don't just affect an individual, they affect everyone and everything around them, that's how charms and curses work, it's why we feel a particular way when we enter a building. Sometimes we feel right at home, other times it just doesn't feel quite right, does it?"

This time Katie shivered. "I know what you mean."

She had searched the house deeds for clues to its history uncovering the last will and testament of a man from 1780. He was the first person to own the current house, or at least the land on which it was constructed. It seems there was something there before, although there is no record of precisely what. What was his connection with Renwick? Had he been responsible for the daisy wheels outside? If so, from what was he trying to protect the house and its occupants from?

Despite Graeme's request not to return to Renwick Hall without him, over the next couple of days, Katie tried to go back several times, yet strangely she could never seem to get there. She either took the wrong turn or it began to rain, or she became lost and disoriented. She texted Graeme telling him, I think forces are working against me, but I feel drawn to the Hall for some reason I can't explain.

Sunday was the night of the full moon. It was bright in the sky when he texted Katie to ask if she could see it. She went into the garden and stared at it in wonder.

You will dream tonight and you will remember. Don't force it, it will come. just make sure you record every impression, no matter how insignificant it feels. You may not like it, your mind is trying to help you remember things, to discover your true nature.

To her surprise, when Katie woke the next morning she did recall a vivid dream about a grand old house. She wrote a note to Graeme about both her feelings on the visit to Renwick hall and her dream.

It was only when I got out of the car that I felt a sense of unease. When you walked ahead, I didn't want to walk alone so hurried to catch up. There stood the gatehouse, looking like the house in my dreams. Always the same house, even though you reminded me it was the gatehouse and the manor had been demolished in the 1800s.

My eyes were drawn to the corner second-floor window. I couldn't see anybody but felt someone was staring down at us. It made me feel uneasy yet I couldn't stop my eyes drifting back up to it. When you said, close your eyes, let your mind go blank and wrapped your arms around me, I did. It was just quiet, peaceful, then when you said, 'come on,' I didn't think much of it. I thought we'd stood there for a few minutes until it was time to leave. I looked again to the window. Although I still couldn't see anyone I still sensed we were being watched, it was a strange feeling.

The house in my dream is far wider than the outline of the gatehouse, it's bigger. Although I don't dream of the outside often, I have walked down the side of it. The gardens are kept beautifully, all very grand, very imposing. It also has a second floor, with wide corridors and very large doors.

Last night I dreamt of a party in the house, full of people, men I didn't know. I was looking after them. There was a huge fireplace with a mirror above. It seems familiar to me as though it's my responsibility to put logs on the fire. I wished people would leave, but they didn't. They didn't talk to me either, they just smiled until I woke.

I have a strange desire to learn more about the people who lived there. I wonder what happened to them all. I wish there was a picture of the Hall itself.

The Fall of Richard Peak

At the outset of the Civil War, Englishmen had been reticent to fight one another. Often the sieges and battles had been endured with minimal casualties, but, over the coming months, the battles would become ever more vicious and cruel. It was becoming a war of attrition. Richard Peak knew that if he couldn't be defeated, it would only be a matter of time before Oliver Cromwell would consolidate his hold on power.

He admired Cromwell's military expertise though, particularly his creation of the New Model Army. Although initially far inferior to the king's forces, they had fought bravely scoring some notable victories. Even Prince Rupert had, with begrudging respect, called them 'Ironsides' because they had fought with the fire of true belief in their hearts. Still, Richard knew a dictator when he saw one. He realised that, while Cromwell may be satisfied with a military victory for now, he was not an ordinary general. He was a skilled politician, puritanical in his drives and beliefs, the time would come when his gaze would turn again to those who had supported the king.

On that day, those closest to Richard Peak would be in very grave danger.

The De Berniers were wily at court, politically astute. Ostensibly supporters of the Crown, with strongholds across the North, although they fought in the name of the king, their castles were often besieged yet strangely never conquered. Honourable surrenders were negotiated, making sure the estates remained intact and afterwards no small number of their men fought alongside the parliamentarians. They manipulated situations on both sides so that when the time came, they could, if it suited their purpose, also be recognised as loyal supporters of the parliamentarian cause. Richard knew that in the end, his beloved daughter Grace would be safer in their household than in his own.

He visited Grace whenever his campaign duties allowed, although these visits became less frequent as the war intensified. When Grace reached the age of consent at twelve years old, she would be betrothed for marriage. Adam Bright, a regular attendant at the masked balls Maria held, had taken an instant liking to Grace. He was a frequent lodger with the De Bernier household and he would attend her, on the pretext of bringing her books, particularly poetry which she loved.

By 1646 the war had turned in favour of the Roundheads. They now controlled two of the major river arteries across the country, the Severn and the Thames, which meant they could move men or supplies at ease. The only other major artery they needed to control in order to choke the entire country and secure total victory was the River Trent. The town of Newark had been strongly royalist from the outset of the war. Surrounded by low plains and reeds, the castle occupied a strategic position on the river which had proved difficult to breach.

Twice it had been besieged yet each time the defenders had fought valiantly until they were relieved. By March 1646 it is again under siege and this time there is no hope of relief. If Newark falls, the war is lost. Both sides know this and the parliamentarians are taking no chances this time. The castle is besieged to the north by almost six thousand Scots in a camp they have named Edinburgh and by nine thousand English and Welshmen to the south in a camp they have named London.

On May 4th, as dusk fell, the fighting subsided. Richard Peak, sat in the courtyard surveying the redoubt they had created inside the castle walls; that final defensible point they would retreat to if they were overrun. In all likelihood this is where the remaining defenders would breathe their last. The outer sandstone walls were already pockmarked by the impacts from musket balls and small cannon fire. Although they held firm, the defenders had also contributed to the devastation by stripping all the lead from the roof and windows as they ran short of ammunition. To make matters worse, the calibre of their weapons was not uniform so along with his men, Richard sat chewing on lead balls until they were reduced to a size useable for the large pistol strapped to his belt.

At least it took his mind off the hunger.

Due to their sheer numbers, after several months, the besieging forces were reduced to scavenging over forty miles of countryside for food. It was even worse inside the castle where even the rats were hunted for the pot. Even though the defenders were less than two thousand in number, the food had run out over a week ago, clean water was in short supply and worse, the plague had arrived. Even if they survived the fighting, to stay meant certain death for them all.

Richard called his page. "James, bring me paper and ink, I need to write a letter."

James arrived, with a small piece of parchment. He was apologetic as he leaned forward to hand it over, "I am sorry sir, it was all I could find." Then he added quietly, so as not to be overheard, "The king has summoned you, my lord."

"Thank you James. Please put these in my quarters."

He headed to the royal apartments.

Realising the hopelessness of their situation, King Charles wanted to spare the town from destruction and sought advice from his commanders. Once they had agreed that surrender was the only logical outcome, Richard Peak offered to accompany the King to the Scottish camp where they would hopefully receive a more favourable welcome.

An hour later, when he returned to his modest quarters, he sat down to write his letter, then settled in his cot in anticipation of a restless night ahead.

Just before dawn on May 5[th,] along with two servants, he accompanied King Charles out of a side gate and discretely crossed the river. Wearing full battle dress, they covered themselves from head to foot in rough blankets so that anyone watching would assume they were simple people fleeing the castle while they still could.

They made their way to Edinburgh camp where the King surrendered to the Scottish commander David Leslie, who in an ironic twist of fate would later become the 1st Lord of Newark.

"My lord," said Leslie, as he greeted the King. "Would you do me the honour of accompanying me to the nearby village of Kelham. The surroundings there are more convivial than our rough camp and we can perhaps speak more freely."

Leslie had been a loyal subject of Charles' father, who as well as being King of England, was also King James VI of Scotland. He had no desire to see the King come to harm, but his years at war on the continent had shown him that the world was changing and one day there would no longer be a place for absolute monarchs.

After several hours of discussion, Leslie turned to Richard Peak. "Sir, you have accompanied the King, he has vouched for your honour and good service, yet you have asked for nothing in these discussions. What is it you seek for your men?"

"Only an honourable surrender," he replied. "They have fought bravely in service to our lord, but with no malice to our brothers."

"Very well, you will carry the letter of surrender back to the garrison to make arrangements to hand over the castle to my men. In return, I will grant you and your men safe passage."

He looked at the King who smiled at him and simply nodded.

Taking his leave, he returned to the castle that evening. The following morning, just after dawn, he led his soldiers out of the town and they set off to their respective homes.

Home, thought Richard. He thought of Maria, of his beloved daughter Grace and he longed to be there. Gathering those of his men who had followed from his estates, they marched together with the rising sun at their backs, making their way westward.

By the time he reached Ashton two days later, having received the letter he had sent just prior to the surrender of the garrison, Grace and her new husband Adam were waiting for him. Now approaching fourteen years of age, Grace was the image of her mother, already her beauty had no equal. He hugged her tightly and kissed her. He asked them both to accompany him to stroll through his estate to the edge of Renwick Manor. As they walked, she told him of how she had worked in the household teaching the ladies sewing, reading and poetry, but now that he'd returned, how much she looked forward to returning home.

"I must talk with Adam," he said, "Would you mind returning to the house and arranging some supper?"

"Of course not," said Grace and she headed back through the glade towards the manor house.

"You cannot bring her home," he said to Adam when she was out of earshot.

"You know she will be devastated. Although she believes you are her guardian, she is the image of her mother and she wields the amulet in the same way, but as yet she does not understand it's true power."

"You must never speak of this to her," he growled. "You learned enough from Maria these past years to teach her without revealing her parentage. She has always believed that Catherine was her mother, to tell her of Maria would only bring her pain.

Cromwell will not rest with a military victory alone. Eventually, they will come for those of us who have supported the king. I am a danger to her now.

"Henry De Bernier is a Catholic and will be safe for now, but he will manipulate himself into the favour of whoever rules in Charles' absence. She is safer in your house, or, better yet, continue to live on the Renwick estate as long as you can. As long as I am in his debt, he will be comforted to have her close to him."

"Can you repay the debt now that the war is over?" asked Adam.

"No, the coffers were depleted with the need for weapons and supplies and the land has been neglected in our absence." For a moment his eyes glazed, then he continued, "were Maria with me, it may have been possible, but I will be further in De Bernier's debt before this is over. Her safety, and perhaps yours, now rests on me *not* repaying the debt. De Bernier needs to believe he has won, then he will fight to protect his new estate and you and Grace along with it."

The shadow people

Some weeks later, Graeme's team met again in Leeds, to say goodbye to a colleague who was leaving to do consultancy work to get some balance back into his life. It was a fun evening but Paul and Graeme went back a long way, so it was also tinged with sadness.

Katie wanted to see Graeme and ardently wished they didn't have to go out.

"It'll be fine," he said. "We won't be late, if you phone your husband before we go we won't waste time later either."

They had cocktails and a few beers at various bars followed by an excellent steak meal in a private dining room, accompanied by plenty of red Rioja and white Albarino. It was an intimate affair, an opportunity for good conversation with some light-hearted piss-taking to say goodbye to an old friend.

Graeme had long since noticed that somehow people of a certain persuasion seemed to gravitate towards Katie. Her colleague Ewan was one such poor soul about to be dragged into her web, or was he? Graeme knew a little of his personal life, that his parents had been swingers for example. Ewan himself had discovered this by accident while watching a TV program about swingers. He was married with children but admitted that his sexual appetites were, in his own words, 'quite varied.'

The next morning, as Katie and Graeme lay in bed re-living the events of the previous evening, he was concerned by Katie's revelation that Ewan had, at one point, proposed a casual sex ring.

Swinging, indeed casual sex in general, wasn't Graeme's thing and frankly, the idea of being the filling in any sandwich involving Ewan was, to say the least, alarming. The secret Santa had been interesting some months earlier where he'd noticed Ewan enjoying furry handcuffs with a gimp ball in his mouth. They had not even been bought for him, they were bought in order to wind up another colleague. Despite this, Ewan had seemed comfortable, he was enjoying himself a little too much, especially in broad daylight in a busy urban office.

Graeme's mind was running riot now. He knew Katie fancied the idea of being tied up, but he most definitely didn't. He had an alarming vision of being handcuffed to the bed, the gimp ball in his mouth, muffling his screams and pleas for mercy as Ewan burst into the room wearing nothing other than a batman mask and a cape. In his mind's eye, he could see Katie standing naked beside the bed, giggling from too much wine, as his eyes bulged and the panic increased. The painful, unpleasant - not to mention unhygienic - manifesto Ewan would have dreamed up would leave him chaffed and possibly with difficulty walking for a while.

Graeme wasn't a prude, still he felt it important that if one was going to engage in any activity, it was essential to have the right equipment. In this case he was fairly sure he didn't have what may be required of him.

Katie was laughing hysterically.

"I'd prefer it if Tyler were here," he said. "It's not the prospect of a supply of drugs to loosen my bits or take away the smarting sensation. Frankly, I'd just want to swap places. I don't begrudge Ewan his fun and Tyler would be unlikely to notice he'd been violated. He'd probably just wake up feeling a little sore, perhaps damp, maybe even a little sullied, nothing out of the ordinary after a drug-fuelled afternoon on the town."

It was still early and they had a few more precious hours together, so they held one another tightly and eventually the giggles faded as they fell into a deep sleep following one another into a new, different, altogether more pleasant dream.

That morning Katie's boss Bruce had wanted to stay in the hotel to complete the team's annual appraisals while he had them all in one place.

Fine, thought Graeme. I can have a lazy morning. Yippee! although the prospect of Katie leaving early didn't appeal. He needn't have worried, as usual, she was one step ahead. Upon finding out about Bruce's plan, she'd already written her appraisal sending it in ahead of time. Although surprised at her punctuality, Bruce simply said 'that's fine.'

For all Katie loved Graeme, she could still not be completely open with him. The closer he got to her, the more she held back. Something inside her still needed to make itself known but she was conflicted.

A few weeks later Graeme had been working in Dublin and he flew back early to spend the night with Katie. She'd made her excuses about attending a dinner, but, as always it was just to spend time with Graeme. Their recent holidays apart, each with respective partners, had hurt them both. After spending the night together, neither was in any rush to depart. They sat in the bar and ordered coffee so that they could talk. During this conversation, Katie again revisited the occasion at the party where she'd been drugged by Tony and this time she was strong enough to tell Graeme what she remembered.

"You know the story of how we ended up there, how I was given drugs?" Tears welled in her eyes as she struggled with the words. Graeme held her hand across the table and she continued. ".....I was carried to the kitchen then laid across the table where they took turns to abuse me."

Graeme wasn't surprised but he could feel his blood boil. It was an important step although he struggled to remain calm. If she could admit to herself what had happened, she was growing stronger. He must have gone white, because Katie gave him a questioning look, checking to see that he had not changed the way he felt about her. He hadn't, but he now realised that time was running out. If he was to help Katie get to the bottom of what was driving the events in her life, he too needed help and he shuddered at the thought of what that would mean. He knew what he had to do, he needed to wait until he was at home alone, for the approach of dusk as the skies darkened when he would be able to sense the presence he sought.

Of all the things Graeme could see that others could not, the shadow people frightened him the most. They exist in the myths of all cultures, they have many names; ghosts, genies, djinn, watchers, dark angels, daemons, dwellers on the threshold. His grandmother had always called them the shadow people, but, from painful experience, he had long ago learned they were not shadows, they were all too real.

They frightened him because he knew that they were drawn to strong emotions. This is the energy that sustains them, it is why ordinary people only tend to see them at time of great stress such as the passing of a loved one, for example. The last time Graeme had spoken with one was when his grandmother Helen had died over thirty years earlier. He had sat by her bedside when the dark figure appeared at the doorway. Like black smoke yet solid, he couldn't see through it. His grandmother conversed with the being in a language he recognised but would never repeat. People seldom realise the real power of words.

It had seemed surprised that he too could see and understand it and it stared at him intently. He had felt as though it was burning a hole right through him, but his grandmother reached out, held his hand, squeezed it tightly, then she left this world.

Without looking down at her, Graeme knew she was dead. A wave of emotions washed over him and, through his tears he asked the shadow, "Will she be okay?"

"Yes." It replied

The being in the doorway faded and again light flooded the room from the corridor outside. He knew that it had taken something of him with it when it returned to the place it had come from and he wanted it back. Little did he know then that the day would come when the debt owed him would be repaid.

Now over thirty years later, there was another soul that Graeme couldn't bear to lose. Waiting until the house was empty, as dusk fell, he sat in his large armchair breathing deeply, slowly, rhythmically. Concentrating on his breathing for a few minutes, he knew instinctively the point at which he could put himself into a trance when the world around him would start to melt away. Everything faded, everything except the doorway which he stared at intently as he called to them, not with words but using his strongest emotions to draw them to him.

The intensity of his feelings for Katie soon drew not one, but four shadowy figures. The doorway acts as a symbol to help our minds make sense of the experience. The doorway they really stand at is what we call death, or rather the veil between worlds. Standing at this doorway, time has no meaning.

They are patient beings, they know that we all pass through that doorway. It's a terrifying thought, but we each pass through it many times. Graeme knew this, and he also knew more about what that journey entailed. It comforted him that they were unable to pass through the doorway without an invitation because, when they did, they could wreak havoc. Some regard them as malevolent, but it's more symbiotic than that, they need us, they envy us for, like the gods themselves, we sustain them. Clairvoyants sometimes contact them without realising it.

They do speak on occasion, they will sometimes answer questions put to them and can provide invaluable help, but they are treacherous creatures making it dangerous to ask about oneself. His grandmother had often warned him never to use the gifts she'd given him for his own selfish purposes. They are particularly helpful when it comes to questions that arouse great emotion or emotional turmoil, she'd told him, because this is what sustains them, but your heart must be true. If the questioner is honest, his questions selfless - to help another for example - then they may answer.

Before Graeme could ask his question, one of the figures stepped forward. It seemed familiar. Was it the same one he had seen all those years ago?

"Why do you approach the doorway?" the figure asked. "It is not your time."

"I need your help." Graeme answered truthfully " My vision is clouded."

"Yes, because of your love for the girl," the figure replied matter of factly.

Oh God! he thought. It knows Katie!

"She needs help," he said.

After a brief pause, it replied, "You cannot save her."

A chill ran through him, as he continued. "I know

that…" he said pausing to emphasis the point. "… but she can."

The shadow moved a little closer and seemed to stare into his soul. Emphasizing its own point it asked, "Are you sure she is the one who needs saving?"

Graeme froze, knowing the price he was going to have to pay, he ignored the question until the shadow continued, "She must complete the journey. She agreed to the terms, as you all do."

"She carries a pain within her, she needs to understand the trigger, what is it?" demanded Graeme. "I have felt it. Her whole life, the whole area where she lives is steeped in a current of sexual energy. When I took her to Renwick Hall, although she didn't realise it, she had felt it too, when she stood almost trance-like staring at the second-floor window."

Graeme shivered at the memory. Magical energy is often channelled through sex and while some may use this power properly, consciously, with consenting like-minded adepts, it's all too easy for it to be distorted into something dark, very dark and dangerous. Kundalini is not something to be summoned lightly.

"Yes, she is drawn to her past lives as you all are," replied the entity.

"Why, this one?"

"To do what all men do." The shadowy figure replied, "To sin, to right a wrong done to them in a previous life, to seek revenge, or to atone for things they visited upon others. You, above all others, know that no soul can have peace from the great wheel until all of their work is done."

Me above all others?, wondered Graeme, puzzled by the comment.

He knew it was taunting him, but he understood that he must not ask about his own journey.

He again shivered involuntarily. He also knew the watchers couldn't hurt him, at least not yet, but they frightened him still. They were the living embodiments of his own subconscious fears and failures, as well as the accumulated sins of all men who pass through the door and they are legion.

"Show me where to look to help her," Graeme said as if bending the figure to his will, commanding it to answer.

"You understand the price you will pay for this?"

"Yes." said Graeme, " I understand."

"Look to the house. She visits it constantly in her dreams and, as you have already suspected, to the mirror."

It turned away, joined its companions then, along with the doorway they seemed to recede into the distance and fade away.

As they evaporated, he seemed to hear it say, "Your debt is repaid, the next time we meet, you will not return."

Graeme awoke from his trance with a start. It was dark and he was sweating from the exertion. He was enveloped in an unearthly cold that seemed rooted in his very bones, his body ached and burned as his circulation slowly returned. Although the encounter had seemed to last for mere moments, several hours had passed by unnoticed.

The shadows are treacherous beings and time works differently in the doorway between worlds. Had he remained there much longer, he would not have returned.

Now he was totally drained, he needed to sleep.

THE CHARIOT.

Changing Tracks

Only a few weeks remained before Katie's annual summer trip to Ayia Napa and she pestered Graeme to accompany her, but they both knew he couldn't.

She would be away camping this coming weekend. It was some small consolation that they managed to spend a night together before she had to leave.

Once in their hotel room, as always, they held one another as soon as they could and kissed deeply, passionately, before they started to catch up and as a prelude to lovemaking, even as she spoke, she was slipping off her bra from under her t-shirt .

The next morning they lay together talking.

"Will you come to the races with me?" said Katie.

"Of course I will, you know I like the races. We're going to see some actual horses though aren't we?"

"Of course, " she said, smiling.

"I know you like the races, you like holding court in the champagne tent."

Katie feigned a hurt look. "That reminds me. I think you're right, there can't be any such thing as coincidence."

"I know that, but what makes you so sure now?"

"Well, I was thinking about the races and remembered when you chose a horse called One for Arthur to win the Grand National? Well so did I. What are the odds of that?"

"I remember," said Graeme, rolling his eyes. "Then you went into town to spend all your winnings."

She smiled, pulling him closer.

"I feel close to you like no other, I look into your deep blue eyes and I'm lost in you. We have found each other.

"I dream of you often. You know how dreams are fragmented, you protect me from something sometimes in the house although I don't remember what. Sometimes I just float, but you're always holding my hand. You told me once that I'm not really lost, I'm just finding my way back home. I like that thought."

He wasn't yet ready to share with Katie his conversation with the shadow people, but he knew that a desire had arisen within her to understand how she could stop this cycle within which she had found herself, one that was growing stronger by the day. She knew she had incredible power to manipulate men but, along the way, she had found herself in situations that she didn't know how to get out of.

"What am I looking for?" she asked.

"I wish I knew. It's like looking through a glass darkly, somehow you hold not just my heart but my soul in your hands. I think you're starting to remember who you really are. You're never lost or alone. You are FAB. Come on, let's have a bath. It's almost lunchtime, we should have checked out by now."

An hour later, they sat across from one another in a booth at the end of the bar, holding hands, as always, neither wanted to let go. As they continued to talk, each played their little game. Katie always tried to get one more glass of wine down Graeme and he in turn tried to get her to eat something.

All too soon, it was time for Katie to say goodbye. "You just put a smile back on my face to take some of the pain away from leaving you. Thank you for lunch, for listening to me rabbit on and for trying to make some sense of the shit I've told you. You're so good for me, you make me feel safe, loved and special. I am one very lucky girl"

"No. You are wonderful. I love making you laugh, it's my privilege to be your very own personal clown. I've had a fabulous time. Thank you. I'm grateful to be able to share your life. Whatever happened before doesn't matter to me. There's more for you to learn about yourself Katie and, if it helps, you have the strength to put a stop to some bad things, then it's worth it. I know it's painful, embarrassing even for you to talk about these things, but there's no shame. You are indeed loved, special and safe with me. I can't believe how soppy I am with you. You consume me."

As she drove away, Graeme's thoughts turned to their coming separation. The impending girls' trip to Cyprus filled him with dread. He hated being apart from her, his imagination would run riot, every moment would torture him as he would constantly worry about her.

Katie, however, had still not given up on the idea of getting Graeme to accompany her and, a few days later, she'd enlist Jenny's help to try to entice him. Even as she did, she was laughing to herself, because she knew he'd hate it.

As the weekend approached, she packed plenty of Fruit Gums then she and Jenny set off to camp in Wales with their partners. They were clearly getting merry when Jenny suggested Katie ask Graeme if he would like to wake up in between them in Ayia Napa. So she texted him to ask.

That's very kind of Jenny, thought Graeme, as he mulled over the prospect of clubbing with lots of fit blokes with an average age of 25. Katie had a body built for sin, whereas he had a body built for... cake.

She already knew he was shy, still his imagination was running wild. He'd never disappointed two women at once before. Might be fun.

He was laughing now. Although it was late, clearly Katie was in the mood for fun, so he replied to her text.

I'll need to consider the physics if I am going to be sleeping between you.

You will be wrapped around me, whatever.

Will my back be warm this time? I'm sneezing now thinking about the aircon. Will I have two big Jenny shaped dimples in my back when I wake up? I hope she doesn't need her hair washing. An allusion to the story Katie had told him when she had returned from New York.

Stop it. She's asking why I'm giggling.

Will my bum be getting a furry massage too?

Graeme knew that if they'd all been out on the town the scene the next morning would be far removed from a gilded Hollywood version, where everyone looks fab no matter the time of day or what had transpired.

Reality wasn't like that for Graeme. He didn't have the manicured life of an Instagram star. He had visions of waking to the sound of Jenny snoring in his ear and the feeling of a big hairy growler masquerading as a warm furry mitt pressed up against him.

I'd probably be wishing I had learned to drink responsibly and wondering why Jenny had fallen asleep with a large piece of pizza stuck to her hair strewn face. Jenny is quite pretty actually, but the tomato sauce would only serve to complement the smudged mascara that she clearly wouldn't have had the opportunity to wash off. Would she look like a sunburned badger, serene as she breathed in and out, gulping for air and snoring as if she was having a dream about catching flies?

I'm usually very thirsty after a night out, ravenous too. I would be looking at the pizza thinking I'd have to pick the hairs out before putting it in the microwave. In all likelihood, I'd be wondering where you were too then most likely find you, due to a rustling movement under a large residue of kebab.

Wow, he thought to himself, my first threesome.

Katie was reading his text, trying to hold it in as everybody would hear, but soon she was crying with laughter. Then it was her turn to tell Graeme how she thought things would play out in her imagination.

Yes I can relate to that. Most likely I would stir wondering why I was surrounded by kebab meat and pitta bread. I'd look around the room wondering where the hell I was. It would soon come back to me once I saw Jenny lying on the bed. Then I'd be wondering why I was on the floor and who was that laying next to Jenny thinking she must have copped off with someone.

Then I'd panic as I recalled the events of the night before, peep again at the guy snuggled close to Jenny then suddenly realise, Oh my god! It's Graeme. What's he doing in bed with Jenny?

Graham giggled as he read her message.

Could you handle it? she teased.

Even as she texted, Katie was making herself laugh, imagining Graeme's expression of horror at the thought of having to drink a pint of vodka diet coke, sipping it slowly through a straw. This is going to get messy.

Now it was Graeme's turn to laugh.

Katie was clearly enjoying her camping trip.

Me and Jenny have now had a few beers. I've just read your text to her, she howled laughing.

A few beers, my guess is that's a bit of an understatement. Graeme surveyed the selfies she had sent. *That HUGE glass looks like the same one Jenny had last night... is it fastened to her hand?*

It would be a good scene for my book. You're just going to have to come to find out, or you'll spend your life wondering how it might have been, although me not liking competition would mean that I'd be in the middle.

Graeme's smiled. *You don't like girls, anyway make no mistake you have NO competition.*

You're mine. I don't share so I don't want you getting a taste for a threesome, even if it was with my bessy mate.

By 1am Katie was past the point of no return, but recent events still preyed on her mind. She sent Graeme a final picture with a comment.

My nose looks long. There's just me Colin left.

Where is everyone else? Why is a man bearing a striking resemblance to Eric Cantona leaning over, feeling your bum?

That's just Colin. He's off to bed now. I am the last man standing. Me and Virgil going to bed, I'm cold.

Are you drunk? I wish I was holding you. I am sorry but I worry about you... I just can't help it.

Only you, I love you. Came the reply, then Katie passed out.

Graeme smiled, he wondered what went on in Katie's head when they were apart and she had been drinking. *Goodnight beautiful,* he said.

A few hours later, she texted Graeme again. *Good morning gorgeous. Why am I camping? I'm cold. Why are you not here to warm me up?*

I don't know. You are a funny onion. You will feel better when you get home later today.

Maybe. But I'm coming to find you. I am lost. You are like a drug that I can't get enough of. You are mine.

I adore you.

I keep telling you Katie, you're not lost, you're waking up, finding your way home.

Take me away, I need you. You are under my skin. I am totally in love with you. I am laid here waiting patiently for you to wake me up properly. Just been reading your story again and laughing in my tent to myself. You are funny.

Is there any chance I could talk to you this morning? Take Virgil for a walk in half an hour or so, he'll love you for it, at least if I can hear your voice you don't seem so far away from me.

The next few weeks soon passed and Katie went to Cyprus. She knew that, had he been able to join her for a few days, it would have hurt him too much to leave her in a place like that. Instead, she consoled herself by torturing him with selfies, dressed to kill, surrounded by gits, as he referred to her multitude of admirers, and incoherent texts in the early hours of each morning. He spent his time worrying and wondering what her mind was still hiding from her.

The summer weeks were strange for both of them. Graham knew that time was running out and Katie couldn't help focusing on their future wherever that would take them, but neither were prepared for the truth that would soon reveal itself.

The Astral Mirror

As the balmy days of late summer passed, things had been going well for Katie with the first two parts of her quest. For almost a year, she had prevented her husband from putting her in any more dangerous situations. On the odd occasion when he had pushed the boundaries, asking her to take off her bra in public, she'd been strong enough to push back and, although she still couldn't remember everything, she was remembering more and more. Her joy was compounded by the best of all bonuses; she had recently become a grandmother for a second time. Another baby girl had arrived a few weeks ago.

Earlier that day, she had received a text from Carly, which, combined with her meeting with Graeme, put her in an excellent mood. Tom's rehabilitation continued to bear fruit. He was getting on better with Carly and the arrival of their new daughter Sophia was helping to cement their relationship. Katie continued to be supportive, as always being a doting grandma and some small distance between their homes was helping.

She had agreed to help them finance a family holiday and Carly had written a charming thank you note.

Katie, I just wanted to say thank you for everything you have done for us. We both really appreciate it so much. Since Christmas especially, I have seen a big change in the way Tom treats us all. He has so much respect for you and the move has really helped. You never once let us struggle, you're such a fab, doting grandma. No amount of words can express what a wonderful person you are . We love you lots. .

"That's great news," said Graeme. "I told you it would do him good to be in his own place. He's managing his feelings for you better now that he isn't under the same roof. You're a very powerful person to be around. I sometimes wonder if you realise just how powerful. I told you Hollins' Brook was important and, being on the opposite side of it, the water provides a barrier, a calming effect for the kind of emotional energy that arises, that's why we're baptised." Changing the subject and trying to lighten the conversation, he added, "How's my mate Tyler?"

"In prison." Katie paused for maximum dramatic effect.

"Really? What for?"

"You remember you said our meeting was a car crash? Well, he ran someone over, although he didn't actually know he'd done it."

"You're kidding. How can you not know you have run someone over? Surely the person shaped dent in the car would be a clue, or maybe the white chalk outline on the road?"

"The police seem to think he may have already been dead when Tyler hit him, but they're not sure."

"Let me get this straight. He may or may not have knocked someone down, but at the very least ran over a dead body in the road? How did the police know it was him? Did they follow the line of white powder to his house? I assume he was off his head again on cocaine?"

Katie had to laugh. "I know, you couldn't make this stuff up. "

She backtracked slightly. "He's not actually in prison yet, he's going for trial next month."

Although they both liked him on a personal level, Graeme sometimes had a dark sense of humour. He couldn't help seeing the comedy in the situation, so, as always when they were about to be separated, he did his best to make Katie laugh, this time at Tyler's expense.

"You know I worry about you being away without me," he said. "It's hard not to worry about all the sex, drugs and alcohol, but this will pale into insignificance when we spare a thought for poor Tyler. It isn't the fact that he would be going to prison for manslaughter, he'll be very popular. People often like to think they can give as good they get. I suspect that for Tyler this isn't going to be true and he'll have to resign himself to being a letterbox rather than the postman... getting a lot more than he'll be giving. Fortunately, drugs are freely available in the penal system, he'll probably need something a little more relaxing at the thought of what may be coming his way.

"What of his victim? Tyler had always thought that the drugs heightened his senses. He even said, `Wow, I can feel every bump in the road'. Unfortunately, he couldn't. Now his sports car has a person size imprint on the underside with two feet shaped dents in the front bumper."

Katie was crying with laughter. "Please stop," she said, so he changed the subject.

"Do you remember the three things you had to do, with your husband, your son and your dream? Are you ready to explore your final frontier?"

"Yes," she said firmly. "Yes, I am."

"You're more special than you know and you have more power than you realise running through you."

"What do mean?"

Graeme contemplated her for a moment. She was truly fabulous and she knew it. She had talked about her power, about how she would routinely keep eight or ten guys chasing her at any one time, trying to have lunch, a drink or a spa day. She always kept them guessing, but she would never understand her true nature if he couldn't make her admit it to herself.

"Have you ever seen a Mandelbrot fractal?" he asked.

"No, I am sure I haven't."

"Think of it as a very complex daisy wheel. You

remember, the thing which captures our dreams and evil spirits in its web. It's a mathematical pattern, no matter how much you zoom in, the same pattern emerges again and again, closer and closer. Holograms are made this way. If you break a holographic image into any number of pieces, every single piece, no matter how small, has within it all of the information required to recreate the whole thing."

"I think I understand. How does that impact me?"

"We are the same. Each of us has a spark of the infinite within us that's never destroyed - ever. What would you say, if I said the stars in the sky are no different to you or I? If we could zoom out far enough, we would see that they are actually a mirror. They shine for you Katie.

"Let me take you back in to your dream about the house."

"Can you go back into a dream?" asked Katie, surprised.

"Yes. I told you, you have no idea what power lies within you"

Katie closed her eyes, laid in his arms as he held her tightly directing her through the doorway in her mind that led back to the house.

"Wow," she said, surprised.

"I'm in the drawing room, there's girl standing by the fire, she's perhaps in her mid-twenties, a servant, I think. She's wearing a cream outfit, like a puritan maid. There's a group of about a dozen men standing around talking. They're wearing masks over their faces, then someone calls to the leader of the group, the tall thin man with the hat, the grey hair and beard, his name is… Robert?"

"Does that mean anything to you?" asked Graeme.

Katie went silent for a moment as if struggling with a deeply buried memory. "I'm not sure why, it just seems to remind me of someone."

"Go on, tell me what else you see."

"He, Robert, looks at the girl, he nods and she pulls down the top of her dress to reveal her breasts. She's a dark-haired girl, with piercing blue eyes, quite petite, perhaps a little over five feet tall, her breasts are full, not large, the crowd of men look on admiringly, ogling her as she takes a goblet of wine from one of them and drinks it, she seems to know what's expected of her.

"Robert leads her upstairs to the second floor where they all follow through the large doors into the bedroom where I can see there are dark wooden panels, mullion windows and a large four-poster bed. The shadows are strange in the dim light, almost alive and..." she hesitated... "the shadows... they're watching.

"The girl's dress is removed, she's instructed to bend over the bed then Robert begins as one by one they take her, roughly, without feeling."

Katie believed she was the girl in the dream as these events had parallels in her recent life. Graeme didn't believe this to be the case although he'd suspected for some time that this was a fragment of a past life, perhaps even the source of her current dilemma.

"How are you watching this?" he asked.

"I... I'm just watching," she said, then suddenly Katie realised that she wasn't the girl and there was something else. "A boy is standing beside her, about twelve years of age, being forced to watch too. The men are eagerly awaiting their turn and the boy is clearly upset by what he sees."

"Is this a regular occurrence?" asked Graeme.

"Yes," said Katie matter of factly. "It happens once a month. The girl seems to know her place in the ritual."

"Ritual?" asked Graeme, intrigued. "Can you go back downstairs, to the drawing-room and the fireplace?"

Katie hesitated, then said, "Yes. I'm looking at the fireplace with the mirror above it. It's the same mirror I have in my hallway at home, the one that I felt compelled to buy soon after moving into my house."

"When you had your dream, many years ago, that you were having an orgasm, and you were in the house alone, was the mirror in your bedroom?"

"Yes," said Katie, wondering where he was going with his questioning.

"Who's face do you see in the mirror?"

But she can't see the reflection in the mirror; her subconscious continues to hide it from her. It knows she's not ready yet and the picture is blurred.

"Come back to me," Graeme whispered.

Katie was startled as if she'd just woken.

"Wow!" she said. "I can feel... something. I never believed in things the way you do, yet there are times when we make love that I just seem to trip over into another place. I have been doing it more and more lately."

Graeme remembered the texts she'd sent him recently about standing in the garden in the evenings. She was starting to see the world very differently.

"I want to go back into my dream in the house," she said.

"Not yet. Let me do some more research, then we'll try again in a few weeks."

Graeme did continue to research the history of the house until they could meet again. When he'd exhausted the traditional, official channels; census, property records and so on, he started to look for esoteric texts that spoke of the period when the house was first built in the mid-sixteenth century and extended at various times into the 1600s.

"I've found out a little more about the time the Hall existed," he told Katie. "It may help us shed more light on what was going on. These were dangerous times. The First English Civil war was not long past, Oliver Cromwell was still Lord Protector of all England, Wales, Scotland and Ireland and his witchfinders roamed the country. The church held sway, although behind the scenes, power could switch between the Catholic and Protestant elements and science was yet to be born as we know it today. Even in the time of Isaac Newton decades later, many people we regard today as scientists were known as alchemists and their interests ranged far and wide into the nature of the universe. Around this time, those curious minds who were rich enough, or clever enough to secure the patronage of powerful people, called themselves Lunar Men."

It had been a long shot but, to his surprise, Graeme had found what he was looking for - an old text on the society of Lunar men. This was a common name for magical groups of the time, and it seems that there was a group in Renwick around that time, led by one Robert

Redman. Although it would hold a clue, Graeme realised that this was unlikely to have been his real name.

He continued. "Although the origin of the story is a mystery, it seems that the local ruling family of the day were unorthodox in their religion, that they used many forms of commerce to increase their wealth and holdings. They coveted the nearby lands of Ashton and, when the opportunity came to hold the owner to account for a debt he was unable to pay, a deal was struck."

"You look puzzled," said Katie

"There is something strange here though," he said. "The nature of the debt is not specified and, although it's not entirely clear, one referred to his daughter Anne, a shy, pretty young girl, not yet of marriageable age. She was indentured to the household. In reality she was effectively being held captive."

"Why is that strange?"

"There doesn't seem to be an official record of the then Lord of Ashton, a man named Richard Peak having children. Anyway, it indicates that somewhere along the way they reneged on the deal, seized the lands and the curse which prevented animals crossing the brook was born."

Graeme knew that such curses would only work when they aroused powerful emotional currents which resonated through time and space. In common parlance, we would call it magic, but he didn't believe it was magical, to him it was just the natural order that was yet to be fully understood.

He wondered what had happened to the young girl?

It would not be long before he had his answer.

On November 1st Katie and Graeme were in Manchester. They were looking forward to meeting business contacts then spending the night together, but this night was to be like no other they'd ever experience. As the train pulled in to the station and he descended to the platform, Graeme shivered. What had the shadow being said to him when he'd asked why Katie found herself drawn to that particular life?

'To do what all men do,' the shadowy figure had replied. 'To sin, to right a wrong done to them in a previous life, to seek revenge, or to atone for things they themselves visited upon others. You, above all others, know that no soul can have peace from the great wheel until all of their work is done.'

All Souls' Day was only a few hours away and, if Katie was to be free of her past, it had to be tonight.

The morning was a routine round of meetings culminating in a lunch with some partners from a large legal firm. After lunch, visiting a couple of pubs and eventually landing in an old fashioned boozer called The Deansgate, they settled down to talk. Graeme ordered a whisky and Katie her usual vodka diet coke. As they talked, the drinks kept flowing.

For some reason, Graeme's mind was drawn back to the tales Katie had told him about her visits to the adult resorts in the Caribbean.

"There is more, isn't there? There's still pain behind your eyes Katie."

Katie was loosening up with the alcohol, she smiled.

"Well," she said as she prepared to make her final

confession, "I suppose I'm quite excitable really and when you have had a fruitful life as I have…" She smiled again, struggling to find the right words. "Look, I've had a great life, if it all came to an end tomorrow, I'd have no complaints."

"Tell me all of it Katie. Then, after tonight, we put the past behind us once and for all."

She took a long drink and her mind drifted back.

"There have been some things I've done that honestly I can't explain, but I seem to put myself in situations that I've not enjoyed. When I was young - maybe eighteen - after a night out in Manchester, I was taken to a car by a guy I met where he forced me to give him a blow job. He was rough and I felt violated but can I complain? Well, I went voluntarily, so I can't can I? My self-esteem was low, and I guess over time, it made me realise that I would use my sexuality rather than be used for it."

He watched as the emotions ran across her face as she recalled the events. She'd always been free in her physical love with Graeme, but he always suspected this one act wasn't something that she relished so he never initiated it, but, until now he didn't understand why. Suddenly it was like a dark shadow was passing across her face as she began to explain how she ruthlessly wielded her power.

"I told you that my husband liked to show me off. Well, at one of the adult resorts we visited, I knew he wanted more, so one night I put on a sex show with a Canadian girl for a small audience, but I'm not attracted to women, I was more interested in what would pleasure me. I met a guy who ran another hotel and we started fooling around in the pool but it stopped short of sex".

"Why?" asked Graeme.

"Only because my husband came back. Whenever there are other guys, he would sometimes be happy to share me, on his terms, though he'd never leave me alone with them.

"Anyway the theme continued. The next day we were talking to some guys, two Italians, maybe in their thirties, drop-dead gorgeous. We'd been out in the sun all day, drinking and we were all naked in the hot tub just chatting. There was a Belgian girl there too, who thought she was more attractive than me. I knew they both fancied me so I flirted for all I was worth. One, in particular wanted me on my own and yes I would have sneaked off to have sex with him, but it turned my husband on to know everyone wanted me and that I was with him.

Shortly afterwards, he said, 'We're going back to our room and these guys are coming too'."

Graeme felt sick at the thought of what was coming. He could feel the anger rising in him again but he remained calm. "So you had sex with all of them, didn't you?"

"Yes!" she replied, spitting out the word, almost proud of the memory of her achievement, yet there was something else too, a tinge of regret and sadness. She had seen off the competition, but...

"I wanted everyone to desire me and they did. I was the centre of attention." She said, in the understatement of the evening, "but I didn't enjoy it. I can remember it clearly, it was totally mechanical, my husband orchestrated it. Looking back, I realise I was being used... abused, a plaything for him to get off on.

"I remember being laid there with one of them while my husband just stood chatting with the other about motorbikes, they were having a cigarette, just watching... I don't like being watched, it bothers me."

Her eyes fell to the floor as she struggled with the emotions that her recollections were dragging to the surface. They sat in silence, Katie almost disbelieving that she had shared that with the man she loved, scared of what he'd think. As for Graeme, he was taking in what she had told him, trying to process the raw emotions.

"You told me once that he'd give you a free pass to sleep with whoever you wanted when you went away with the girls, as long as you told him about it so that he could get off on it. You may have hurt him Katie, but he has exacted his revenge and he has been slowly stripping your dignity away, one layer at a time. No more.

"I can't pretend it's not painful to hear these things, but tonight it will be over, the past will no longer have a hold on you, Katie, if you choose to be free of it."

She pulled herself into his chest, clinging to him tightly.

"Let's go back to the hotel, I've had enough," she said.

THE HANGED MAN.

The Awakening

In the first minutes of November 2nd 2017, All Souls Day, Katie and Graeme lay in bed in their hotel room. A full moon shone through the gap in the curtains.

Graeme was feeling feverish, so he sat on the edge of the bed, naked, with the windows open trying to find some relief. It was cold, the temperature only a little above zero and even Katie had wrapped herself in the quilt. His mind raced with the fever and the recollections of the things she'd told him.

It's time, he thought, turning back to Katie. "Are you ready to go back into your dream for the last time?"

"Yes," said Katie and she began to breathe slowly, rhythmically as he'd taught her. Focusing her attention inwards, she approached the door in her mind's eye and stepped through into the drawing-room where the men were gathered in groups talking.

"Is the girl still standing by the fireplace?" asked Graeme.

"Yes."

"Go over to her, what's she doing?"

Katie replied, "She's playing with her necklace, she's... smiling at me."

"Can you see the mirror above the fireplace?"

"Yes."

"What can you see in the mirror?"

"I'm wearing a mask under a hooded red robe."

"Can you take off the mask... slowly?"

She paused, then started to remember, slowly at first, then the memories came unbidden. Momentarily she screamed. "Oh no! please, no! I can't have done those things!"

As she turned her head into Graeme's chest he could feel her tears on his skin. Even through her sobbing, she knew it was true and the events over the last two years with Graeme had eventually led her to this understanding. She was not the girl in her dream, nor was she an idle spectator. The face staring back at her in the mirror was the tall, thin, grey-haired leader of the group - Robert.

"He's... not called Robert," she said.

"He's... I am... called Adam... Adam Bright."

"Of course," said Graeme, "Adam means man of red earth and Robert means bright. I should have known it would've been a blind to protect his real identity from the witchfinders. And Anne, her name means grace. Do you know what your first and second names mean? They mean grace and pure, there are no coincidences, you were meant to remember her."

She continued sobbing for a few moments then suddenly Katie woke, as if from a dream, to her real life. Helen, the shining light, had brought them together, guiding their journey. The sexual energy which ran through her core was otherworldly and, as one of the primordial forces of nature, she had once before used it to explore those other worlds - consciously - as the master orchestrator then, unconsciously in this lifetime, as the abused, but it wasn't that simple. It coursed around her and, as the Devil in the tarot had warned them all those months ago, they were without understanding.

When she started to write her story for Graeme in London he had performed another reading, the final outcome had been the Magician. The cards had hinted at her true nature whilst Helen's symbol of the moon had guided her to self-reflection, revealing her true nature in her dreams. Katie's memory of her past life suddenly became clear, her tone turned distant, cold even, as she began recounting the events of that night in Renwick Hall.

"It is the year 1658, All Souls' Day. We are the Temple Society of Lunar Men seeking hidden knowledge in these are dangerous times. There are thirteen of us, all bar one, men good and true." She spat the words. "Nobles, clergymen, teachers – some, do indeed search for knowledge to feed their souls, although most seek only to feed their greed, for land or power. We are gathered for a ritual to explore hidden worlds, some would call it a séance to contact the dead, but the entities we seek are not ghosts. They live alongside us, but at a frequency we can scarcely detect.

"You know this land as Cheshire, or to the north Lancashire - recent names. It is an ancient land with a much older name. This land is called Amounderness and, for the last sixteen years, we've used the dream paths to explore the power that this land contains. The knowledge passed down to us predates what you would call history.

"We are all now in fear for our lives. If we are revealed to Cromwell's witchfinders, none will survive, no influence will save us, but I have a more pressing matter.

"We require a sexual offering to raise the powers we need, one sensitive enough to channel the emotions in order to contact those who live in the borderlands between worlds.

"We put on our masks, to hide our true faces from them, our robes to emphasise our power and nobility. Mine is the white tunic and red cloak of the Magus, the Magician, I will direct the energies we awaken, for it is I who have called forth the powers we seek to control.

"Grace is taken upstairs where a pentagram is inscribed inside a circle on the bedroom floor. Lit candles are placed at each point then a young boy is brought to the room, he stands just inside the circle. I point my ceremonial dagger upwards, call down the blessings of Adonai and then point to the East, the South, the West and the North to claim the protection of Raphael, Michael, Gabriel and Uriel. These powers you call archangels we, in the Temple of Lunar Men, through our founding priestess, have come to know them much more intimately.

"The rhythmic chanting begins, and, one by one, the participants defile the sacrificial girl. She is more than just a simple sacrifice. She wears a small stone pendant, an ancient relic passed down through her own family for centuries; she is the focus, the Nexus. When she has surrendered herself completely, the stone will allow her to walk between worlds. She does not struggle, she knows her fate as the young boy watching, no more than a child, becomes increasingly unbalanced at what he sees. The incense, chanting and emotional energy sends him into a trance; involuntarily, he follows her on her journey. He accesses something we cannot, as his mother walks beside him on the other side.

"There is a rare alignment of the full moon this night. The combination of vibrations, energies if you like, start to break down the barriers between worlds, it will not last long, our time is short."

"Why?" asked Graeme.

"The power of the amulet was intoxicating and we sought to learn more. To begin with, to explore other worlds... we wanted simply to *know*. Tonight things are different, more urgent, I can feel despair rising within me." She sobbed. "I feel... afraid... of losing something... of approaching death. My health is failing, I am not strong enough to resist, but it is not for myself I seek the bargain.

"You were right about Grace. She was held as ransom for the debt of Richard Peak by the De Bernier family. Richard was a good man, he had been a fierce warrior and loyal to the King, but now such allegiances, even old ones, are dangerous. The De Berniers are born of noble blood, they understand court intrigue much better and there are scores to be settled even though they too have secrets to hide. Initially, they sought simply to protect themselves, but for years they had looked with envy at the pastures of Ashton so, when their chance came, they tricked Richard Peak out of his estate which he agreed to willingly for Grace's sake.

"He was by now a broken man, never having truly recovered from Maria's death. He had grown weaker as the long years of war at his king's side took their toll, but he knew their secrets so he was still dangerous to them. It was for this reason, rather than as security for the loans they had made, that they took Grace to make sure he caused them no trouble. He could not expose them without risking her life but at the same time, he knew they would protect Grace.

"As soon as I saw the stone amulet she wore, I knew that she was his illegitimate daughter with Maria. Like all who met her as she grew to womanhood, I fell in love with her. During my visits to the house, I fell under her spell, as we all had with Maria. In time my love for her became all-consuming. I used what little influence I had with Henry De Bernier to persuade the family to release her from her bond so that we could be married, even if it meant staying as virtual captives on his estate.

"Despite her young age, Richard had given me his blessing during his leave from the campaigns he fought. Partly because Maria had been my mentor and he knew Grace would need help to control her power, but mostly because he realised that when Cromwell became vengeful, as he inevitably would, that she would be in grave danger.

"By 1649 he was proved right. When King Charles was beheaded, there was a state of panic amongst the nobility.

"Having guessed Grace was his daughter, when I asked him, it was he who unwittingly gave me what I needed. He told me of the ritual Maria had used when she had saved his life and how he had brought her back to England. She had never told anyone the secret of crossing the great divide but, with what I had learned from the masked balls, I now came to realise how the amulet's power worked.

"He was the simplest of men, honourable brave and true. He had never sought to understand her powers as we had, but he knew that Maria was no ordinary woman and that Grace would inherit her power as well as her beauty.

"She may be English by birth, but she was also descended from the same Berber tribe. Their tribe worshipped far older powers. They were often punished by both the Muslims and the Christian Spaniards. Had they not been useful, they would have been wiped out centuries ago, but they had ancient traditions, shamanistic rites that made them adept at what we call dream walking.

"The Lord of Ashton should never have survived that night in the Tajo gorge in 1625. Maria had often told Richard that she was a 'bruja', a witch from a long line of witches and that only her magic had saved his life.

She could walk between the worlds of the living and the dead. He had actually died that night and she had brought back his soul. He had never understood the source of her power, but I did. I recognized the stone charm she had always worn, which now hung around Grace's neck, for what it was. I recognised the divine feminine sexual energy that coursed through her and with it, the ability she inherited to direct the power of the stone.

"It was I, not Richard Peak who called down the curse on the parish of Renwick, but it was Maria who made it effective. She had always known her destiny was to be his protector and she continued even in death. You see, death is not the end, there is no country where love cannot reside. I crossed Hollins' Brook to her grave where I removed the daisy wheel from the headstone. They would have killed him otherwise, but even the fools amongst us, who only sought money or influence, recognised true power and, when their horses refused to cross the brook even when harshly whipped, they were afraid.

"That same blood now flows through her daughter's veins, she is the key. Grace is now twenty-five years old, the boy at her side is our son Henry. He is approaching puberty, but he is dying. Years ago, we saw the tide turning against King Charles, our home was under virtual siege because of our loyalty and the plague ravaged every living thing. It has returned and our son is showing the first signs. Hard to understand now perhaps, the plague is something common in these times, with no cure. He will not live to see manhood without intervention from the other side yet, in trying to save him, the infection may spread, he may take us all to our deaths.

"It is not death I fear. I know I will return, but the pain of separation from the soul of my wife Grace is too much to bear. It is rare beyond imagination, yet I have found the one my soul adores and I am afraid that I will not remember in the next life. I have to find her when the time comes to follow, I must speak with those who guard the doorway."

Graeme recoiled in horror. Behind the ritual, he recognised the signature of the same shadow being he had encountered on two occasions separated by thirty years.

"You knew what it would do to her yet you made a deal with them, the shadow people, to save your son and to let you pass through the gate without drinking the water of forgetfulness so you could be with Grace again?"

"Yes," said Katie. "You understand how they feed, the power of the emotions required to bend them to your will, but there is always a price. A price both Grace and I had agreed to, without hesitation for our son's sake."

"Did it work?"

"Yes, it did. There was never another recorded case of the plague in Amounderness. Our son Henry grew to be strong, eventually realising his inheritance, he became the lord of the lands of Ashton. Henry was named in honour of Henry De Bernier. Although it stuck in my throat, it was the price I paid for the gift of him agreeing to my marriage to Grace.

"It was too late before I realised that it was the amulet, not the dark ones who had done this. Henry returned from the other side, but his mother Grace did not and, when my time came to pass through the veil, I forgot, as all men do."

"So you have been a victim in both lives?" said Graeme. "You were not abusing Grace, they tricked you, so this sexual power has followed you through the centuries, whilst they have watched you and fed on it."

"Yes. The amulet is very powerful, it is made of Moldavite, rarer than diamonds. The green stone fell from the sky millions of years ago. It resonates with a frequency that affects the laws of nature and the Berber shaman revered it, they imbued it further with their own power. Sexual energy is part of our primal creativity yet it courses through Grace's family line more strongly than in most."

"What happened to the amulet, how is it that it affects you so strongly?"

"After Grace died, I buried it with her, next to Hollins' Brook, on the opposite side to where her mother still lies."

"Oh my God! It's beneath your house, isn't it?"

"Yes. The daisy wheel on Maria's gravestone across the brook was indeed a magical charm for protection, but the ones built into the house had a different purpose, they were placed there to remind me of its presence.

"I realise now that it was the stone that drew me to the house, that's why I risked everything to buy it. It was the stone that channelled the raw sexual drive within me that caused all of the subsequent events. The dark ones knew, they watched and they fed again on the power it reawakened in me"

She sobbed. "Please forgive me Grace. It has taken three hundred and fifty-nine years for this realignment to occur, for me to awaken from my sleep. Do you know the significance of the number?"

"Of course," said Graeme. "Adding all the numbers then reducing until you get down to one digit equals 8. It means dominion, the symbol turned sideways that floats above the Magician's head depicted on the tarot cards."

Finally, they both understood that it was *she*, Katie, who was the Magician, she who had spent many lifetimes, including much of this one, paying the debt she was tricked into from a previous life, lived centuries earlier, all for one terrible mistake.

"Yes," said Katie. "But it's also a symbolic reference to the mid-winter festival of the pagans. Christmas day, when we celebrate the return of the sun. When the earth turns on its axis once again, perhaps I may finally be free."

The sexual power she had raised still flowed through her and she could still be ruthless in its application. Katie had never understood where her power came from or that it needed to be harnessed. She had always used alcohol to instigate it and, in the mistaken belief this was how she could control it, it had got the better of her on many occasions leaving behind a trail of destruction.

She was Maria's spiritual heir, but she needed another to help control the power within her, without it creating chaos and consuming her. Graeme had shown her how to activate her power naturally, making love, not war. She would no longer need the alcohol, it would become nothing more than habit.

He whispered to her gently, "The burden of the stone was never yours to carry."

"No, but on Grace's death with no female heir, I couldn't let the stone pass to Henry."

"So you took on that danger yourself, knowing it couldn't be controlled?"

"Yes, I thought that burying it would be the end, but it needs another guardian."

"Now that you understand, you can choose to be free Katie. You have paid your debt, it's up to you, let the house go."

She let the words wash over her. Suddenly she saw the world the way Graeme did. He had told her once that souls seek one another from lifetime to lifetime but, as the shadow being had warned him, he had indeed been blinded by love.

Katie realised that Graeme had also been present in that house in 1658. Should she tell him?

She was about to speak, but hesitated. No, she thought. Now I understand, he is on his own journey, he has to find out for himself in his own time.

Feeling a wave of love wash over her, she looked at Graeme and she knew, their journey was not over. They were bound together, for them, it would never be over.

THE END

A little while, a moment of rest upon the wind,
and another woman shall bear me.

Kahlil Gibran 1883 – 1931

www.ingramcontent.com/pod-product-compliance
Lightning Source LLC
Chambersburg PA
CBHW020930260626
47169CB00006B/1655